'The moment ... knew that boy ...

'I was holding him ... saw the look on yo... thought you were looking at me.'

'I was,' he admitted. 'As certain as I was in that first moment that he was my son. I also knew you were his mother. And I found myself very attracted to you.'

'Because of Georgie. And I was stupid enough to think you wanted me for me and Georgie because he was mine.'

'Lauren, please. I'll always—'

'Don't say it,' she demanded. 'I don't want to hear how grateful you are.'

He writhed in frustration. 'Isn't it enough that I want to marry you?'

'I *don't* want to marry *you!*' She laughed, not that it was funny.

A muscle ticked in the hollow of his jaw. 'Well, you have no choice.'

Dear Reader,

Take a look at what's in store for you this month:

Baby Boy Blessed from Arlene James is our **That's My Baby!** title and little Georgie apparently has more than a bit of the author's own son in him!

A Royal Baby on the Way comes from Susan Mallery, now a very established writer of Special Editions, and it kicks off an absolutely breathtaking set of five linked books about a royal family with a missing prince. These five books go across Sensation™ & Desire™ as well as Special Edition™, so do keep your eyes open if you want to catch them all—although each book does stand alone!

Cathy Gillen Thacker is back with another of her **McCabe Men** in *His Cinderella*; it's Wade's—the oil millionaire—story.

Three more fantastic books: *Daddy by Surprise* by Pat Warren, *Pregnant & Practically Married* by Andrea Edwards, and *Yours for Ninety Days* by Barbara McMahon complete this month's absolutely stellar line-up.

Enjoy!

The Editors

Baby Boy Blessed

ARLENE JAMES

SILHOUETTE

SPECIAL EDITION®

*First published in Great Britain 2000
Silhouette Books, Eton House, 18-24 Paradise Road,
Richmond, Surrey TW9 1SR*

© Deborah Rather 1999

ISBN 0 373 24285 9

23-1100

*Printed and bound in Spain
by Litografia Rosés S.A., Barcelona*

ARLENE JAMES

grew up in Oklahoma and has lived all over the South of
the USA. In 1976 she married 'the most romantic man
in the world.' The author enjoys travelling with her husband, but writing has always been her chief pastime.

Dear Reader,

My children are grown. I can't imagine how it happened. One day I was marvelling over the latest tiny miracle I had wrought, the next we were bombarding one another with balls made of wadded-up newspaper while it poured rain outside, and then suddenly I was being escorted down the aisle of a wedding not my own but every bit as evocative. The last of my darlings will marry this fall, and I'm thrilled about that. (They have demonstrated exquisite taste in mates.) Nevertheless, I treasure those baby days that were so fleeting. We had such fun. Yes, it could be troubling, frustrating. Exhausting. I *know* all about that, but I struggle to retain that knowledge, while those mystical joys of parenthood linger unaided in my heart, a permanent warmth and fulfillment that shall never leave me.

Writing about children is the next best thing to experiencing them, especially when it allows you to indulge shamelessly in warm remembrance. Georgie is strongly based on my own youngest son. But then, so is Colin in a way. And, like Lauren, I was one of those mums who learned to work in the company of babes. (Are you aware, my dears, that you can write whole books sitting sideways while a toddler plays 'cave' in the kneehole of your desk?) I guess we authors inevitably inject a little bit of ourselves and our lives into our work. As in this case, it can be such fun. I hope you enjoy it as much as I did.

God bless,

Arlene James

Prologue

One moment Lauren was smiling proudly and wishing a Merry Christmas to the snow-dusted couple who had just come through the foyer of the newly refurbished and re-opened Eagle Nest Mountain Lodge, and the next she was staring at the ceiling, telling herself that she couldn't possibly have heard a blood-curdling scream. Just as she'd convinced herself that she'd imagined it and turned a limp, apologetic version of her former smile on the wary couple, it came again, unmistakable and chilling. Unmistakably Maria, who screamed at her own shadow, and definitely chilling as far as its effect on her clientele.

"Excuse me," Lauren told the couple smoothly, her teeth set in her most welcoming smile. "I'm sure it's nothing. The maid is young and nervous." She turned toward the rustic log-and-stone stairwell.

Other faces greeted her, some appearing in the wide doorway to the great room, where a majestic ponderosa pine, decorated in vibrant red, stood sentinel over gleaming white adobe walls and rough-cut beams hung with chandeliers made of antlers. As she climbed the wide, open stairs—trying to hurry without appearing to dash madly— still other guests ventured from the dining room where two glass walls offered a breathtaking view of Eagle Nest Lake, the smooth grassy bowl of the Moreno Valley and the mountain range that stretched toward Angel Fire and beyond. Lauren smiled and nodded and climbed on with a sure, steady tread, while visions of her guests checking out en masse blurred her inner eye.

She had worked so hard, sunk every penny into the lodge. Her first summer had proven marginally profitable, but much depended on Christmas and the ski season. If Maria Herrera's silly little superstitions cost her even one guest... Lauren sucked in a deep breath and steeled herself. Maria was only fifteen. Her father, Juan, and brother, Ponce, had proven invaluable to Lauren. One foolish incident was not likely to wipe out all the good work she had done preparing for this Christmas.

Lauren reached the landing and glanced left, finding nothing amiss with the half dozen rooms that opened onto the foyer overlook. Straight ahead, the door to the spa remained closed. Turning right, she moved down the hall that cut between another dozen rooms of Spartan, Southwestern elegance. Maria was hunched against the wall, staring into the opened doorway of Room 17. Her father, Juan, whose graying hair belied his relatively young age, appeared at the top of the back stairway that led down to the dining room and kitchen. Being closer, he reached his daughter first.

She crossed herself and muttered something in Spanish as she pointed into the room. He went to investigate, and Lauren followed.

"On the bed," Maria told her shakily, but before she

could see what it was that had reduced the little maid to near hysteria, Juan stepped into her path, his face a hard, set mask.

"What is it?" Lauren asked, sensing that Maria would receive no reprimand, after all. She held her breath, praying that she wasn't about to hear the death knell, tolling for her lofty expectations for the lodge.

"Call the village marshal," Juan said solemnly. "Better tell him to send to Raton for the sheriff. And don't let anyone leave."

The marshal listened quietly to Maria's gasped, teary explanation. She had worked her way down the hall, changing the beds and cleaning. When she'd reached Room 17, she'd known immediately that something was wrong because the small hairs on the back of her neck had stood up and a dark cloud hovered at the edge of her vision. Nevertheless, she had unlocked the door and entered the room, mindful of her promise to Miss Lauren to ignore these frightening portents. She had seen immediately that the bed had already been stripped and the sheets wound into a tight ball. Only as she'd ventured closer had she realized that the sheets were streaked with blood.

The tall, lanky marshal nodded and turned his black felt cowboy hat in his hands. In a village of two hundred permanent residents, he didn't have a lot of call to investigate crime scenes—or much else. "No body?"

Juan stepped forward then, his fingertips tucked into the front pockets of his faded jeans. "We didn't really look. Figured we ought not to go poking around before you got here."

The marshal considered that, then lifted his hat to his head and carefully positioned it just so. "Yep," he said. "Well, I reckon I'll just go and have a gander."

Lauren swallowed. Had someone killed the plump

blonde who had rented this room? Could she have committed suicide? The woman known as Doris Drew had seemed friendly enough. She had hardly spoken to anyone but Lauren, and even then her conversation had centered upon the lodge, the village and the valley.

"A lovely place," she had said wistfully. "So far off the beaten track. The kind of place where children can grow up safe and healthy."

"About the greatest danger in these parts are icing roads," Lauren had told her, "and we're pretty good at keeping up with those."

Had that safety been an illusion for Doris Drew? Or had Doris Drew been the murderer? Lauren shivered and crossed her arms protectively over her chest.

Lauren, Juan and Maria crowded into the doorway, watching as the marshal ambled toward the bed. He stared down at it for a time, his hands tucked safely into the pockets of his tan suede jacket. Moving around the foot of the bed, he slowly cast about him. At one point he stopped and crouched down, staring at something on the carpet. Silently he rose again and turned away. Gradually he moved out of sight. Maria craned her neck, then settled back in a huff of disappointment.

After several tense moments, the tall, slender marshal returned again, a white hotel towel bundled in his arms. Lauren thought achingly of the sum she'd spent on those big, fleecy towels. Would she ever see a return on her investment now? Or were her brother and mother right, after all? She had been so sure that she could make a success of the old lodge Grandpa George had left them. Was she going to lose it all now over some gruesome crime?

"I found a body," the marshal said evenly. "Wanna see?" He lowered and held out the bundle.

Lauren squeezed her eyes shut reflexively as Maria gasped and Juan gusted a whistle. Suddenly Maria giggled.

Lauren's eyes popped open. Frowning, she leaned forward to see for herself what had Maria cooing like a dove.

The tiny face was crusted with drying, whitish matter, the features scrunched together beneath a fringe of black hair. One little fist crowded a dimpled chin. Lauren felt her jaw dropping. She was unaware of elbowing Juan and Maria out of the way, so caught up was she in the child nestled in the towel. It seemed wholly natural to reach out and take the baby into her own arms.

"It's a boy," the marshal announced proudly. "No sign of the mother. She probably hightailed it. Better ask around."

Lauren could not tear her gaze away from that tiny face. "I just thought she was overweight," she muttered, fascinated as the big eyes blinked, then squeezed tight, one side of the pink mouth crooking up.

"We better get him examined by a doctor," the marshal said.

"Should I call an ambulance?" Juan asked.

"Naw, it'll be faster just to drive him over to the doc in Angel Fire instead of waiting for the ambulance to come from there. Think y'all can take care of that while I ask around after the mother?"

"Ponce can drive Lauren and the baby," Juan suggested.

"I'll give the doc a call, let him know you're coming," the marshal said. He went back into the room and used the telephone there.

"I'll get some clean hand towels to use for diapers," Maria said, hurrying away.

Lauren registered none of it. She was much too busy falling in love.

Chapter One

Lauren put aside the depressing letter, the latest in her brother's campaign to convince her to sell the lodge. It seemed so unfair. When they'd inherited the lodge it had been little more than a ruin, and Larry had been completely uninterested then. Now that she'd invested her life savings, including her retirement fund, and two years of unremitting hard work, the lodge was worth considerably more than anyone had ever dreamed. And Larry seemed to think that he was entitled to half the proceeds even though he had wanted no part in putting the lodge back into operation. Sighing inwardly, Lauren put on a smile for the thirty-something couple approaching the counter.

"I hope you enjoyed your stay," Lauren said.

The couple looked at each other and smiled, stars dancing in their eyes. "Oh, yes," the woman said, sounding a little breathless, "especially canoeing in the moonlight."

Lauren chuckled. "Well, you were lucky, then. We always stop the canoeing at the end of September. Another week, and the canoes would have been stored away for the winter.''

"We even had a full moon," the husband said with a wide grin.

"Definitely lucky," Lauren pronounced, indicating with the tip of a pen where he should sign the checkout form.

"I've been reading your winter brochure," he commented, taking the pen and scribbling his name. "It says the ice fishing is best in January and February."

"That's right."

"And since you do have children here," the wife prodded hopefully.

Lauren glanced down at ten-month-old Georgie, who looked up at her placidly from the playpen crammed behind the counter, all four fingers of one hand crammed into his mouth. The other was wrapped around the neck of a flop-eared dog so bereft of stuffing that it was little more than a rag. Lauren's heart turned over with pure love. Even the stubborn cowlick of inky hair that swirled up from slightly to the right of the center of his hairline charmed Lauren. He was the most beautiful little boy in the world, and if the adoption didn't work out she'd just die. Surely if she was good enough to be his foster mother...

"What my wife means," the man said, breaking into Lauren's reverie, "is that our boys will be seven and eight in January, and we thought we might bring them for the ice fishing."

"That sounds wonderful," Lauren said, reaching automatically for the reservation book. "Would you like to reserve your rooms and book the guide now? A 10 percent deposit will hold them for ninety days, after which we require another 40 percent. I should warn you that our winter rates are slightly higher due to the increased demand of the ski season."

The wife gripped her husband's wrist, saying excitedly, "We could take the boys skiing, too!"

Lauren was still explaining the ski packages when a tall, dark-haired man pushed through the heavy, rough-hewn door into the Mexican-tiled foyer. He plucked leaves from his flannel jacket and tucked them into his pocket before smoothing back his short, black hair. Lauren flashed a welcoming smile. "I'll be with you in just a moment," she said.

He nodded and hunched his shoulders. "No problem."

As she dutifully fixed her attention on the couple standing before her, Lauren noted with disgust that her heartbeat had sped up just a tad. She'd promised herself that she was through with men, but it was only natural to notice that the new arrival was an uncommonly handsome fellow. Tall and broad-shouldered with long limbs, he made a commanding presence, but it was that chiseled face and startling blue eyes that could jump-start a woman's heart. Beside her, Georgie finally grew tired of chewing his fingers and pulled up to clutch at her leg. By the time she got the booking recorded and the money collected, her jean leg was damp at the knee.

"See you in January!" she called a little too heartily as she hefted Georgie into her arms and the excited couple crowded past the man waiting patiently in the foyer. Georgie dropped the flop-eared dog and got a death grip on her ponytail with one hand, making a grab for her nose with the other. She caught the hand aiming for her nose and carried it to her mouth, where she smacked kisses into the chubby palm before addressing the man who now stood on the other side of the counter. "Sorry that booking took so long. Can I help you now?"

The man smiled at Georgie, winning her instant approval, and glanced up at Lauren with those devastating blue eyes. She found herself wondering if Georgie would have this effect on women one day. "I have a reservation," the man said in a deep, thick voice. "Name's Colin Garret, one *T*."

"Garret," Lauren mumbled, pretending that her heart did not flutter as she flipped through her book. "Yes, here we are. Welcome to Eagle Nest Mountain Lodge, Mr. Garret. I'm Lauren Cole, the proprietor. Do you mind if I ask how you heard of us?"

Colin Garret tugged his gaze from Georgie and fixed her with a smile so devastating that she felt it all the way to her toes. "From a friend, actually. He said that if I came to Eagle Nest off-season I'd have a quiet, relaxing weekend away from the chaos of the office."

"One quiet, relaxing weekend coming up," Lauren promised, turning the book and offering him an ink pen.

As he began writing his name and address in the space provided, he asked idly, "Is this just a clever, old-fashioned touch or a real necessity?"

"Both," she said. "I'll enter you into our computer later. Why do you ask?"

"Habit and curiosity," he said, flashing her a smile. "It's what I do."

"It's what you do?" she echoed, and he chuckled.

"I'm a business consultant. People hire me to tell them how to make their businesses more profitable and efficient."

"Ah."

"If I do it again, remind me that I'm on vacation, will you?"

She laughed, devastated by the twinkle in those blue eyes. Land sakes, she was a sucker for blue eyes. How often did Georgie defuse a righteous dudgeon with a teary flash or a happy twinkle? And his sweet baby eyes lacked the depth and inner brightness of Colin Garret's.

Garret plucked his wallet from the back pocket of his

corduroy jeans and produced a credit card. "I trust plastic is okay."

"Absolutely. We like to evoke an old-fashioned feel, but we aren't stupid."

Chuckling, he leaned on the counter while she swiped the card with one hand. Georgie immediately reached for his nose. "I'm sorry," she apologized, dipping in order to derail Georgie's grasp. "He seems to have this fixation on noses lately."

"Aw, that's okay," Colin Garret said, snagging Georgie's hand with two fingers. "I like kids."

Georgie immediately tugged Mr. Garret's fingers to his mouth.

"Sweetheart, no," Lauren scolded gently. To Mr. Garret she explained, "He's cutting teeth. Wants to chew on everything."

"I understand," Garret said, addressing himself to Georgie. "He sure is a jewel." His gaze switched abruptly to Lauren. "Is he yours?"

"Yes," Lauren answered firmly, as if saying it could make it so.

Colin Garret's voice dropped into the low range of silkiness. "Your husband must be very proud to have such a family."

Delight suffused Lauren. "Oh, I'm not married!" she blurted, only belatedly realizing that such a declaration would require explanation. "What I mean is, o-officially I'm Georgie's foster mother."

"Georgie?" he queried softly, letting a small fist wrap around his long forefinger.

"That's what I call him," she said, brushing down the cowlick at his hairline, which immediately sprang up again. "His real name is George Dalton. George Dalton Cole, after my grandfather."

"It's a fine name," Colin Garret said, tugging playfully against Georgie's fist, "a solid, man's name. George."

Lauren noted that his hands were large and capable but employed with a measured gentleness guaranteed not to injure so small a child.

"It's kind of old-fashioned," Lauren admitted, "but it seemed appropriate since he was born here at the lodge I inherited from my grandfather."

Garret looked up, an odd intensity in his very blue eyes. "The boy? The boy was born here at the lodge?"

"In Room 17," she confirmed. "It was the darnedest thing. This woman checked in and then disappeared, leaving this little angel behind. No one heard a thing, and you know she must have suffered, giving birth alone like that. But how she could just abandon her own child?" Lauren shook her head. "I can't conceive of such a thing."

"I absolutely agree," he said coldly.

His finely sculpted face suddenly appeared set in stone, and Lauren shivered. Mercy, he was fine, but she wouldn't want to be on the receiving end of his indignation. That look could freeze lava. Still, like a seething volcano or a cracking ice floe, he was fascinating to observe. Electric-blue eyes, set deeply beneath straight brows that curved only on the outer ends, were fringed in thick black lashes that any woman would covet. High, prominent cheekbones offset a straight, longish nose, beneath which a wide, mobile mouth that could only be called beautiful topped a square, utterly masculine chin. The combination of soft and hard features was breathtaking. It was a wholly masculine, yet profoundly sensual face. Suddenly he relaxed.

"Well, he's a fine boy, and you've obviously taken excellent care of him," Colin Garret said huskily.

She smiled, feeling oddly warmed by his praise. "Believe me, it's been my pleasure. He's the best little thing you've ever seen." She smoothed Georgie's hair again. "I can't imagine my life without him anymore." She hugged him tight and received a messy kiss in return. Laughing, she wiped her face. Colin Garret laughed, too. Lauren heard herself asking, "Do you have any children?"

His smile faded. Finally he said, "I'm not married, either."

"Ah." Her heart pounded a little harder. To hide her interest, she addressed her son. "Guess everyone can't be as lucky as us, huh, Georgie?"

Colin Garret straightened, saying, "I'd better get my bag."

"Would you like some help?" she asked, reaching toward the bell at the end of the counter.

"Not necessary, thanks. It's just a single bag. I'll need a room key, though."

"Oh." Heat suffused her face. "I'm so sorry. Georgie does tend to distract me."

"Completely understandable," he said.

She snatched the key from the drawer and slid it across the counter. "I hope you enjoy your stay with us."

"I'm sure I will."

"We're serving dinner until nine in the dining room. Tonight's specialty is trout."

"Great." He moved toward the foyer. "I'll be seeing you around, I'm sure."

"Oh, I'm always here," Laura said by way of confirmation. "Both of us are, aren't we, Georgie?"

"Then I'll be seeing you, too, George," the delectable and single Mr. Garret said, waving his key. Georgie waved his fist in return, and Colin Garret went out, smiling broadly.

"Well," Lauren said, pressing her forehead to the baby's, "he's just about good enough to eat, don't you think?" She drew back and smoothed that stubborn cowlick again—to no avail whatsoever. "You know what?" she whispered. "You could almost be his own little boy. Did you know that? Blue eyes, black hair. Yes, indeed. No one would ever know that he wasn't your real daddy. And my chances of keeping you would certainly improve if I was married, don't you think?" She sighed, aware that she was dreaming—dreaming up trouble.

It was an old habit. She used to sit in the park in Santa Fe and dream up romantic scenarios around the attractive men who passed by her. But she'd long ago given up waiting for Mr. Right to come along. It had been part and parcel of her decision to try to make a go of the lodge. To that point it had seemed as if her whole life had been geared toward finding someone to love and to love her in return, only to be disappointed time and again. Even her degree in accounting had been more an unconscious product of her desire to meet that right man than a love of the profession. Eventually she'd realized that she couldn't waste her life waiting for love to come along and sweep her off her feet. Things were different for her now. She had real purpose to her life, and that was more important than any silly dream.

It hadn't been an easy decision, though. She'd known that leaving Santa Fe and moving north to the sparsely populated Moreno Valley very likely meant giving up any thought of husband and family. But then, at twenty-seven, she hadn't trusted herself to make a decent marriage and start a family. Yet, here she was at twenty-nine, living in one of the most beautiful spots on earth, a mother to the most darling little boy in the whole wide world and proprietor of a charming inn.

"Who needs a husband?" she asked Georgie. "You're all I need, little man. You and this place. That's all I'll ever need."

Now if she could only keep them. Didn't her selfish brother understand that giving up the lodge could damage her claim on Georgie? She'd convinced the Child Welfare

Office in Taos that Georgie's mother must have meant for
her to care for the boy and that running the lodge made it
possible for her to do so with ease and constant attention.
Almost any other job would have required her to find day
care. This way she could keep Georgie with her every minute. She hugged his little body close and kissed his temple
while he softly babbled baby words that no adult could
understand. With one hand she opened a drawer and swept
the offending letter from her brother into it, then slammed
the drawer shut with a thrust of her hip. She would keep
them. Somehow she would keep them both, the lodge and
Georgie. She dared not think otherwise.

Colin let the door to the inn silently swing closed behind
him before he put back his head and sucked in a deep,
relieved breath. He hadn't let himself believe it until he'd
actually seen the boy, but there could be no real doubt now.
His son. He'd finally found his son.

Thea had done her best to ensure that he would never
know where she had left the infant, taunting him with the
knowledge that he, who valued family above all else, would
never know where or with whom his son was. Not even
court-ordered commitment for mental instability had convinced her to reveal the child's whereabouts. In the endless
months since she had returned to Albuquerque, no longer
pregnant, to taunt him with the loss of his child, he'd spent
a fortune, tracking her across three states until finally he'd
gotten wind of a newborn abandoned at Christmas in the
high, remote Moreno Valley where reporters rarely trav-
eled. After discovering the child's whereabouts, he'd made
arrangements to see for himself if the baby might be his.
Now that he was convinced, he could hardly wait to get
back to Albuquerque and take the paternity test.

A sudden vision wavered before his mind's eye. Her face
was almost triangular with a broad brow and a delicate,

almost pointed chin. Likewise, her golden hazel eyes were enormous, her mouth a small, perfect bow with just a snub of a slightly upturned nose between. Her long, wavy hair worn with thick bangs combined shades of gold and sand with a warm, medium-ash brown. Lauren Cole was not a classically beautiful woman, but she was unique and radiated an intrinsic warmth that attracted him, especially when that warmth was focused on his son. He hadn't expected that, hadn't even considered it. He'd assumed with great relief that the child was receiving adequate care through the welfare system, but his own experience with foster care had prepared him to expect a limited, almost impersonal fondness at best on the part of the care giver. He hadn't reckoned on Lauren Cole. She was a complication he hadn't counted on, but he was grateful for the loving attention she obviously lavished on the boy.

Taking out his cell phone, he punched a couple of buttons, only to hear that his call could not be completed. He'd have to dial Jeff from the room. Anxious to speak with his best friend and attorney, he put away the cell phone and hurried toward the popular model of sport utility vehicle that was his chosen transportation. The sooner he spoke with Jeff, the sooner he could rest easy. He felt certain that it was just a matter of staking his claim now, but he could see no reason that Lauren Cole should be unduly hurt by it. He could afford to move carefully. He had found his son, and the child was well and happy. Suddenly yanking him away from the only mother he'd ever known would do none of them any good, though Colin would like nothing more than to wrap his arms around the boy and hold him close from now on.

Patience, he counseled himself. The difficult part's over. You'll have your son home in Albuquerque by Christmas. His son. What a Christmas this would be! His son. Georgie.

George. George Garret. Yes, he liked that. George Colin,
perhaps. George Colin Garret. What fun they would have!

But it wouldn't be all fun and games, of course. He had
some very real concerns to address. He'd have to start in-
terviewing nannies, fixing up a nursery. The state had already revoked Thea's parental rights, for abandonment, but
Jeff was working on making the revocation permanent once
her identity—and his—was made known. He needed to
make a list of supplies necessary for caring for a child of
Georgie's age. Excitement pumping through his veins,
Colin made short work of depositing his bags in his room
and reached for the bedside telephone.

Lauren made her way through the tables scattered art-
fully about the dining room, Georgie perched on her hip.
One tiny hand clutched the front of her sweater and the
other clamped around her ponytail, pulling her head straight
even as she walked with her occupied hip thrust to the side.
It was a posture she'd mastered over the months, one to
which she hardly gave a thought until her spine began to
ache.

The dinner rush was over, most of the inn's guests having taken their meals an hour or more earlier. What tables
were occupied were filled with walk-ins from the village,
some of them residents, some tourists. One inn guest whom
she seemed aware of no matter his location occupied a
small table placed against the glass wall overlooking the
lake. Trying her best to pretend ignorance of Colin Garret,
she smiled at one of the town councilmen and his wife.

"How's your meal?"

"Y'all got the best food in town," the councilman declared, forking up a taste of enchilada.

"I'll tell Shelby you said so."

"That boy is growing so fast," the wife commented

kindly, nodding at Georgie. "Before long he'll be tall as you."

"That ain't saying much," the councilman teased. "She can't be more than an inch or two over five feet."

"Three inches, actually," Lauren informed him with false hauteur.

"Theee!" Georgie echoed, showing his teeth in a pleased laugh.

"We're learning to count," Lauren explained over the chuckles. "However, at the moment everything begins and ends with three." She chatted a moment longer, proudly accepting praise for Georgie's aptitude with numbers, then turned once more toward the kitchen.

Colin Garret came almost instantly to his feet, a smile splitting his handsome face, his white linen napkin clutched in one hand. A butterfly cut loose in Lauren's chest, but she did her best not to show it. Colin Garret had been everything solicitous and attentive in the past forty-eight hours, seemingly content to laze around the lodge and engage her in conversation whenever she had a moment. He paid particular attention to Georgie, as if knowing that was the surest, swiftest way to her heart. Lauren reminded herself yet again that he would be returning to Albuquerque in the morning, very probably never to return. Meanwhile, however, she didn't have the strength of will to deny herself his company.

"Colin, are you enjoying your meal?" she asked as she drew to a halt next to his table.

"Very much," he assured her. "I've just finished actually. Why don't you and George join me for a few minutes?"

Not wanting to appear too eager, Lauren addressed herself to the child. "What do you say, Georgie? Want to sit with Colin for a little while?"

Colin held out his hands imploring to the baby, and to

Lauren's surprise, Georgie responded by reaching for him. Colin started to take him into his arms, but aborted the effort at the last moment, casting a look down at her. "May I?"

"Sure. If Georgie's comfortable with it, so am I."

Smiling, Colin reached out again, and the boy went easily into his arms. Colin chuckled. "I've read that babies are sometimes clingy and fearful at this age, but he seems quite trusting."

Lauren slipped into the chair opposite his and waited for him to sit with the baby in his lap. "He may be more trusting than the average child his age," she conceded. "I think the fact that so many people come in and out has something to do with it."

Colin turned the boy in his lap and lifted him to a standing position. "Well, I think he's just a very bright and confident young man. You're smarter than the average baby, aren't you, George? That's what I think, and I'm right, aren't I?" He nodded his head encouragingly, and Georgie mimicked the movement, nodding his own dark head obediently. Colin laughed and hugged him tight, addressing himself to Lauren. "He's just a delight, an absolute delight. You've done very well with him."

"Thank you."

"I wish I'd had a foster mother with half your concern and affinity for children," he said lightly.

Lauren was shocked. "You were in foster care?"

Nodding casually, he turned Georgie in his lap and seated him, grasping his tiny hands in his own huge ones.

"I was older than George when the state took me from my father. My mom died when I was four, and Dad was not the most conscientious of parents. He sometimes forgot where he'd left me for days at a time. When I was six, one of the so-called sitters grew impatient and called Child Welfare. He didn't fight them when they decided to terminate his parental rights, didn't even show up for the hearing, and I was terribly angry about that for a long time."

"Oh, my," Lauren breathed, imagining what he must have gone through.

"I hated the whole world just then," he went on conversationally, "and that included the foster parents to whom I was assigned. Before long I was transferred to another family, where I was literally lost in the crowd. They had eight kids there, and I acted out just to get attention. By the time the state assigned me a counselor who really connected with me, I was fourteen and had been through four more placements. I spent the next three years in a group home, but by then I'd figured out that I could help myself with a positive attitude and some hard work. I graduated high school with honors and went to college on a scholarship."

"That took a lot of personal strength and gumption," Lauren told him.

"Thanks," he replied tersely.

"Do you know what happened to your father?" she asked gently.

He nodded, looking down at Georgie's little fingers wrapped around his own. "I found him when I was twenty-one. He was living on the streets, old before his time. I tried to take care of him, but it was no use. He died of pneumonia when I was twenty-three. At the end he told me how proud he was of me and how sorry he was for the way he'd turned out. He told me it would all have been different if my mother hadn't died, that family was everything to her and she was everything to him."

"Do you know what took her?" Lauren asked quietly.

He nodded. "It was a fire, a short in an electrical appliance, I think. Neighbors pulled me through a bedroom window, but she didn't know that and went back in after me. When Dad realized what she'd done, he tried to go after her, but it was too late by then. They had to hold him back. I think maybe he blamed me, but he never said that, of course.''

Lauren couldn't help reaching out to him. Leaning forward slightly, she sent a hand across the table toward him. He let go of one of Georgie's hands and gripped her fingers in his. ''You've been through so much,'' she said softly.

He shrugged. ''Everybody's got a story to tell, something that hurts them. Most of mine is in the past. In fact, the last decade or so has been very rewarding, with one notable exception.''

''And that is?''

For a moment she thought she'd overstepped, that he wouldn't deign to answer. They were little more than strangers, after all. If it seemed that they shared some sort of innate affinity, well, it was very likely all in her dreams. But then he began to speak again.

''I've made some mistakes in the romance department,'' he said bluntly. ''I guess everyone does.''

''Some of us more than others,'' Lauren muttered.

He chuckled. ''Well, I'm definitely one of those. You know what, though? Sometimes even our mistakes bring blessings with them.''

''There goes that positive attitude again,'' she quipped, and he laughed.

''Hey, it works! Don't knock it unless you've tried it.''

''I'll remember that.''

Grinning, he removed his hand from hers and turned his full attention to Georgie again, whispering nonsense that made the baby screw up his face in a toothy grin.

Lauren watched them indulgently, delighted that someone else could be so easily charmed by the boy. Suddenly Georgie yawned broadly.

''Whoa!'' Colin Garret chuckled delightedly. ''You're apt to turn yourself wrong side out there, buddy.''

"It's his bedtime," Lauren explained, quickly getting to her feet. "We were just headed to the kitchen for a snack. It's kind of a ritual with us."

"Is that so?" Colin asked in a musing tone.

Lauren stepped around the table, reaching for Georgie. Colin Garret got to his feet and delivered the boy into her arms. "You sleep well, youngster," he said almost yearningly.

"He always does," Lauren informed him happily. "Sometimes I sit at night and just watch him, sleeping the sleep of the innocent, you know, without a care or a fear in the world."

Georgie laid his head on Lauren's shoulder and wrapped his arms around her neck. Colin patted his back, but his blue eyes sought out hers. "I imagine you can take credit for that," he said. "If he's content and untroubled, it must be because he feels secure and loved. He's lucky to have you."

Lauren smiled. "Thank you. I hope so, because I know how lucky I am to have him."

Something very like pain flitted across Colin Garret's face, but then he cleared his throat and put on a smile. "I'll, um, be leaving in the morning," he said unnecessarily. "I'd like to take this opportunity to tell you how much I've enjoyed my stay—and meeting you, both of you."

"That's very kind of you," Lauren replied. "I hope you'll visit us again."

"Oh, absolutely," he stated. "You can count on it."

He sounded so certain, so sincere. Lauren felt those butterflies take off again, despite her every effort to squelch them. "Well," she finally said, "we'd better say goodnight."

He smiled warmly. She sensed just a touch of something else in that smile, a reluctance or envy or…she couldn't be sure what it was, but it struck a chord deeply within her. He shifted his gaze to the boy. "Good night, George."

Lauren started toward the kitchen, but suddenly his hand shot out and collided with her forearm and hip. "Colin?"

He jerked his hand away, seeming embarrassed. "I, uh, I just— Thank you. F-for everything."

Something about the way he said it lifted the hairs on the back of her neck. What was she missing? There was more here than met the eye. Wasn't there? She shook her head. No, of course not. Countless others had said those very words to her. It was almost a given. She made herself smile and make the standard reply. "You're very welcome. Thank you for choosing to stay with us. We look forward to seeing you again soon."

She left him then, quite certain that she would never see him again.

Chapter Two

She took the call herself, eleven days after he'd left them, and recognized his voice instantly.

"I'd like to make a reservation, please."

"Colin? Colin Garret, is that you?"

He laughed. "Lauren? I hoped I'd be speaking to you. How are you?"

"Fine. And you?"

"Ready for a little relaxation. How's George?"

She smiled to herself. "Georgie's great. He has a new tooth, and he's finally showing some interest in walking, but it's almost analytical. He stands there, and he looks at his little feet, and he looks at the floor, and he looks where he wants to go, and then he looks at me as if to say, 'Show me again.' You really ought to see him."

"I'd love to," Colin said, his voice husky and rough. He cleared his throat. "And maybe I can. How about that reservation?"

She pulled the reservation book from its cubbyhole behind the desk and opened it. "When were you thinking?"

"As soon as possible, actually." His tone dropped a notch, warm silk sliding across her nerve endings. "Something at your lodge keeps tugging at me," he said. "I've wanted to tell you about it, but I convinced myself that it was too soon."

Her heart suddenly in her throat, she gulped. Too soon? Oh, if only he knew how she'd fantasized about him! Could he have feelings for her, too? Why else would he be returning so soon, hinting about his interest? She searched the book, her hands eagerly turning pages. "How's the twenty-third?"

"That's almost two weeks."

The sound of disappointment in his voice made her ecstatic. Eager, was he? Well, he wasn't the only one. Facts were facts, though. "I—I'm sorry, but we're booked solid, and from the moment the ski slopes open we have a waiting list. October twenty-third is the best I can do, unless someone cancels."

He sighed. "Okay. Put me down for the twenty-third."

She quickly jotted down his name in the required space, asking, "And how long will you be staying with us?"

"Through the weekend at least."

She smiled, writing. "That's five days."

"Only five?"

She laughed and inadvertently gave herself away. "You can't have worked hard enough to warrant that much vacation in only eleven days."

"Has it only been eleven days?" he asked softly.

She gulped. And lied. "Th-that's what my book says."

"Seems a lot longer to me."

She bit her tongue to keep from agreeing with him. Finally she said, "I'll let you know if anyone cancels."

"Please do. Let me give you my personal cell number so you can be sure of reaching me."

She quickly jotted the number down and read it back to him.

"Right," he said, adding, "but you don't have to wait for a cancellation to call, you know. In fact, if young George should figure out the theory of walking and manage to put it into practice, I'd love to know."

Warmth spread through her chest. "I think he's still got a few weeks of thinking to do, but there's no telling what brilliance he'll demonstrate in the meantime."

He chuckled. "Maybe I'd better call and check up on him from time to time."

Ka-whump went her heart. "Maybe you'd better."

"Great. Tomorrow too soon?

She couldn't keep the smile from her voice. "Not at all."

"Talk to you tomorrow, then."

She hung up feeling as though she'd just won the lottery. It hadn't been her imagination; he really was interested. And he was absolutely taken with Georgie. Or was that just a means of getting close to her? If so, he couldn't have chosen a more certain route to her heart. Not that she really doubted his sincerity. His joy in Georgie's company was as obvious as her own.

An errant thought burst into her consciousness, winning consideration before she could discipline it. What if they should marry? Her chances of actually adopting Georgie would be greatly enhanced. But how ironic would that be? She'd given up on men, put away thoughts of love and marriage and family when she'd decided to make this old lodge her life. Who could have imagined that she'd find those very things in this remote mountain hideaway?

She was getting far ahead of herself here. She could be reading this situation all wrong. After all, how likely was it that a drop-dead-gorgeous man like Colin Garret would be interested in plain, little old her? And yet, she couldn't quite convince herself that he wouldn't be glad to see her.

Suddenly the world seemed rife with wonderful possibilities, and on October twenty-third, if not sooner, she'd know what those possibilities were.

The order came a few days later. Mercedes Alonzo, the social worker from Taos drove over the mountain to deliver it in person.

"I'm sorry, Lauren," she said, balancing her coffee cup on her knee. "It came from the state office. Nothing's certain, you understand, but you have to take the boy to the lab to have blood drawn. I've made an appointment on the twenty-sixth at 2:00 p.m. I hope that's convenient."

Lauren swallowed the bitter lump that burned the back of her throat and set her own coffee cup and saucer on the low table between them. "We'll be there."

"It could be nothing," the caseworker said, trying to ease the blow. "These tests turn up negative all the time. Some of these women have no idea who fathered their children, and since we don't even know the mother's true identity in this case, we're just drawing straws here. But it has to be done. You have to take Georgie for paternity testing."

"I understand," Lauren whispered, glad that she'd brought Mercedes into her private apartment for this meeting. "At least you gave me some time to get used to the idea. I appreciate that."

"You've done exceedingly well by the child," Mercedes assured her. "There can be no question of that. But we're required by law to give the natural parents precedence."

Lauren nodded. "I know I have you to thank for being named Georgie's foster mother in the first place," she said honestly. Looking over at the child playing quietly on the rug with a set of nesting cups, she added, "Whatever happens, I'll have had these last ten months."

"Don't give up hope just yet," the woman told her. "It'll be weeks before we know anything, and no one can predict what the outcome will be."

Putting on a determined smile, Lauren stiffened her spine. "You're right. I won't worry until I know I have something to worry about." *And in the meantime, Colin is coming,* she added silently. Why that should offer such comfort she didn't know, but somehow it did, and she clung to the thought with all the strength of a desperate mother clutching a helping hand. She'd learned to look forward to their daily chats, even though they often spoke of only the most mundane things. Colin was coming, and she still had hope. Somehow she had to believe that it was going to be all right.

The weatherman had predicted isolated sleet around Taos, particularly in the mountains, so he bypassed Santa Fe and took I-25 up almost to Raton, cutting across 64 to Cimarron. The lodge was on the Cimarron side of the valley, after all, so the route cost him only about thirty extra miles. It was worth it just for the view. Coming down off the mountain and around the final curve, he was struck to awe by the sight of the lake nestled against the mountain slopes, a slick piece of sky fallen to brown earth. And there, right in front of him, tucked up against the sheer cliff atop which the silver road curved, stood the white chimneys of the lodge, rising like sentinels from the red tile roof. His heartbeat quickened.

It had been less than a month, but it felt both like yesterday and an eternity since he'd first set foot in the place where his son waited and flourished. He turned left at the foot of the hill. Fresh gravel had been laid over the drive, and it shifted and crunched beneath the tires of his SUV as he eased it through the gate posts and found a parking place between two rental cars. Yanking his bags from the trunk, he hurried toward the lobby door.

She came out from behind the desk to welcome him personally, both hands held out to him. He noted with appreciation that her hair was down, falling in a sleek, straight curtain across her shoulder blades, the bangs tousled becomingly and calling attention to those big gold-speckled green eyes.

How pretty she was, how completely unique with her golden coloring and piquant face. He found himself glad that his son had been able to look upon that arresting face all these months, to see the fondness and concern glowing in those enormous eyes. How much better that Georgie should know the gentle kindness of a stranger than the vagaries of his own mother's emotional instability. But Lauren wasn't really a stranger, not to Georgie—and in an odd way, not to him, either. She was the woman who had given his son the best start in life that she could, and he was overcome with gratitude at the sight of her again.

Dropping his bags, he took her hands in his and pulled her close, bowing his head to kiss her cheek. She smelled of vanilla and violets and baby powder. Pushing her off to look down at her, he said, "You're a sight for sore eyes."

She beamed. "Thank you. So are you. I'm sorry we couldn't get you in earlier. Foiled by our own success, I'm afraid."

He chuckled. "Hey, don't knock it. Success is a good thing." He couldn't keep himself from looking around the terra-cotta foyer. "Where's Georgie?"

"Ponce and Maria have him in the break room. He's taken to mugging Ponce's every expression, and they get a big kick out of that."

"Ponce, he's that kid who works around here part-time, isn't he?"

"And Maria is his sister. They've been around Georgie

since the day he was born. He adores them both. Let's get you checked in and go reclaim him, shall we?''

Colin smiled. ''I'd love to.''

Georgie was a little reticent at first. After all, he couldn't be expected to remember everyone who came to the inn, but once Ponce and Maria returned to work, Colin soon coaxed him into his lap. A few minutes later Georgie was bouncing happily on Colin's knee.

''Giddy-up, giddy-up, all fall down!'' Colin sang, straightening his legs so that Georgie tumbled gently backward, much to the child's giggling delight.

Lauren joined him, unable to resist as she crouched down to smooth his cowlick with the tips of her fingers. ''It's nice to have our friend Colin back with us, isn't it?''

Georgie fought his way up into a sitting position once more, tugging on Colin's hands to right himself.

'''Gin,'' he demanded.

Colin promptly lifted his knees and began the game again. This time when Georgie went ''tumbling down,'' Lauren bent forward and kissed him noisily under the chin, loving the way he giggled and wiggled.

''My dad had a cleft chin like that,'' Colin mused absently.

Lauren looked up in surprise. ''Did he?'' Colin himself had only a slight depression in his chin.

''I take after my mom—well, except for size. She was a small woman. But I got her dark hair and blue eyes. Though, in fairness, Dad's eyes were blue, too.''

''They must have been attractive people,'' Lauren heard herself saying.

''Why, thank you.'' He lifted a dark eyebrow, a slight smile on his lips. ''Some people,'' he said, ''believe that the combination of black hair and blue eyes are not to be trusted.''

She pushed up to her feet, helping Georgie sit up again with a hand at his back. Colin lifted his knees and protectively locked his big hands together in the small of Georgie's back. "I don't put much stock in old wives' tales," she said meaningfully, and Colin smiled up at her.

"Good," he said. "Then you and Georgie won't mind joining me for dinner?"

"Actually," she countered, folding her arms, "I thought you might join us—in our private apartment."

The warmth that blazed in those blue eyes threatened to melt her bones. "I'd be delighted," he said through a wide smile. He turned that smile on Georgie. "Just delighted."

Colin lay on his back on the floor, Georgie atop his chest. Suddenly Georgie lunged forward and captured Colin's nose in his pudgy fist, squealing with delight while Colin laughed. A deep and amazing contentment settled over Lauren. She curled her legs beneath her on the couch and sipped cocoa from a steaming mug, happily tired. Suddenly she remembered the appointment.

"Oh, gosh. I've been meaning to tell you something," she said, sitting up straight.

Colin looked past Georgie's dimpled knuckles. "Wha's dat?" he asked in a nasally tone created by Georgie's grip on his nose.

Lauren giggled, despite the severity of her situation. "I have to take Georgie into Taos tomorrow afternoon."

Colin sat up then, dislodging Georgie's grasp. "Oh? Aren't the roads iced in that direction? I came in through Cimarron because the weatherman was predicting sleet in the mountains on the other side of the valley."

"That was two days ago, silly," she told him. "The sand trucks have been out repeatedly since then. Besides, I don't have a choice." She looked down at the mug in her hand.

"I didn't want to say anything, but I got a court order to take Georgie for paternity testing."

She had the definite impression that his facial expression was carefully schooled. "What time do you have to be there?"

"Two o'clock."

"Have you thought what you'll do if…*when* his rightful parent comes forward to claim him?"

She shook her head. "I can't. I'll come apart if I do."

"Lauren—"

She sat forward and placed the mug on the coffee table, cutting him off. She didn't want words of comfort. She wanted to forget. "The caseworker says it will be weeks before we know anything for sure. No point worrying about it now."

He opened his mouth as if he would argue, but then he closed it again and looked down at Georgie, who had struggled to his feet and was trying to climb Colin's chest like a wall. Colin swept him up into the crook of his arm, and Georgie promptly got a death grip on his ear.

"Errr," the baby said.

"It's part of a matched set," Colin teased, easing the grip of those tiny fingers, "and I'd like to keep it that way." He tickled Georgie to distract him, and Georgie virtually collapsed in giggles, confident that Colin would catch him and ease his descent.

Lauren watched the play with burgeoning gratitude. It was easy to forget tomorrow when tonight was so sweet. Suddenly Colin looked up at her. "I'll take you tomorrow," he said. "My truck has four-wheel drive."

She smiled and nodded. "I'd like that. We both would."

He mumbled something that sounded like, "The least I can do," but Georgie's giggles suddenly erupted into belly laughs as Colin captured his stocking feet and pretended to gobble them. Lauren sat back and curled her knees up once again, content for now to do nothing more than watch the two dark heads bob as they played together on the floor. Tomorrow would be soon enough to begin to worry.

"Oh, man," Colin whispered, "just look at that."

"Were we ever that innocent, do you suppose?" Lauren asked softly.

Georgie wrinkled his nose, then smiled in his sleep, eyes fluttering behind his lids.

"Not me. Wonder what he's dreaming about."

"It's happy, whatever it is," Lauren said.

"I could watch him all night."

Lauren smiled and picked up one of the receivers from the dresser. She pressed it into Colin's hand, whispering, "I'll let you carry this into the other room, then, and if he cries, you can deal with it."

An introspective smile crept into place. "Deal." He clipped the monitor receiver to his belt.

She pushed him gently into the hall, pulling the door closed behind them. "Adult time," she said, ushering him down the hallway. When they reached the kitchen, she made a detour. "How about a glass of wine?"

"Sounds great." He leaned a shoulder against the door frame, watching as she moved behind the blue-tiled counter.

The kitchen in this apartment was barely functional with a two-burner stove, a bar-size refrigerator and a small microwave, but with a restaurant in the same building, it was adequate. She decanted the bottle on the counter and let it breathe while she took down two glasses, explaining, "This is the house red, a fruity little wine with a gentle bouquet and a rosy cheek, at least according to the review in the Taos paper."

Colin chuckled. "A rosy cheek? What does that mean?"

She filled a glass and carried it to him. "Well, as best I

can figure, when you hold a swig in the pocket of your cheek, it tastes rather like roses.''

He tried that, first swishing the wine around in his mouth. Finally he swallowed. "Hmm, can't say I've ever tasted roses, but the wine is definitely good.''

She smiled at that and took up her own glass. "How about we take this into the living room in front of the fire?"

"Sounds good.''

He led the way, strolling into the living area and the pale, tweedy sofa positioned in front of the beehive fireplace. Gentleman that he was, he waited until she picked a spot and sat down, then lowered himself into place beside her, leaning back and crossing his long legs in front of him. "I could get used to this,'' he said after several moments of watching the flames.

She sighed. "I know what you mean. It's as though this valley is imbued with a stress-relieving aura. I've never been busier, really, and it isn't as if I don't have a few worries, but they're hard to remember in this place. Whatever it is that makes the burdens seem lighter, they ought to bottle it.''

He cut her a look while casually sliding an arm around her shoulders. "Ever heard of fresh air?"

She laughed. "You may be right. I know I'd hate to be fighting my battles in some place like Albuquerque or Los Angeles, anyplace like that.''

"Albuquerque hardly equates with L.A.,'' he said, "but I'm more interested in these worries and battles you speak of. Something heavy going on?''

She struggled for a moment with the thought of telling him all her woes, but then she shook her head. "I don't want to talk about it.''

"You sure?''

"It'll work out,'' she insisted. "I don't want to ruin this moment by rehashing my problems.''

"Fine by me," he said, and sipped his wine. "Just remember I'm here if you need me."

A warmth that had nothing to do with the wine or the fire spread through her, and she heard herself blurting, "I thought men like you were figments of the collective imagination."

He seemed genuinely surprised. Leaning forward, he placed his wineglass on the coffee table and turned slightly toward her. "Whatever do you mean?"

She rolled her eyes. "You know exactly what I mean. You're handsome, successful, kind, gentle, affectionate. And you're wonderful with Georgie. Every woman's dream man."

He took one of her hands in his. "You don't know everything there is to know about me. Don't assign me too many virtues until you do."

"You aren't married, are you?" she asked teasingly—although, he couldn't know that it wasn't a joke.

He drew back. "Absolutely not. Never have been."

She tried not to let her relief show. "Have you wanted to be?"

"Yes. And I've made some mistakes because of it, frankly."

"Well, we're both members of that club," she said wryly.

He chuckled. "I guess everyone our age is."

"Speak for yourself, old-timer," she teased. "How old are you, anyway?"

"Thirty-six, at least a decade older than you. I only meant that we're both single adults."

"One of us is more adult than you think," she quipped. "I'm twenty-nine. Thirty in June."

"My birthday's in September."

"Would you kiss me?" she heard herself asking. The astounded look on his face must have equaled her own.

"Oh, heck," she said, figuring she might as well take the bull by the horns now that she'd let it out of the chute. "Just don't run."

He didn't run. He fell back into the corner of the sofa as if in he'd had the props knocked out from under him. Licking her lips and bolstering her courage, she leaned forward. His eyes grew wide as her face drew near, but then the lids dropped down like shades with weights attached. She closed her own eyes and pressed her mouth to his.

At first his lips were incredibly soft, but then they firmed and moved beneath hers, accompanied by a faint moan. Suddenly his arms came around her and pulled her down against his chest. He sent a hand into the hair at the back of her head, tilting it just so as he parted her lips with his and slid his tongue into her mouth.

She shivered at the sweet invasion and melted into him. His tongue plunged deeply, his hand tightening the pressure on the back of her head, grinding their mouths together. Something hot and liquid burst low in the pit of her belly, shocking her. Instantly she became aware of the hard ridge cradled against her. With a mixture of awed delight and sheer terror, she realized that she'd awakened a passion with depths heretofore unknown to her—and she wasn't the only one shaking with the effort to leash it.

Suddenly he scrambled up into a straighter sitting position, his mouth clinging to hers even as he withdrew bodily. She levered her weight away from him. At the last moment, before their mouths parted, his hands came up and gently stroked her face. Then he pulled his head back and let it drop to the edge of the cushions.

Embarrassment at her audacity heated her face. Seemingly sensing this, he cupped the back of her head and pulled her facedown into the hollow of his shoulder, holding her lightly against him. She sighed and closed her hands in the fabric of his sweater. He let out a deep, gusting breath, and she gradually became aware of the rapid beat of his heart, which matched her own.

She turned her face, resting her cheek against his shoulder, and slid her feet down to the floor, twisting so that she was once again sitting beside him. He wrapped his arms loosely about her and simply held her until their breathing evened and their hearts slowed. Finally he reached for the hand that she'd allowed to fall to his thigh and threaded his fingers through hers.

"Life is more complicated than this," he said gently. "I have to keep reminding myself of that when I'm with you."

"Maybe it doesn't have to be," she mused. "Maybe we're making it more complicated than it really is."

"If I let myself believe that," he whispered, "I'll be making love to you before either of us has a chance to think logically."

She smiled at that, more than content at the moment. "You're right. Our lives are centered three, four hours apart."

"There is that, yes."

"And Georgie has to be considered."

His hold on her hand tightened, but he said nothing to that.

She sighed. "We don't know everything about each other yet."

"We need time," he agreed.

"But at least we know the basic attraction is real," she said smugly, turning her face up.

His grin was quick and honest. "We do know that," he admitted, and kissed her quickly before beginning to disengage himself. "I'd better go before all my good intentions disappear."

She didn't argue. She loved that he was so much the gentleman, especially when he so obviously did not want to be. "Will I see you in the morning?"

"I'm not sure," he said, getting to his feet. "I brought work with me, and I haven't even looked at it yet. I promised myself a full day tomorrow, but if I'm going with you to take Georgie for the test tomorrow, I'd better see how much I can get accomplished tonight and in the morning."

"I understand. I'll be pretty busy myself."

"Let's plan to meet for lunch, at least. How's twelve-thirty?" He reached down a hand, and she placed hers in it, letting him pull her to her feet.

"That ought to work."

"Walk me to the door?" he asked softly, and she nodded, sliding her arm about his waist as he looped his about her shoulders. When they reached the door to the outer hallway, he unclipped the monitor from his belt and handed it to her, saying, "I guess you'll be needing this."

She nodded and dropped the receiver into the pocket of her cardigan. "Good night," she whispered, lifting up onto her tiptoes. He bent his head and kissed her once more, his mouth lingering tenderly against hers.

"Good night, Lauren."

He opened the door and slipped out into the dimly lit corridor that led to the great room. Lauren closed and locked the door from sheer habit. Then she wrapped her arms around herself and sighed. She had never expected to have such hope again, and certainly not with a man like Colin Garret.

Colin ricocheted off first one wall and then another, literally reeling. He wondered if the soles of his shoes were smoking. His toes were certainly still curled.

He felt as if he'd been hit with a sledgehammer. He was aware of the attraction, of course, had been from the first moment he'd laid eyes on her, but nothing had prepared him for the wallop carried in her kiss. Not that he hadn't been aware of the kind of possibilities wrapped up in that little woman. Not so little, he mused, remembering the feel of her breasts against his chest, the lushness of the curves that had pressed against him. His head was still spinning, and he could only hope that he hadn't said anything harmful.

He groaned, thinking of the secret he was keeping. What had possessed him to keep quiet until after the test proved his paternity? Had he really thought that would make it easier for either of them? Oh, God, what should he do now?

He had to tell her, he decided.

He didn't dare tell her, not now!

Then when? After he'd lost all control and made mad, passionate love to her? Just before he showed her the court order and walked out with Georgie?

Lord, she had to know that he would never keep her from his son. Georgie belonged with him, but no one could doubt that Lauren should remain a large part of the boy's life. She was the only parent George had ever known, after all, and such a good one. Georgie was healthy and happy and well adjusted because of her, and that would make the coming changes all the more easy for him. But what of Lauren? What was this going to do to her?

He'd thought this all through, and now everything had changed. What was happening? What did he want to happen?

Groaning again, he shoved away from the wall and moved toward the door at the end of the corridor. A neatly lettered sign on the other side read Private, and Colin couldn't help thinking that it was a monumental understatement, considering what had just happened. Pausing, he looked around the great room, barely noting the impressive antler chandeliers and rough-hewn supports and beams. One couple snuggled on the immense leather sofa in front of an equally immense fireplace that literally roared heat into the room. When he'd told Lauren that he could get used to this, he hadn't meant just relaxing in the modestly appointed private apartment beyond the door at his back. He'd meant the whole thing, the lodge itself, the valley, and yes, her, too.

He rubbed a hand over his face, resigning himself to the need for some hard thinking. Sighing, he started off across the room.

It was going to be a long night, a very long night.

Chapter Three

He woke up groggy but determined. A glance at the clock on the bedside table told him that he'd slept all of four hours, but that would have to do. He wanted to speak with Lauren at the first opportunity. The sooner he told her the truth, the sooner they could come to terms with it and decide what to do next. With luck, understanding and a little generosity on Lauren's part, they might come out of this friends, anyway. Throwing back the covers, he went to the closet and yanked down a pair of jeans and a sweatshirt. Jumping into them, he dragged on socks and athletic shoes, then brushed his teeth and ran his hands through his short, straight hair. Shaving and showering would have to wait. He wanted this monkey off his back as quickly as possible.

Halfway down the stairs he heard the shouting and recognized Lauren's voice immediately. Taking the remaining steps three at a time, he vaulted past the curious faces gathering outside the dining and great rooms. He came to a quick stop at the end of the counter in the foyer. Lauren was in place behind the counter, just as she had been the first time he'd seen her. She had faced off against a couple on the other side, a slightly built man and a pregnant woman displaying her slightly rounded belly like a weapon. None of the three seemed to even notice his arrival.

"This is the reason, Miss Stingy," the woman was saying spitefully. "We have a child to support now!"

"So do I!" Lauren shot back. "Georgie is—"

"That's a crock," the man said. "They give you money for keeping him."

"A stipend, Lawrence," she pointed out, "and there's a very good reason it's called that. Besides, it's only until I adopt him. Once he's legally mine—"

Colin gaped at her, horrified. She was actually trying to adopt George? Why hadn't he known she was trying to adopt George? Lawrence stated bluntly what Colin already knew—and Lauren couldn't possibly. Yet.

"You have about as much chance of actually adopting that kid as a snowball has in hell."

"That's not so!" Lauren insisted. "The court will consider my petition when Georgie's one year of age, and even the social worker says I'm a wonderful mother."

"You're fooling yourself, Lauren," the woman said. "They don't give babies to single parents, especially not single women with your track record."

"What's that supposed to mean?" Lauren demanded.

"You know perfectly well that you're not cut out for motherhood," the woman mumbled evasively. "If you were, some man would have married you by now."

"That's enough," Colin said, not quite prepared for the impact his carefully modulated statement would have. Utter silence descended. Every eye turned in his direction. Lauren's were filled with tears. He caught his breath.

"And what would you know about it?" the man demanded.

Colin instantly bristled, disliking the man's tone immensely. "I know that she's been an excellent mother to Georgie," he said firmly. "I know you're making a fool out of yourself in public."

The man's neck turned red, but he shot a look past Colin through the doorway. Colin turned to look at the curious faces gathered there. "You folks can go on about your business now," he said calmly, the tone of his voice brooking no argument. People began to drift away. Colin turned back to the trio in the foyer. "What's this all about?"

"Who is he?" the man hissed at Lauren.

Lauren lifted her chin. "His name is Colin Garret, if it's any of your business." She turned to Colin then, a little shamefaced. "Colin, this is my brother, Larry, and his wife, Randi."

"Miranda," the woman said. "I'm Miranda, and he's Lawrence. Why can't you get that straight?"

Lauren closed her eyes and literally bit her lip. Colin didn't blame her. What a brother and sister-in-law! He looked at Lawrence Cole. "I don't care whose brother you are," he said bluntly, "you're not talking to Lauren like that with me around."

Larry didn't even grace him with a reply. Instead he smiled grimly at Lauren. "Another one of your men, is it?"

"Probably married," Miranda muttered quite audibly.

"He is not!" Lauren hissed. "And you know that wasn't my fault! I had no idea Ford was married until his wife turned up at my office."

"So you say," Miranda scoffed, despite Lauren's wobbling chin and falling tears.

"That's it!" Colin exclaimed, no longer concerned with being reasonable. "I want you out of here!"

"You can't throw us out," Miranda began.

"Now!" Colin barked, stepping around the end of the counter. Lawrence jerked as if he'd been hit and stumbled backward toward the door, snagging his shrewish wife by the arm and towing her with him.

"You aren't going to get away from this, Lauren!" her brother cried, now that he'd put sufficient distance between him and Colin. "Granddad left this lodge to both of us!"

"And you wanted no part of it," Lauren exclaimed. "I built this place by myself, and you know it! You have no right to demand half of it now."

"We have every right," Miranda countered. "Our lawyer says so!"

"And Mother agrees!" Larry stated pompously, as if that ought to settle it.

"Well, you can just go tell Mother that I'm not giving in on this!" Lauren shouted.

"Don't think I won't!" Larry promised, hauling his wife from the building.

Despite her defiant stance, Lauren immediately crumpled, forearms on the countertop, hands shielding her face. Colin lifted a hand to the back of her head, smoothing the lustrous hair that she'd rolled into a smart chignon.

"It's all right," he said. "They're gone."

Lauren sniffed and raised her head, brushing at her tears with her fingertips. "But they'll be back. When Larry decides he wants something, he doesn't give up, especially when it's something of mine."

"Is it true that your grandfather left the lodge to both of you?" Colin asked gently.

She nodded morosely. "Yes. The will names both of us. Larry wanted to sell the place, but I wouldn't hear of it." She looked at Colin pleadingly then, adding, "I've put my life savings into this place. I even cashed in my retirement and used that. I've begged and borrowed the rest, but not one penny of it came from my brother, and now he wants half!''

Colin sighed. She was in a hell of a pickle, but he needed the answer to an even more important question. ''And are you really trying to adopt Georgie?''

She nodded again, knuckling tears from beneath her eyes. ''The social worker says I have a pretty good chance as long as neither of his natural parents comes forward before he's a year old. I can petition the courts then.''

Colin grimaced before he could stop himself. Fortunately she misunderstood.

''No, really. The fact that Georgie was born and abandoned here indicates that the mother intended for me to keep him with me, and since no one knows who his father is…''

''Lauren,'' he began, and then he purposefully bit his tongue. He couldn't tell her now, not when her brother had just essentially threatened to sue her to gain a share of the lodge, *her* lodge. Why hadn't he realized that she would want to adopt Georgie? Why hadn't he even considered it? He took a deep breath, trying to order his thoughts. ''Uh, did you get anything in writing, a-about the lodge, I mean?''

She shook her head. ''Didn't think I needed to. He's my brother, for pity's sake. He told me that if I wanted to risk my neck on restoring this place, so be it, but he'd have nothing to do with it. That was over two years ago, of course, before I put everything I had into the place to make it work.''

Sighing, she slumped over the counter once more. ''You don't know what it was like, how much I've done. And now that it's really starting to pay off, Larry wants half! It's just not fair!''

''I agree,'' he said, stepping around the counter to take her into his arms. She snuggled against his chest, warm and womanly. He took a deep breath, steeling himself against the rise of desire. "I'm sure I don't have to tell you that life isn't always fair," he said, "so I won't. I'll just say that if we each got everything we deserved, I'm sure you'd have all your heart's desires in short order."

She tilted her head back, looking up at him. "I don't know about that, but I'm glad you think so."

He smiled down at her, feeling helpless and uncertain. Worse, if he stood here a moment longer, he'd kiss her, and neither of them could really afford that just now, though she couldn't know it.

She lifted a hand to his cheek. "You haven't even shaved, and you still look good enough to eat."

He burst out laughing. He couldn't help it.

She laughed, too, and the smile transformed her face to one of perfect beauty. "Thank you for riding to my rescue," she said softly.

"My pleasure, ma'am," he drawled, pretending to doff a hat. "I'd best saddle up now and get back to my real work. If I don't corral them papers they're liable to multiply and stampede."

She giggled and let go of him. Just then the monitor clipped to her belt crackled and transmitted a yell. "Ma-a-a-a!"

"There's my boy, awake at last," she said gaily, pushing past him to head for the apartment. She drew up at the end of the counter and pointed a finger at him. "We're still on for lunch, right?"

He nodded, smiling, and she rushed away. Colin closed his eyes and lifted a hand to massage his temples with middle finger and thumb. Lord help him. What was he going to do now?

Why couldn't she have been like that smug Miranda, he wondered, or poor, crazy Thea, instead of the sweet, loving, hardworking woman that she was? But no, that would mean

Georgie wouldn't have had the tender care that she'd lavished upon him. He was grateful beyond words that Thea
had possessed the good sense to abandon his son in this
place with this woman, though—despite what Lauren might
think—he was quite certain it had been nothing more than
happenstance on Thea's part. She'd simply been looking
for the most remote place she could find in hopes that he
wouldn't stumble across the child. In fact, she'd taunted
him with that knowledge once she'd returned to Albuquerque. It was just God's grace that she hadn't been proven
right. If Jeff hadn't overheard a conversation at a table next
to his in an Albuquerque restaurant about a baby born in a
lodge at Eagle Nest at Christmastime, Thea might have
accomplished her goal.

He'd nearly gone insane himself during those awful
months of searching, wondering where his son was and
who was caring for him. No, he couldn't begrudge Georgie
the months spent in Lauren Cole's capable care. For that
reason alone he had to be very careful how he played this
out. The problem was that he had no more idea how to go
about telling Lauren the truth now than he'd had the night
before.

Scratching his chin, he turned toward the stairs and his
room once more. Maybe he could think better after a hot
shower and a cup of coffee. Maybe some miracle would
save the heart of a good woman who deserved better than
she was likely to get.

The roads were clear except for small patches of ice in
the shady spots. Colin drove with care, however, coasting
into each hairpin curve and gently accelerating out of it.
Lauren couldn't quite bring herself to look at him. Lunch
had been an awkward affair, with Georgie providing the
only moments of normalcy and levity. Without him to focus
upon, silence had reigned, as it did now, Georgie having

succumbed to sleep within moments of being belted into his safety seat, as was his habit. A vehicle was like a big cradle to him, rocking him instantly to sleep. For once, Lauren heartily wished it was not so. She would have liked to have given Colin something to think about other than the ugly glimpse of her past that her family had revealed earlier.

The dense forest outside flowed by her window, green firs and pale cottonwoods displaying sparse, red-gold leaves. Soon the first heavy snowfall would blanket the valley and dust the mountain forests, creeping down the peaks and slopes until the ski resorts opened for business once more.

"I meant it when I said I'd made some serious mistakes in my past."

The sound of his voice jolted her. "I—I beg your pardon?"

He kept his gaze trained out the windshield, his hands lightly gripping the steering wheel. "You aren't the only one with regrets, you know."

"You just haven't heard the whole story," she said forlornly, shaking her head in hopes of putting an end to the conversation before she embarrassed herself further.

"About two years ago," he said, "I met a woman named Thea. A few months earlier I'd ended a long-term relationship with another woman." He slid Lauren a rueful glance. "Gina was a flight attendant. It took me way too long to realize that she wasn't ever going to settle down to hearth and home." He tightened his grip on the steering wheel. "Anyway, Thea and I seemed to have a lot in common. For one thing, we met at a seminar at the university in Albuquerque. I wrote a book some time ago, *Entrepreneurship and Small Business Management for the Average Income Investor*—"

"I didn't know you'd written a book!" Lauren exclaimed, her interest firmly caught.

He chuckled and shook his head. "It hasn't exactly been a bestseller, but it's opened a few doors for me, gotten me on a few panels. That's what I was doing at the seminar, chairing a discussion panel. Thea asked some astute questions, and after the meeting she sought me out to ask a few more. One thing led to another, and we became involved."

"It must have been flattering," Lauren prodded gently, "that she wanted your advice."

He nodded. "It wasn't just that, though. She really seemed to be everything I was looking for. I mean, she loved kids, adored them. She was an elementary school art teacher, after all. And, like me, she grew up in the system."

"The welfare system, you mean."

He nodded. "We talked for hours, sharing our sad stories. What I didn't know, what I didn't realize until it was too late, was that it was all lies."

"Oh, no."

He looked at her then, making sure that she understood. "Thea was never in foster care, never abandoned, never abused. She has parents and siblings in Oklahoma, an ex-husband in Texas, all of whose lives she's made a living hell."

Lauren closed her eyes, deeply moved. "Oh, Colin, I'm so sorry. What is it about people like that?"

"You can't blame Thea," he said. "She can't help herself. I'm the one who rushed headlong into catastrophe. By the time I figured out how serious her problems were I was in way over my head. When I suggested at lunch one day that she might need counseling, she broke into my house and destroyed my bedroom. Beat the furniture with a hammer, ripped the drapes and bedding, destroyed appliances. She even piled my clothing in the yard and set fire to it."

"Dear God," Lauren breathed. "What happened to her?"

"She's in a mental hospital in Oklahoma now," he said. "I tried to help her, but nothing I did made any difference. She won't take her medication for any significant length of time, and without it she's simply psychotic. I understand that she was heavily into illicit drugs as a youngster. It's really sad. At least she's close to family this way."

Lauren turned her face away, unwilling to let him see that her eyes were swimming with tears. After a moment the tears receded. "I guess I'm not the only one who was duped."

"I suspect it's your nature to trust," he said softly. "Maybe too much so."

She sighed and propped an elbow on the window frame, her head resting on the heel of her palm. "You're right. I know you're right. I should have made Lawrence sign papers. I should have insisted on seeing Ford's place."

"Ford. He's the man you thought was single?"

She nodded glumly. "The husband of one of my best friends asked me to meet him. That's what made it so difficult. They knew all along, you see, my friend and her husband, but they let him talk them into introducing us, and then they kept quiet."

"With friends like that who needs enemies?" Colin muttered.

"It wouldn't have been so bad," she said reluctantly, "but I introduced him to my family and neighbors, even the people I worked with."

Colin lifted a brow at that. "You must have dated for some time, then."

"About four months," she admitted, "and in all that time, I never knew where he lived. I mean, he gave me an address, but I never went there. Every time I suggested it for one reason or another, he always had an excuse. I never suspected a thing until his wife showed up at my office demanding that I leave her husband alone. Even then, I was sure it had to be some kind of mistake.''

"What'd you do?"

"I called him at his private number."

"Ah, the convenience of a good cell phone."

"That's exactly right," she admitted. "At least I had sense enough not to let on that this woman had been to see me until I had him face-to-face."

"Did he cave or bluff?" Colin asked succinctly.

"Caved. Like a house of cards."

"So that was that?"

She shrugged. "Actually, he tried to convince me that he'd leave his wife for me—as if that was what I wanted."

"Why didn't you?" he asked, sliding her an enigmatic look.

"I don't want some other woman's man," she said indignantly. "I'm not, *wasn't,* that desperate. Besides, if he'd cheat on her, why wouldn't he cheat on me?"

Colin smiled. "Smart woman."

"Not smart enough apparently," she muttered.

"Like I said, you're not the only one who has regrets."

For a moment they drove on in silence. Then Colin asked, "Is he why you decided to take a go at the lodge?"

"More or less," she admitted. "I just figured that I was never going to find the right guy and that maybe I shouldn't even try anymore. It was embarrassing, you know, after everybody found out. I mean, his wife came screaming into my office, accusing me of trying to steal her husband. She even called my mother."

Colin rolled his eyes. "Of all the immature stunts!"

Lauren sighed. "I'm used to it, actually. It's just the sort of thing my brother does constantly."

He shook his head. "I guess family isn't the answer to all the world's ills, after all, is it?"

"I think it can be," Lauren said hopefully. "In my case my brother was ill a lot when he was an infant. Then my dad died unexpectedly before Larry was a year old, and Mom just sort of fixated on him, you know? I think at some point she realized that she'd ignored me much of the time, and she feels defensive about it now. Does that make sense?"

He nodded. "Yes, I'm afraid it does."

"The way I figure it, though," Lauren went on, "I can be a better mother because of her mistakes." She looked over her shoulder at Georgie sleeping so peacefully and trustfully in his safety seat. "In a way, since my grandfather died, Georgie's the only person in the world who has loved me unconditionally and without reservation, but I know I can't let myself become fixated on that. I have to think of what's best for him. Otherwise, I'll have another Larry on my hands—and I'll wind up as bitter and lonely as my mother.

"Not that I don't love my mom and brother, you understand. It's just…they're not happy people, and I don't want to be like that. I'm determined to be happy with what I have—but then, just look at all I've got." She turned another glance over her shoulder, smiling.

Colin made no comment to that, seeming to fall into a silent reverie, as if trying to figure out certain things.

"You have to turn here," she told him as they drew near the intersection on the outskirts of Taos. "The lab is just a few blocks over."

He checked the road, put on the signal and made the turn.

Two blocks down he spotted the lab building. "This it?"

"Yes. You'll have to circle around and park in back."

He followed her instructions to the letter, silent all the while. When he'd parked the car and turned off the engine, he cast a glance over his shoulder. "I hate to wake him up to get stuck with a needle."

"Don't worry," she said. "He'll snap awake the instant we open a door. As for the other, I've come prepared."

He looked doubtful but didn't argue. She reached for her door handle, motioning toward the back seat with a jerk of her head. "Watch."

Colin leaned forward, turning a look between the bucket seats. Lauren pulled the handle and swung open the door with just a whisper of sound. Georgie sucked in a sudden breath and popped open his eyes, rubbing at them with his fists. Colin laughed.

"I don't know what it is," she said, "some kind of personal sensor. You drive, he sleeps. You stop and get out, he's wide awake in a snap."

Colin focused on Georgie. "Was that a good nap, buddy?"

Georgie pointed at Lauren and her open door, demanding, "Ou'."

Colin yanked his own door open. "Okay, we'll get you out right now."

They went into the building, reading signs on doors as they walked down a wide corridor. "This is it," she said, pointing to a sign that read Blood Draws.

Colin paused, then reached out and pushed the door open. Lauren carried Georgie inside, Colin following with the diaper bag. She went straight to the window at the end of the narrow waiting room. A heavy-set man behind the glass greeted her with a smile, then quickly checked his book.

"George Cole?"

"This is him," Lauren said, hefting Georgie higher on her hip.

"Paperwork's all done. Bring him on back."

Colin appeared at her shoulder, asking, "Can I come, too?"

"Sure." The man waved them toward a door to the left, getting up from his chair.

Colin stepped up to open it, holding it back so Lauren could carry Georgie through. The man gathered papers, vials and a fabric-covered board fitted with what looked like a straight jacket. "This is what we call the papoose board," he said. "We strap the child in, immobilizing him, so we can get the draw."

Lauren grimaced. "Georgie hates to have his arms held down."

"If he moves, we could pop out of the vein," the big man said. "Then I'd have to stick him again."

"Maybe I could just hold him in my lap," Colin proposed hopefully.

The technician eyed him. "Think you can hold him still enough?"

"I think so." He looked at Lauren. "Is that all right with you?"

"Better you than me," she answered honestly.

"Let's use that tall chair over there," said the man.

Colin walked over to the chair, put down the diaper bag and sat, holding out his arms. Lauren handed him Georgie, then quickly removed the child's coat. The technician was pleased that she'd had the foresight to put Georgie in a short-sleeved T-shirt.

"That'll make my job a little easier," he said good-naturedly, pulling up a rolling stool. "A little distraction, if you please, Mom," he went on, extracting a large rubber band from his lab coat pocket.

Lauren pulled the ragged flop-eared dog from the diaper bag and set it on Colin's shoulder. Georgie laid his head back against Colin's chest and looked up at the toy. Lauren began making barking and woofing sounds. Georgie smiled and babbled, reaching up with his unoccupied hand. Colin wrapped his arms around the child and held on.

"Look at that silly dog sitting up there," he crooned.

The technician swabbed the baby's arm, and Georgie momentarily looked that way.

"Look at that silly dog," Colin crooned again, and Lauren barked and wiggled the toy.

"Here we go," the technician said, and Colin tightened his hold, literally hugging Georgie into stillness.

Georgie screamed like a banshee and kept on screaming long after the ordeal was over and they were back in the waiting room, no matter what Colin did. Lauren felt a little guilty, playing the comforter after Colin had played the heavy, but she couldn't bear to hear Georgie cry any more than Colin could. She stepped around in front of them and held out her hands. Georgie clambered up into her arms, complaining loudly as he pointed at the bandage on the inside of his elbow.

"I know, I know," she told him, reaching into a pocket. "Maybe this will help." She drew out a red sucker, and Georgie's pathetic sobs turned to greedy chuckles.

"No fair!" Colin said, laughing as Georgie's tears became slobbers of anticipation.

"You unwrap it and give it to him, then," she offered, holding it out.

"Okay, I will." He took the sucker, winking at Georgie's sudden frown, and squeezed off the cellophane. He held it out by the soft looped handle. "Here you go, pal, a reward for heroism in the face of a needle."

Georgie reached for both the sucker and Colin.

"You traitor," Lauren said, laughing as she delivered him into Colin's arms.

"Hey, you're cheap," Colin teased, letting go of the sucker before Georgie engulfed it in his mouth. "Don't swallow it, though, just suck on it." He pulled on the handle, only to have Georgie clamp his teeth, the head of the sucker caught firmly behind them, pink drool leaking onto his chin.

"You're going to need these," Lauren warned Colin, holding out a packet of wipes.

"I'm going to need a raincoat," Colin said, shaking sticky drool off his hand.

"That, too," Lauren confirmed unrepentantly. "That's what happens when you're determined to play the hero."

Colin stuck his tongue out at her. Georgie generously yanked the sucker out of his own mouth and swiped it across Colin's, who was too surprised to react until he had sucker all across his jaw and chin. Lauren chortled behind her hand. Colin shot her a look meant to intimidate, then ruined it with a smiling grimace as he wiped his face with his free hand.

"Oh, great," he muttered, looking at his sticky hand.

Lauren laughed again and opened the packet of wipes, taking pity on him. Carefully she cleaned his face—and then his neck, where Georgie inadvertently hit him with the sucker.

Colin took it all in stride, the very essence of patience. He really was a hero, Lauren decided, of the daddy kind, and as far as she was concerned, that was the very best kind of all.

Chapter Four

They spent the remainder of the day in Taos at Colin's suggestion. Lauren was only too happy to let him entertain her with the standard tourist attractions, anything to keep from dwelling on the significance of what they had just done with Georgie. She couldn't let herself believe that the blood test would prove the paternity of some stranger in Albuquerque, and the best way not to believe it was just not to think about it. So she called Juan and explained that they would be later returning to the lodge than expected. He assured her that everything was under control.

They drove downtown, parked and walked around the square, poking around in the shops and enjoying the variety of merchandise available.

Some of the shops were gaudy and cheap; some of them exclusive and swank, stocked with one-of-a-kind artwork, antiques, handmade jewelry and clothing. Lauren bought some chili pepper Christmas lights from the specialty store on one corner and a set of luminarias from another. With the holidays coming, she had to think about decorating. Colin bought a hat from Peru for Georgie and a hand-painted scarf for Lauren, despite her protests. They spent the most time oohing and aahing over a line of accessories and jewelry. Lauren was especially taken with a pair of small hoop earrings, silver and copper inlaid with turquoise, but the price was enough to send her in the opposite direction fast. Colin bought himself a shirt at a Western-Wear store and changed out of his damp, wrinkled one so they could have dinner at one of the nicer restaurants in town.

Lauren wasn't so sure about the idea, frankly. Georgie always behaved wonderfully in the restaurant at the lodge, but he was on home turf there. She couldn't vouch for his behavior in unfamiliar surroundings. Colin wouldn't take no for an answer, however, so off they went for cheese soup, fresh salads and blue-corn tortillas stuffed with mesquite-grilled chicken. Georgie made do with potato slices baked with cheese and bits of ham and tomato and served with avocado mashed with orange pulp.

It was a leisurely, fun dinner, seasoned with light banter and whipped with baby antics. Colin got a genuine kick out of the way Georgie tried to follow the adult conversation and eat at the same time, his little mouth continually gaping open for another bite, even when the spoon was waiting in the other direction. When he'd eaten his fill of food, he lost interest in the conversation, too, and thereafter occupied himself by charming the other patrons with flirting smiles and comical faces. One couple even stopped by the table to tell Lauren and Colin what an adorable son they had.

Neither seemed of a mind to correct the mistake; it just seemed more trouble than it was worth with two strangers they would likely never see again. But it woke in Lauren a longing that she had been trying to hold at bay ever since

Colin Garret had walked into her inn with his windblown black hair and vibrant blue eyes, smiling at Georgie with the same indulgent adoration as she herself felt for the child. It was the longing for a partner that she felt, a need for the mating of like minds and dissimilar bodies, a joining of forces and lives and hearts. It troubled her, that longing, as much as any of the other problems that beset her, because she feared that she couldn't trust her own judgment when it came to Colin or any other man to whom she was so strongly attracted. It troubled her, and it gave her an odd, unwanted hope at the same time. Now she only had to decide if that spark of hope was worth the chance of getting her heart broken once again.

"We had a lovely time," Lauren said, strolling slowly along at his side down the corridor toward her office.

"Yes, we did," Colin agreed, clasping his hands behind his back. "Think George will sleep through the night? He had two good naps in the car today."

"He always has two naps a day," Lauren said. "Besides, he was worn out by all his adventures. He'll be fine."

Colin nodded, relieved to know it. He was learning more and more about his son—and the delectable Miss Cole.

"Well, good night," she said, when they reached her office door.

"Thanks for letting me tag along today," he said, reluctant to go.

"Oh, it was my pleasure," she told him, bowing her head as if suddenly shy. "I'm not quite certain how I'd have gotten through it without you, frankly."

The wobble in her voice alerted him. He'd been expecting it since they'd left Taos, winding home through the dark in near silence, and he was glad that she hadn't waited until he'd walked out the door to let the tears come. He gently shoved her back against the wall and lifted her face with a hand curled beneath her chin.

"Now, you listen to me," he said. "Whatever happens, you'll always be a big part of that little boy's life. I know that for a fact."

She shook her head and blinked away the tears. "You don't understand. That isn't how it works. I-if they give him to someone else, they'll want m-me out of the way to be sure he bonds. I'll be f-forbidden ever to—"

He shook her, her shoulder bones feeling small and delicate beneath his hands. "No! That won't happen. I won't let you believe it will."

She bowed her head again, but then she lifted it and laid it back against the wall. "You're right. There's no point in thinking negatively. The blood test won't match. We'll celebrate Georgie's first birthday on Christmas Eve, and right after the New Year I'll petition the court to adopt him. And that will be that."

He wanted to kick himself. He meant to comfort her, true, but not mislead her further. He had to tell her the truth. Now. He opened his mouth. But then she smiled softly and lifted a hand to his chest, her small, delicately tapered fingers splayed over his heart, and he lost everything but the thought that her mouth had never seemed so compellingly kissable.

He covered her mouth with his. Her mouth curved slightly, as if she smiled, but then her hand slid up and around his neck, and she tilted her head, parting her lips. Something wild and ungovernable broke free in him, something primitive and demanding. Deepening the kiss, he instinctively pressed her back against the wall, thrusting a knee between hers. She went up on tiptoe, winding both arms around his neck so tightly that his breathing felt threatened. He fixed that by placing his hands at her waist and simply lifting her against the wall. She was heavier than he'd expected, and that pleased him, because his needs at that moment were anything but delicate. She wrapped her legs around him, as if afraid he might drop her, and suddenly he found himself right where he most wanted to be. The position was electrifying—and dangerous—and try as he might he couldn't keep himself from thrusting against her, feeling her sweet core yielding to his rigid desire.

What would it feel like to sink into her? To feel the soft pillows of her breasts against his chest without the barrier of clothing between them? To taste the skin on her belly and lick the insides of her thighs? He wanted to hear her gasp and moan and sob his name. He wanted to make her claw his back in mindless need and scream in helpless release. He wanted to explode inside of her.

Shoving a hand up inside her sweater, he cupped what he'd only been able to imagine, exulting to find that her breast overflowed his hand. Gasping, she let her head fall back, allowing him to sample the delicate curve of her neck. Gasping again, she threaded her fingers through his hair. Pinning her with the pressure of his thrusting pelvis, he covered her other breast with his free hand. And it was precisely then that the door at the end of the corridor opened—and closed again—right after the little shriek that told them in no uncertain terms they'd definitely been seen.

Disentanglement was instinctive. Suddenly they stood staring at each another in shock. Lauren covered her mouth with her hand, her eyes wide. Colin tried to clear his reeling head with fresh air, lungs pumping like a bellows. Suddenly their frantic gazes collided, and in the snap of a finger, it was all right, completely in perspective. As one, they burst out laughing.

"Poor Maria," Lauren grasped.

"I guess we must have shocked her," Colin said, grinning. "We certainly shocked me."

"And me," Lauren admitted, sobering slightly.

He put his back to the wall and sucked in one more deep breath. "I guess it'll be all over the lodge in a matter of minutes."

Lauren smiled apologetically. "Probably. Do you mind?"

He shook his head. "You?"

"No. It's not as if I've been caught kissing any other of the guests."

"None?" he heard himself ask, and winced.

She fixed him with a level, frank gaze. "Not that I haven't had opportunities, but weekend affairs are neither to my taste or my best interest."

"I'm sorry," he said. "I knew better than to ask that."

She smiled slightly. "I assumed you did."

He wrung his hands together, trying to get a grip. "I don't seem to be thinking clearly, so you'll forgive me if I ask another stupid question?"

She nodded.

"I guess taking up where we left off is not an option, is it?"

She laughed again, even as she shook her head. "I'm afraid not. As you said, you aren't thinking clearly, and neither am I."

He had regained enough control, he hoped, not to show his disappointment. "I'll say good-night then, before I embarrass us both further." He started toward the door.

"Colin," she called.

He paused and turned to face her, half in fear that she'd changed her mind and half in fear that she hadn't.

She smiled and said, "Thank you."

He cocked his head. "For what exactly?"

"For kissing me," she said, pulling closed the front of her cardigan with both hands, "and then for not kissing me."

He bowed his head, smiling. "You're welcome."

"And for the record, I'm not embarrassed."

He chuckled. "I'll see you tomorrow."

"Tomorrow," she repeated. He left her there, leaning against the wall as if she needed it to hold her up, smiling dreamily even as her wispy brows drew together in concerned thought. He knew exactly how she felt. Exactly.

He didn't see her, actually, except flitting from one room to another or at a distance as she conversed with someone else. Occasionally she tossed him an apologetic smile or called out that she'd only be a moment longer, only to be called away by some new crisis. After lunch, during which he never laid eyes on her, he set up his laptop in the dining room and tried to get some work done, but he couldn't help wondering if she was really as busy as she seemed and, if so, who was watching George. He stayed with it long enough to type some notes and put together a preliminary prospectus for a couple intending to open a boarding house for students near the University of New Mexico. Then he got up and walked back to the apartment.

Maria answered his knock on the apartment door, George on her hip. Her face flamed a dusky red when she saw him. "Mr. Garret."

"Hello, Maria. Hello, George. Maria, do you know where Lauren is?"

Maria shook her head. "She's got the monitor with her, though. I can call her, if you want."

"Ask if she minds if I spend some time with Georgie."

Carrying George with her, she turned and hurried into his bedroom. Colin heard her speaking a few moments later, and then she reappeared. "Miss Lauren says if you can watch him a few minutes, I'm to come help clean up a big mess in the kitchen."

Colin felt an absurd spurt of relief. So she was busy, and he was to mind George. He held out his hands, and Georgie came easily into them. Colin snuggled him close. "How are you today, buddy? No lingering effects from that nasty old needle?"

Georgie pointed toward the little kitchen and gibbered purposefully.

"I was just about to get him a drink," Maria said. "He has a sippy cup of juice in the refrigerator, and he'll need a bib."

"I'll take care of it," Colin assured her, wondering where to find that bib.

"You're to call Miss Lauren on the monitor if you need anything."

"Will do."

She slipped past him, literally escaping through the door.

Colin looked at his son. "Okay, George, let's have some juice."

It turned out to be a messier affair than he'd imagined. For one thing, George didn't like to sit still while he sipped his juice, and for another, that bib proved truly elusive. Colin tried tying a dish towel around George's neck, but George managed to rid himself of it with amazing promptness, and even when he didn't, the juice soaked right through it to his shirt.

When he seemed to have had his fill of juice, Colin wiped up after him—the floor, the counter, the stovetop, even the sink—then wiped up a fiercely protesting George himself with a soft, wet washcloth and changed his clothes. Afterward, George seemed sleepy, so Colin sat down with him in the rocking chair in his room, and soon George was sleeping like, well, a baby. Lauren came in just as Colin was attempting to transfer him to his crib.

"I was confident you could get him down by yourself," she said softly, "but I thought I'd better check just to make sure."

Colin finally managed to get George down on his side

in the crib. The moment he took his hands away, the baby flopped over onto his back and sprawled. Lauren squeezed in beside Colin and quickly removed George's shoes, then pulled up the covers and laid them lightly atop him.

"Shouldn't we, like, *tuck?*" Colin asked, demonstrating with his hands how he expected to shove the edges of the blanket down against the sides of the bed.

"He hates to have his arms and legs restricted," she reminded him.

"Oh, right. I should've remembered that."

She chuckled, as if to say that he wasn't expected to remember all the idiosyncrasies of her son's character. "You don't have to stay any longer," she told him, leading him out into the hall. "I'll be close by in the office, trying to catch up on my computer entries and get the payroll ready. I have the monitor with me."

He lifted a hand to scratch the back of his neck. "Well, I do have some work to do."

"Tell you what," Lauren said indulgently, "you can set up your laptop in here, if you want. I saw that you were working in the dining room, and that's fine, but you'll have fewer disturbances in here. Unless you'd rather go back up to your room?"

"No! I'd love to set up in here."

She beamed at him. "Good. Well, I'll leave you to it, then. If you need me, you know where I am."

With that she slipped back into Georgie's room, placed a gentle kiss on his forehead and slipped out again, hurrying away to work. Colin leaned against the doorjamb and folded his arms, splitting a look between Lauren's retreating back and his son's sleeping form. He didn't know which was the more interesting sight, Georgie sleeping as though cradled in the outstretched arms of a legion of guardian angels or Lauren's swaying hips. For a short, curvy woman, she sure could wear a pair of jeans. He straightened suddenly, realizing which picture his body found more compelling.

How, exactly, had this happened? he wondered. He'd been absolutely focused on his son when he'd come here, and yet from the first he'd felt the lure of Lauren Cole. Shouldn't he have been able to put that aside, though? Was it merely because she had given George such a fine start in life that he couldn't quite ignore the pull between them? He just didn't know. And he wasn't even certain that it mattered. He hadn't counted on an entanglement with Lauren Cole. He'd come prepared to consider her feelings while claiming his son, but now his own feelings were quickly becoming tangled up with hers, and he no longer knew whether to grab Georgie and run fast in the opposite direction or give this thing time to play out between them.

Perhaps it wasn't even his decision to make alone. Maybe he ought to just tell her the truth and let her decide whether to throw him out on his head or try for something genuine between them. Briefly he considered the possibility that she might fight him for George, but that wasn't really likely. For one thing he had the law on his side—or would as soon as his paternity was proven—and for another she knew very well that he would be a good father to George. No, he couldn't see her fighting the inevitable, but losing Georgie would hurt her deeply. If her brother was successful in forcing her to sell the lodge, too... Colin shook his head. No, he couldn't let that happen.

He couldn't walk away with Georgie in his arms knowing that he might have well left her with nothing. She had to know the truth eventually, but he could make sure she understood that she was to remain a part of Georgie's life. And a part of his own. What part, exactly, he wasn't sure, but time would tell them both that. Somehow he had to convince her to give them that time. Meanwhile, he needed to find a way to help her with Lawrence, too. Perhaps that would prove his good intentions and be enough to convince her not to write him off just because he was Georgie's father.

Lauren went over the figures one last time and entered them, ready to instruct the computer to print out the checks, when Colin spoke to her through the monitor.

"Lauren, you better get in here!"

Shoving back her chair, she ran from the room, careening down the hall and into the apartment. A glance showed her that the living area was empty. Colin's laptop blinked at her from atop the bar separating kitchen and living room, papers strewn around it.

His voice came to her from Georgie's room. "That's it, buddy. You can do it. Come on. Stay with it. Stay with it."

Alarm gave way to curiosity, tugging her toward the nursery. Colin sat on the floor, toys scattered every which way, and in the midst of the chaos stood Georgie, his little knees wobbling, his arms thrust out before him, his eyes glued to the hands that Colin held out to him.

"Come on, son. You can do it," Colin coaxed. "Just lift up one foot and put it down again in front of you. I won't let you fall, I promise. Come on. Come on."

Holding her breath, Lauren went down on her knees beside Colin. Georgie switched his gaze to her, a smile lighting his features and proclaiming, "Look at me, Mom! See what I can do!" Abruptly he looked back to Colin, and then he stepped off, wobbled dangerously and steadied. Grinning, he tried again—and nearly fell on his face. Colin reached forward and swept him up in strong hands.

"You did it!"

"Yeah!" Lauren clapped her hands, absolutely delighted, and Georgie joined in, applauding himself.

"Was that his first step?" Colin demanded excitedly. "He hasn't done it before?"

"His very first one!" Lauren exclaimed. "Unless he's been toddling around the room by himself."

"I don't think so," Colin chanted, lifting Georgie over his head. "Your first step! Man, I wish I'd had a camera!"

"Well, I sure won't forget that," Lauren said, smiling up at Georgie and tickling his chin. "I've got a snapshot right in here." She tapped her chest.

"I was afraid you'd miss it," Colin said. "I was afraid *I'd* miss it!"

"I'm glad you didn't," she told him honestly. "These milestones are even more special when they're shared with someone who cares, you know?"

"I know," he replied softly, holding her gaze with his.

Was it insane to hope for a future with him? she wondered. The way he had kissed her last night had melted her bones. The way he handled Georgie, seeming to take pleasure in his every little move, melted her heart. But she'd been burned before. Somehow she tended to forget that when he was around.

Georgie spied his flop-eared dog and applauded it, then twisted out of Colin's lap and swiftly crawled over to it. Colin's smile seemed permanently implanted in his face.

"I can't believe he's walking."

Lauren sat down beside him, legs folded crosswise. "I wouldn't say he's exactly walking. Yet. But he did just take his first step, so it won't be long."

"How long, do you think?"

She chuckled. "I don't know. Two months. Two weeks. Probably by Christmas, anyway. There are no written laws for these things."

He grimaced. "You must think I'm a real ninny, asking such stupid questions."

"Not at all."

"It's just that I don't know much about babies," he said.

"I mean, I can take care of him. I just don't know all the details."

Disciplining a smile, she leaned forward and covered his hand with hers. "I understand. Everyone's that way in the beginning. It's mostly instinct, though, and yours seem to be very good where Georgie's concerned."

He smiled at that and turned his head to watch Georgie bite the nose of the flop-eared dog. "I just want the best for him."

"Spoken like a real parent," she quipped, and then wondered if he thought she was trying to draft him for the job. "I—I just meant that you'll make a good father. Someday."

He looked away, muttering, "I hope so."

Well, she'd embarrassed herself enough. "I have to get back to work," she said quickly, getting to her feet. "Want me to call Maria or Ponce to watch Georgie?"

He shook his head, saying lightly, "I'll look after him."

"You're sure?"

"Absolutely."

"I wouldn't want to take advantage," she pressed. "We can take the playpen into the office. We've spent lots of time together that way, trust me."

"But I want to stay with him," Colin insisted, looking up at her.

"You're supposed to be on vacation, not baby-sitting."

"Listen, spending time with George has been a blast. Come on," he wheedled, "I'll be going home tomorrow. Let me spend some time with him, and help you, while I can."

She felt a shiver of uncertainty, as if she was missing something, but she pushed it away, smiling. "All right. Thanks."

Printing and distributing the checks required more than an hour. Then one of the dishwashers called in sick for the evening rush, and she spent another hour finding someone to replace him. Once she got back to the apartment and finally had time to sit down with Georgie, it was easy to push aside other concerns in favor of cuddling him.

When Juan buzzed the apartment a few minutes later to say that Colin had a call and Colin excused himself to take it in his room, Lauren was almost relieved. She didn't let herself think about Juan having assumed that Colin was with her or the kiss that Colin automatically dropped on her cheek as he was leaving the apartment—or why she purposefully avoided him again by failing to answer the phone the next time it rang or the knocks that fell on her apartment door later.

She told herself that she was taking time to spend with Georgie, that she was making up for an unusually busy day that had caused her to neglect him, but she knew that she was hiding, hiding from fear and temptation. Perhaps she was even hiding from hope. Or perhaps she was hiding from the decision that she knew she had to make. On one hand, she wanted desperately to throw herself at Colin Garret before it was too late, arms and heart wide open. On the other hand, he seemed almost too good to be true. She couldn't help wondering when the facade would slip, exposing secrets and destroying illusions.

Maybe if she ignored him, Colin would just go away and never come back again. Then she could tell herself that he had been the one who ended it, that she was wise to draw back and had lost nothing of real importance. Was that what they called a self-fulfilling prophecy? For fear that he would not stay, she pushed him away? But was that really what she would be doing? Was it the same if she simply turned her back and pretended not to notice as he drifted farther and farther from her?

But she couldn't take that easy route. She had to think, really think, about Colin Garret and his significance in her life. She had to decide whether or not to take a chance on him. No longer could she career through life, welcoming whomever came her way and mourning their absence when they disappointed her and left. She had Georgie to think of now. Those who impacted her life also impacted his. She'd been a fool to let Colin in so easily. The question was, Would she be an even greater fool to push him away before she even had a chance to know if he would truly stay?

It took a long, quiet dinner in her apartment with Georgie to make her see that all the pleasures she had so enjoyed before Colin Garret had come along were not the same now. He had changed everything, whether she wanted him to or not, and now she had to think, to reason, and to make some wise, concrete decisions about what she wanted from him and how far she was willing to go to get it. She had to decide what she was willing to risk to keep Colin Garret in her life, and she had to decide now, tonight, before he left this place again. She needed some undisturbed tranquillity.

"Let's get you bundled up, handsome," she said to Georgie resignedly. "We're going to take a walk. It's time I showed you Granddad's little getaway."

Chapter Five

Lauren sat beneath the small, three-sided shelter, staring at the deep black canvas of the lake. Moonlight shimmered in wide, metallic strokes, all the way to the shoreline. The mountain peaks across the valley gleamed white against the black, jagged silhouettes of the pines, the silk of the skies and the diamond pinpricks of stars.

The sound of footsteps crackling amongst the fallen leaves and needles reached her ears. Unsurprised, she turned her head toward the point of land that hid the lodge from view. The unmistakable form of Colin Garret strolled into view. Lauren smiled to herself. She should have known. Perhaps she had.

Colin walked toward the lake, tossing a twig and some pebbles he'd picked up into the inky water and watching the shimmers from each ring of entry widen and widen into nothingness. Finally, his hands empty, he slid them into his coat pockets.

"It isn't just my imagination, then," he said loudly. "You really are avoiding me?" He turned and looked at her, piercing the shadows with an almost tangible gaze.

Lauren made no apology. "I was," she admitted. "Now I'm just soaking up the night. And remembering."

He started up the gently sloping bank toward her. "Remembering?" he echoed politely, just a touch of acid in his tone. "May I ask what memories you're entertaining, if they aren't too personal?"

She wasn't offended. He had a right to feel slighted. Pulling up her knees, she rested her forearms atop them, gazing out at the lake again. "My grandfather used to bring me out here. It was our camping spot, within shouting distance of the lodge—to please my mother—but out of sight, so we could pretend we were out in the wilderness."

"Sounds perfect," he said, the acid tone leaching away.

She smiled. "It was. We'd fish and watch the sunset over the mountains, then cook our dinner over a campfire. Later we'd tell stories and make jokes before bedding down on pine boughs or piles of leaves, our heads under the shelter, our feet to the fire." She sighed. "That was the best sleep. And waking with the dawn was such an exhilarating experience, the birds singing, the sunshine like delicate crystal."

"Sounds like your grandfather sure knew how to show you a good time," Colin commented wistfully.

"Oh, yes, he did. Of course, Mom thought it was insane, sleeping out under the stars. She was sure I'd wake up with pneumonia every time. That's why she never let Larry come along. He was too delicate. Asthma, bronchitis, allergies."

"Poor Larry. He missed out on some wonderful times, I imagine."

"Yes." She smiled up at him and patted the blanket next to her. "Want to sit down?"

"I thought you'd never ask." He dropped down beside her, crossing his legs and getting comfortable. "Where's George?"

She turned a look over her opposite shoulder, indicating the corner of the shelter where Georgie slept soundly, wrapped in a blanket atop a pile of leaves, a light blue stocking cap covering his dark hair. "I told you, it's the best sleep imaginable."

Colin chuckled. "I have a feeling that boy can sleep anywhere and through anything."

"So true. I've vacuumed floors with him sleeping on my back in a sling."

"You're so good to him," Colin said, softening his voice. "I hope he knows how good one day."

"Oh, I'm not worried about that," she told him offhandedly. "Speaking of his sleeping habits, though, it's the strangest thing, what wakes him."

"Like the car door opening?"

She nodded. "And the blinds. In the mornings I always go in and open the blinds over his window, and he wakes right up."

"What about nap time?"

"Depends on the circumstances, but usually he just wakes up on his own. Sometimes, though, if he's sleeping with that old stuffed dog, he wakes up when I move it aside."

"I've noticed he's awfully fond of that thing," Colin said, a note of vicarious pleasure in his voice. "He treats it almost like a person."

She smiled. "So did I. There's something about that old flop-eared dog that is just…real."

"It was yours then?"

"My dad gave it to me," she confirmed, "bought it in the gift shop at the hospital where I was born."

Colin looked down at his hands. "I never had anything

like that," he said thickly. "Or at least if I did, I don't remember it. I, um, like the idea of passing on something like that, so I'm really glad you had it to pass on to George."

"So am I."

"Why were you avoiding me?" he finally asked. "Was it because of George?"

She tilted her head, wondering just why he'd asked that, and decided that he was either worried she considered him an inferior baby-sitter or was jealous of his obvious affinity with Georgie. Neither was true, of course. "No, it wasn't because of Georgie."

"Then was it the way I kissed you?" he asked huskily, and she smiled at his astuteness.

"Yes. And the way I kissed you."

He took a deep breath through his nostrils, squaring his shoulders and straightening his spine. "All right. What if I said it wouldn't happen again? What if I promised—"

"But I want it to happen again," she interrupted gently, placing a hand on his forearm so that he pivoted his head. "You see, that was the problem all along, this intense attraction that I've felt for you from the very beginning. And then there's the way you treat Georgie, like he's one of the great wonders of the world. And the way you routed Larry and Randi when they came to browbeat me about selling the lodge. And the way you laugh and look and smell and taste and—"

He leaned over and put his forehead to hers, an arm looping about her shoulders. "Lauren," he whispered, "you pull me. You draw me like a kid to candy."

She giggled. "Like Georgie to his suckers?"

Chuckling, he pulled back enough to gaze into her eyes. "Sweets are habit forming," he said, and she lifted a hand to his cheek, letting her eyes target his mouth.

"Yes," she whispered, "that's why I had to be sure."

"And are you?" he asked, threading his fingers into her hair. "Are you sure? It's important to me that you trust me."

For answer, she lifted her mouth to his. Heat shimmered through her as he dropped his legs and twisted slightly, tightening his arm to bring her closer. His hand slid from her hair down her neck and around to the hollow of her throat, his kiss pulling gently at her mouth until she melted and parted her lips. His tongue stroked inside, flicking and sweeping. Her head reeling, she lifted her arms around his neck, anchoring herself. He pressed her head back, plumbing deeper and deeper, until her heart hammered in her chest and the blood in her veins literally steamed.

She was wearing too many clothes. The insulated nylon jacket that she wore over a snap-front flannel shirt and a quilted silk camisole was suddenly stifling. She shrugged it off one shoulder and then another. Colin seemed to sense her dilemma and helped by shoving it further down, forcing her arms from around his neck. Frustrated, she broke the kiss long enough to strip the sleeves off over her hands and flung her arms back where they belonged. Colin toppled gently backward, pulling her with him and capturing her mouth along the way.

It was amazing how well their bodies fit together when they stretched out side by side like this, and amazing how she became aware of parts of her body that usually seemed to hardly exist. Her skin felt sensitized. Her breasts were heavy and full. She tingled and shimmered from head to toe, but the center of her existence had become her mouth, where her body joined his. Swollen, questing lips could not get enough of one another. As they struggled to taste and feel and fit together, clothing became an unbearable impediment.

Hands tugged and shoved at offending barriers. His coat fell away. Shirttails came untucked. Snaps opened. Buttons popped free. Finally his fingertips found the clasp of her bra, and her skin prickled as the night air cooled flesh heated by passion. In the instant before he covered one breast with his hand, her nipples tightened painfully.

Suddenly her breasts felt absurdly large and an embarrassing wetness gathered between her legs. She could not seem to get enough air or find a comfortable position. She thrashed, needing something she couldn't even name, seeking it in his mouth and skin, digging her fingertips into the muscles of his shoulders.

Bowing his head, he looked down at her. ''My, you're beautiful!''

Only then did she fully realize that she lay half-naked upon a blanket on the ground, cold air assaulting her flushed skin, her young son sleeping nearby. Gasping, she scrambled back and into a sitting position. Crossing her arms over her chest, she gaped at Colin, who twisted around and sat down next to her. So fast. How could it all happen so fast? He plucked her black silk camisole from the jumble of clothing around them and tossed it into her lap.

''Get dressed,'' he rasped, ''before I lose what little sense God gave me and finish what we started.''

Beginning to tremble in the cold air, she put on the camisole. ''Aren't you going to dress?'' she queried mutedly.

He slid her a cryptic smile. ''When I cool off.''

She reached for a shirt, discarded it and reached for another. Shrugging into it, she watched him hang his head. ''Something's wrong.''

''Everything's wrong,'' he said harshly. ''I knew what I had to do when I came out here, and I let you distract me. Again.'' He sighed. ''I'm out of my depth here, you know. Nothing like this has ever happened to me before. I want to do this right. I want…so damned much.''

Her shirt decently closed once more, she slid a hand

beneath his elbow and into the crook of his arm. "Tell me."

He pushed a hand through his hair, then dropped it to cover hers where it rested in the crook of his arm. "Lauren, I…I don't know how to do this."

"Just say it. Whatever it is, we'll deal with it, work it out. That's the conclusion I came to, you know, that you, *we,* are worth striving for, hoping for."

He looked at her then, and it seemed to her that the sheen in his eyes was more than moonlight. "Lauren, you're the best person I've ever met."

Even as she smiled, she sent him a doubtful look. "You know how stupid I've been. With Ford and even with Larry—"

"We all make mistakes, Lauren. I've told you about my worst one."

"The point is, I don't believe that *you* are a mistake," she said. "I believe you came here for a reason."

"Yes."

"And I'm going to be brave enough to discover what that reason is."

He smiled at that and leaned sideways to kiss her quickly on the mouth. "You're an incredible woman," he whispered. "I thank God it was you there the day I walked into the lodge."

"Me, too."

"I'd never do anything to hurt you," he went on. "Please believe that."

She laid her head on his shoulder. "I do. I really do."

"Good." He laid his cheek against the top of her head. "I know this is coming out of left field at you. I know I should take more time, but I…I just can't leave here without saying this." He took a deep breath, and the words seemed to rush out on his exhalation. "The thing is, I just know that *I'm* George's daddy. I knew the instant I laid eyes on the two of you that day. I knew I'd found my heart, my reason for being in this world. I knew it as surely as I drew breath.''

"It was like that for me, too," she exclaimed, lifting her head. "One look at that tiny face, and I knew without any doubt that I was meant to be his mother."

He shook his head. "No, you don't understand. I'm not saying this right, and it's important that I do, because you're such a wonderful woman. You've been a wonderful mother, too. I knew that instantly. And I love you for it."

She threw her arms around his neck. "Oh, Colin, I love you, too! I think I have from that first moment!"

"Wait!" he insisted. "Let me try to explain. I'm so grateful that it was you I found when I walked into the lodge that day. I can't imagine that any other woman would have been so loving and generous, and I can't imagine my life without you in it now. From this point on, you'll always be a part of everything I do. Always."

Lauren was reeling. It was almost too much. It was as if they'd shared an elemental experience, an innate knowledge of who they were and where they belonged, side by side and hand in hand. Tears filled her eyes. "Oh, Colin! I'd given up. I thought this would never happen. When I moved up here and took on the lodge I gave up all hope of love and a family of my own. Then I saw Georgie, wrapped in a towel, hours, maybe only minutes, old, and I knew—I just knew—that he was mine. And that day you first showed up at the lodge, so handsome and so sweet, I thought then that you could be Georgie's dad. The coloring's the same. No one would ever know that you aren't blood kin if we didn't tell them."

"But that's just it, Lauren—"

She pressed a kiss to his mouth. "I know. Love *is* what matters most. Georgie is as much my son as any child of my body could ever be, but people don't always understand that because they haven't felt that instant kinship, that jolt of recognition and love that rocks the foundation of the world. But you and I have, for George and for each other.'' Pulling his head around, she put her forehead to his. "I'm so glad you didn't wait until your next visit to speak up. I know now that everything is going to work out. Georgie belongs with us, and I know that God won't let him be taken away now. Why else would he have brought you to us like this?''

His mouth appeared to work over words that wouldn't come out, but when she lifted her mouth to his once more, words became unnecessary. He kissed her with deep poignancy, almost desperation. A shudder passed through him. Sliding her arms around him, Lauren realized that he was chilled, dangerously so. Pulling back, she demanded that he dress.

"I'd better go now," he said faintly, after donning his coat. She couldn't blame him. Everything had happened so fast! One moment she'd been struggling with the idea of hoping for too much and the next her wildest dreams were coming true!

"Maybe you should," she conceded. "As much as I want you, I'd like to wait until after—" For some reason she couldn't quite bring herself to say it first.

"Until after we're…married?" he asked, his voice going up a notch at the end.

There. It was said. Beaming, she nodded and threw herself into his arms, snuggling against his chest. "Yes. Until after we're married.''

He sighed, sounding frustrated and impatient and wonderfully anxious. She wanted to throw her arms wide and embrace the world, laughing with sheer joy. Instead she closed her eyes and held on to him, reveling as his arms came around her in a warm, protective embrace. Yes, this was right. She hadn't made a mistake in opening herself to him, in letting herself love him. She put her head back, inviting him to kiss her once more. He obliged, brushing her lips with his in studied restraint.

"We'll talk again in the morning," he promised softly. "I...I need some time to figure everything out."

"No hurry," she told him. "I know it's going to take weeks to work out the details. I just want you to know that I'm open to all possibilities. I love the lodge, but you and Georgie are more important than anything else."

"Oh, Lauren," he said, sighing. "If only you knew how complicated this is!"

"But it isn't really,". she insisted. "I meant what I said."

"I know."

"We'll figure it out."

"Somehow," he whispered.

She lifted her arms about his neck and kissed him with all the pent-up longing of the weeks to come. "I love you," she breathed against his mouth. Suddenly he set her back from him and sprang to his feet.

"I have to get out of here," he said, "before I wind up in real trouble."

She laughed, loving that he was so eager. Leaning back on her elbows, she smiled up at him. "Good night, darling."

"Good night."

He stood staring down at her a moment longer, then he abruptly turned and strode off in the direction from which he'd come. Lauren watched him until he'd rounded the point, then she lay back with a sigh and pulled her coat up around her.

"Thank You," she whispered up to the stars. "Thank You. Thank You. Thank You."

Colin leaned against the sink in the small bath attached to his room. He didn't know whether to be sick to his stomach or hysterical with laughter. How on God's sweet earth had he gotten himself into this? What other nitwit could begin to confess to a woman that he was about to take a child from her and wind up engaged to be married? Groaning, he stared at his image in the mirror over the sink.

You could be Georgie's dad. The coloring's the same. No one would ever know that you aren't blood kin. Love is what matters. George is as much my son as any child of my body could be.

Maybe she did have as much right to George as he did. Maybe he was supposed to understand that he couldn't take that baby away from her. But marriage?

He closed his eyes and was instantly swamped with the sensations that had made him a raving madman out there by the lake. All right, he wanted to have sex with her. The world was full of women about whom the same could be said.

But he didn't lose control at every opportunity with other women. And no other woman had laid claim to his son's heart.

Still, was he seriously thinking of marrying her? He must be. Otherwise he would never have left her without making it clear that she had misunderstood him.

And who could blame her for that? He'd confused everything, said it all wrong—and after he'd almost made love to her right there on the edge of the lake! What else was the poor woman supposed to think?

Wandering into the bedroom, he plopped down on the foot of the bed and put his head in his hands. What was he going to do? She didn't deserve to be hurt; she deserved just the opposite. And it was up to him to see that she got it. He owed her. She'd loved his son as if he were her very own. Without her, only God knew where and how Georgie would be. Yes, he definitely owed her.

Sighing, he collapsed upon the bed. Maybe it was the

best thing for everyone. Georgie needed a mother. Why not the only mother he'd ever known? Marrying Lauren wouldn't be a hardship. Better her than Thea! The logistics were the big problem, but those could be worked out—somehow. Why not at least let her think that they would marry, until he could figure out what to do next?

All right, so he was engaged. He could be engaged. And maybe, just maybe, he could be married as easily. Or not. Maybe by the time the blood tests came back, everything would be resolved. Time was what he needed. Well, he had time. Jeff himself had told him that it could take weeks for the paternity tests to be definitely concluded. He'd use that time to either let Lauren down easily or prepare himself for marriage.

Relaxing, he told himself that it was a good thing that he was going home tomorrow. He could think clearly back in Albuquerque. He'd work this all out, and everything would be fine. It had to be. Somehow, it just had to be, because hurting Lauren wasn't acceptable.

"When will you be back?"

"Soon," he promised.

"I'll miss you. We both will."

"I'll miss you, too," he said, kissing her quickly between the eyes. Then he pulled Georgie to him and kissed his cheek. "Daddy will be back as soon as he can, son, I promise."

Lauren laughed and threw an arm around his neck, Georgie poised awkwardly on her hip. "I love you, Colin Garret."

He kissed her again. "Take care," he whispered, breaking away. "I'll call tonight."

"Tell Daddy bye for now," Lauren said to Georgie, lifting his hand to flop it in a wave. "Bye-bye."

"Bye," Georgie whispered, putting his finger in his mouth.

Colin turned, grabbed his bag and his computer case and literally fled the foyer.

Lauren watched him drive away. She turned in a dreamy circle, Georgie balanced on her hip, only to straighten at the sight of Juan leaning against the end of the counter.

"Leaving awful early, ain't he, your Mr. Garret?"

Lauren smiled secretively. "He has a lot to do today."

Juan scratched an ear, ruffling his thick, graying hair. "Did I hear someone calling him 'Daddy' before?"

She maintained her composure, carrying Georgie around Juan and the end of the counter to slip behind it. "Maybe. I guess you could have."

Leaning forward, she set Georgie in the center of his playpen. He immediately flopped down, crawled over to the side and pulled himself up. Lauren busied herself filing forms. Juan slid around the end of the counter and came to stand across from her. "So Maria is right," he mused.

Lauren shot him a skeptical glance. "Not if she's predicting gloom and doom again."

"Who said anything about premonitions? I'm talking about her seeing you kissing that Garret guy."

Caught. Lauren laughed. She'd been laughing since last night. "Oh, that." She could feel herself blushing.

Juan grinned. "So? What's with you and him?"

Lauren weighed the pros and cons of telling him, then chucked it all and came out with it. "We're getting married!"

Juan reeled back. "¡Madre de Dios! That's sudden! How many times you seen the guy? He's been here maybe twice now?"

"Oh, I know it's sudden," she said, "and so does he. That's why we aren't rushing into anything. We're going to take our time and make absolutely sure that all the various issues are worked out. So you can relax. We're not going to do anything stupid, I promise.''

Juan leaned against the counter, looking down at Georgie, who was holding on to the top rail of the playpen as he toddled around the perimeter. ''You ain't done nothing really smart since I've known you,'' Juan said to Lauren. ''Like with this here boy. You with a lodge to run and you decide you got to have him, too. Oh, well, why start being smart now, eh?'' He grinned at her. ''It usually comes out okay. It's just, I worry about you. A heart big as yours can trip a girl up, you know?''

Lauren chuckled. ''Look who's talking.''

He shrugged. ''Me? I ain't got no troubles. Got me two good kids an' an okay job,'' he teased.

Lauren felt compelled to ask a question she'd long wondered about. ''Your wife died a long time ago, Juan. Don't you ever get lonely?''

He shook his head. ''Not so much, no. Concetta, she is with me always, here and here.'' He tapped his head and his chest. ''We are never apart, my Concetta and me. But Maria—and Ponce, too, sometimes—for them she is too much a shadow. This is what makes me sad.''

Lauren smiled. ''I think I know what you mean. It makes me sad that Georgie will never know my grandfather. He was so wonderful.''

Juan nodded. ''Yes, Mr. Cole, he was a good man. He would know exactly what to make of your Mr. Garret.''

Lauren stiffened. ''Do you have reason to doubt Colin's sincerity?''

Juan shook his head. ''No. Do you?''

''Of course not,'' Lauren scoffed. If a little voice in her head whispered that Colin Garret was still too good to be true, she refused to listen. That was the old Lauren talking, the desperate, purposeless Lauren. Her life was completely different now. *She* was different. And she knew in her heart of hearts that she and Colin—and Georgie—were meant to be together.

Chapter Six

"Hey, I'm glad you called," Jeff said, dumping his overcoat on an extra chair at the table and plopping his briefcase on top of it. "You've been scarce around here lately. Good to see you."

Colin signaled the waiter with an uplifted hand before greeting his old friend. "Good to see you, too, counselor. How have you been?"

"Busy," Jeff said. "Can't tell you how much I'm looking forward to a quiet dinner." The waiter appeared with menus, placing them on the table before the men.

They ordered drinks—bourbon and branch water for Colin, scotch for Jeff—and quickly perused the menus. "What are you having?" Colin asked idly.

"Prime rib, as usual. And you'll be having the salmon."

"As usual," they both said, and laughed.

Colin closed his menu and laid it aside, grinning widely. "It really is good to see you again. I'm just a little distracted tonight, though. I'm swamped at the office, and all I can think about is getting back to Eagle Nest.''

"How is the boy?" Jeff asked, leaning his elbows on the table.

Colin marveled at the smile that broke out across his own face. Just the thought of George lifted his spirits dramatically. "He's fine. He took his first steps day before yesterday. Of course, it'll be a while before he's actually walking, but Lauren says by Christmas for sure. He'll be a year old on Christmas Eve, you know."

"Man, a whole year," Jeff said, shaking his head. "Seems like it was just yesterday that you were telling me Thea was claiming to have had your kid."

"Seems like forever to me," Colin said.

"I don't mind telling you, I didn't really believe it at first. I mean, after all those months of hang-up calls and veiled threats and weird packages in the mail, I just thought it was another one of her wild ploys."

"That's because you didn't see the gloating way she told me that I had a son I'd never find," Colin mused darkly.

"She probably thought that leaving him in a remote little place like Eagle Nest would ensure that you'd never hear of him."

"She didn't reckon on the popularity of the valley or the success of the lodge," Colin said, nodding.

"She had to know you'd move heaven and earth to find him, though," Jeff commented.

"I have no idea what she thought or thinks," Colin said resignedly. "Even if she were completely sane, I'm not sure I'd ever understand her."

"I'm not sure we're supposed to understand women, anyway," Jeff muttered, "even the little ones. Every time I think I know how Meg and the girls are going to react to something, they totally confound me—and Meg and I have been married seven years now."

Colin thought of pretty Meg Locke and her two golden-haired daughters and grinned. Jeff was a sucker for all three. They wrapped him around their collective little finger like twine on a stick. Jeff groused about being the only male in a female-dominated household, but Colin knew that he secretly loved it. Colin himself wouldn't mind a little girl of his own one day. On the other hand, every man needed a son, and Colin was proud to say so.

"So maybe I'll just borrow yours from time to time," Jeff quipped. "Meg and I are out of the baby business, trust me."

"You wouldn't say that if you could see George," Colin told him confidently. "He's got my daddy's cleft chin and my hair and eyes. He doesn't talk much yet, but Lauren says that's normal. She says he's the best kid ever, too. I held him in my lap when they took the blood for the test, and he wailed like he was ready to rip somebody's arm off, but he didn't move a muscle, not one. And he sleeps like all the angels of heaven are watching over him, like the world is a really safe, sane place, you know? The sleep of the innocents, I never understood that term before, but that's what it's like. It's amazing. I could just stand and watch him all the time."

"You could stand and watch him sleep all the time?" Jeff mused. "Spoken like a parent who never prayed for ten minutes of uninterrupted silence. Besides, standing over either one of my girls is tantamount to asking them to wake up screaming. They have, like, bat radar or something. Every little creak and sigh startles them."

Colin shook his head. "Not George. He could sleep through an earthquake, except for these certain little signals, like opening the car door or the window blinds. Lauren says she used to vacuum with him strapped to her back and he'd sleep through it."

They chatted about children's sleeping habits until the

drinks arrived and their dinners were ordered, at which point Jeff changed the subject somewhat. "So it's George, is it? Where'd that come from?"

Colin shrugged. "It's a good name."

"Uh-huh."

"I like it," Colin said a little defensively. "It may not be trendy right now, but it's a solid man's name."

"I agree," Jeff said lightly. "I was just wondering how you came up with it."

"If you must know," Colin said, slightly irritated, "it's Lauren's grandfather's name."

Jeff nodded nonchalantly and sipped his scotch, rankling Colin further.

"George Colin is a better name than Colin James, Jr.," he insisted. "Besides, it fits him."

"It's a fine name. It just sounds a little mature for an infant."

"Lauren calls him Georgie," Colin grumbled.

Jeff nodded. "That'll work."

George was an excellent name, Colin thought. Come to think of it, George Colin was an excellent name, but a man could be forgiven for wanting his son named after him, couldn't he? Lauren would understand that, surely. The question was, would she understand how a man could botch something as simple as identifying himself as a father and accidentally get engaged? Would that same man be forgiven for breaking the heart of the only mother his son had ever known? Such thoughts were weighing heavy on his mind.

"For a man who's very likely found a long-lost son, you sure are troubled," Jeff noted, sobering. "What gives, Colin?"

Reluctant to explain the fix he was in, Colin shrugged. "I don't know what you mean."

"You were positively walking on air the first time you

came back from up there," Jeff pressed. "You having doubts about the boy's identity?"

Colin tossed back at least half his drink and grimaced as it slid down, shaking his head. "No doubt," he said breathlessly. "I'd stake my future on it." In fact, I may have done just that, he thought.

"So what's the problem?"

"Does there have to be a problem?" Colin asked, exasperated at his friend's astuteness. Shouldn't such a perceptive fellow know when somebody didn't want to talk about something? He made a face, aware that he was being unreasonable. "I'm just impatient, that's all. I want him with me. You can understand that."

"Sure. It's just that you're not quite yourself. Want to tell me about it?"

Colin resorted to a half lie. "I just want it settled."

Jeff reverted to his lawyerly self. "When the test results come in, and providing they tell us what we expect them to, we'll file for custody. Thea's custody has already been terminated by the state, and based on her mental condition we'll ask for that termination to stand, but there's still the matter of protecting you and the boy from her. Have you decided how you want to handle that?"

Colin shook his head. "It seems heartless to prosecute her."

"If she contests, you may have no choice."

"I realize that, but we can cross that bridge when we come to it. You just concentrate on getting me legal custody of my son."

"Will do," Jeff said, lifting his drink in an unspoken toast.

Colin shifted forward in his seat and lifted his own drink. "What're we drinking to?"

"To George Colin Garret," Jeff said, and Colin clinked his glass with Jeff's, smiling.

"Hear, hear."

"I'll petition for the name change when I file our custody claim."

They tossed back the liquor and plunked their glasses onto the tabletop. Salads and rolls arrived then, along with yells from the bar that signaled a favorable score in the evening's ball game, and talk turned to sports, then movies and books and business. Not once during the evening did the topic of unexpected and unintended engagements come up, so Jeff departed none the wiser—and Colin continued to agonize alone about what he was going to do.

It had all happened too quickly. Lauren was sure of it. Now. Now that he was gone and she hadn't heard his voice in some forty-eight, okay, forty-five, hours. He was gone, and he hadn't called in nearly two days, and it just wasn't real. They'd rushed into this. A few kisses, and suddenly it was forever. Where was her head? What had she been thinking?

She stared at the television that sat atop the chest of drawers at the foot of her bed, sadly unaware of what she was watching, certain now that she was going to get her heart broken. Yet, when the phone—which was automatically routed through the front desk at night—rang on her bedside table, she pounced rather than let the answering machine get it.

"Eagle Nest Mountain Lodge."

"Lauren, it's me."

The sound of his voice was a soothing balm that at once quieted her worst fears. Sitting up, she pushed her hair out of her face and braced her forearms on her knees. "Colin. How are you?"

"Fine. How about you?"

"Oh, I'm fine." She smiled because suddenly it was true.

"And George?"

"He's fine, too. We're both just fine."

"That's good. I'm glad. I can't help worrying a little, you know."

"I know. I'm thinking about you, too. Did you have dinner?"

"Sure. With my friend Jeff. You know, the attorney. I think I've mentioned him."

"Maybe so. I don't remember right now. Doesn't matter. How was it?"

"Dinner? It was fine. Everything's fine."

"Oh, good."

The line was silent for a moment, as if they'd momentarily run out of words. Then she heard herself saying, "I miss you, Colin. When are you coming back?"

He gusted a great sigh through the phone. "I don't know. Soon. Maybe you should check your reservation book for me."

She laughed at that. "You don't need a reservation, Colin. If nothing else is available, the couch in the living room folds out into a bed. A-and there's the cabin. No one's been there in quite a while, but it isn't far from the old campsite, and it's livable. In fact, I was thinking…I mean, the cabin could be converted into a really comfortable home…i-if someone was interested."

"I didn't know there was a cabin on the property," Colin said noncommittally.

"My grandfather actually lived there the last few years, after the lodge closed."

"I see."

"I thought about fixing it up and renting it out as a vacation home," she went on brightly, "but I guess it's a good thing I never got around to it. This way you're assured of a place to stay even if the lodge is full, although the only access from the cabin to the lodge is by foot right now. We closed the road a few years ago, not that it couldn't be reopened.''

''The couch then. Unless you're uncomfortable with that.''

''Not at all. We're both mature, responsible adults.''

Another pause followed. She twirled a lock of hair around her finger, wondering if he was aching for the sight and feel of her as much as she was aching for the sight and feel of him.

''I'd better go,'' he said then, softly. ''I have a lot to do tomorrow.''

''So do I,'' she said gaily, in order to hide her disappointment. ''You know what it's like around here. In fact, I've had to hire on some extra help for the ski season. We've had our first snow, by the way. You should have seen Georgie's face when I took him out in it to play!''

''Oh, I wish I had,'' Colin said fervently.

''He misses you,'' Lauren said. ''We both do.''

''Will you do something for me, hon?'' Colin asked. ''Will you tell him that I miss him, too?''

''I'll tell him.''

''And Lauren—''

''Yes?''

For a long moment he said nothing, and then, ''I guess I just needed to hear your voice.''

She smiled, and tears filled her eyes. ''It's so silly, this being in love, isn't it?''

''Oh, I don't know,'' he said roughly. ''I think I could get the hang of it.''

She laughed again. ''Me, too.''

''Well,'' he said, ''good night.''

''Sleep well, darling.''

''I'll try,'' he said, and he hung up.

Lauren wiped away the tears and chuckled to herself. Everything would work out. They were going to be fine once all the details were worked out, once Georgie was legally their own. It was silly to worry about unknown perils. No one ever knew what the future held, but whatever it was, they could face it together. Yes, that was what counted, that they would be together, a team, a unit. Her and Colin and George. A real family, a dream come true, her very own miracle of the heart.

As he did every morning, Colin greeted with a hearty hello the secretary that he shared, along with a suite of offices, with an independent real estate appraiser and a pool cleaner.

"Good morning, Mr. Garret," she returned, reaching for a pile of bright yellow notes. "You have several messages."

"Thank you, Mrs. Wilmon." He shuffled through the stack, making mental notes on some and dismissing others. One in particular spiked his interest. The university press that had published his book was interested in doing another. "Did you finish that typing I gave you?" he asked distractedly.

"Yes, sir. It's on your desk."

"Efficient, as always," Colin said, smiling as he gave her his undivided attention. Then he did something he didn't know he was going to do. "Would you ask Don and Jason to give me a few minutes? Oh, and could you start gathering some cartons."

"Cartons?" the surprised secretary echoed.

"Cardboard boxes," he clarified, "for packing. And I'll need the client list."

"You're leaving us!"

Colin chuckled, feeling absurdly giddy. "I'm afraid so, but never fear. Financial guarantees are in place, and Don and Jason will find someone to take over my responsibilities quite soon."

"I knew there was more to this Eagle Nest thing than vacationing," Mrs. Wilmon exclaimed. "You just aren't the sort to go off impulsively like that."

Colin leaned into her desk, bringing his face close to hers. "I thought that, too," he confided mysteriously. "Guess we were both wrong." He didn't tell her that the decision to pack up and head for Eagle Nest—and very likely marry a woman whom he barely knew—had hit him like a sledgehammer just moments ago. But it was the right thing to do. It was the right thing to do for his son and for Lauren, so it was the right thing for him. Feeling much lighter than he had in months, he straightened and carried his messages and briefcase into his office. He had much to do, and the sooner it was done, the sooner he could get on with the new life awaiting him.

His office mates, Don and Jason came in together. Both were shocked at his sudden announcement but also supportive—and curious. He told them only that fatherhood had impressed him with the need to simplify his life in order to spend as much time as possible with his son. They congratulated him and sounded flatteringly disappointed to be losing him, then took the hint and left him alone. Despite his morning appointment, which consisted of apologies, a lot of free information and a recommendation for another consultant, Colin was able to begin weeding through his files before lunch, determining what had to be done to close as many accounts as possible. Some could go with him. Others would have to be returned to the client or forwarded to a colleague. It would take weeks to clear it all.

Having canceled the next day's appointment, he devoted the morning to listing his house with a Realtor, then spent the afternoon and the evening in the office. He intended to spend Friday and the weekend the same way, but by Thursday evening he knew that he wasn't going to do that. He had to see them, both of them. No, that wasn't totally honest. The truth was that he wanted to see George, but he had to see Lauren. He had to know if what he was planning to do was workable. He left a message for Mrs. Wilmon, then called Jeff to break a Sunday dinner date with him and the family. Jeff sounded concerned.

"If you're worried about the care the boy is receiving, we do have some legal recourse—"

"No, no, it's nothing like that. I just want to be with him."

"You haven't been back home two weeks yet."

"Well, it's partly the place, I guess," Colin said, realizing it was true. "It's hard to come back to the rat race after spending time there. And I have been under a lot of stress."

"And for a long time," Jeff conceded. "So when will you be back? We'll reschedule dinner."

"I'm not sure," Colin hedged. "I'm taking some work with me. I'll let you know."

Jeff sighed. "I knew you'd be a devoted father, but I didn't expect you'd be so unpredictable about it."

Colin chuckled. "You're the second person to tell me lately that I've developed a disturbing tendency toward predictability. Maybe it's time I made some changes."

"Change can be good," Jeff said carefully, "but what if the boy turns out not to be yours? What then?"

"That won't happen," Colin said firmly. "Now wish me farewell and be a good lawyer."

"Easy roads, old buddy," Jeff retorted flippantly, "and I'm a better lawyer, and friend, than you may know."

Colin doubted that. He knew how far Jeff would go for the sake of friendship and what feats he'd pulled off in the name of justice.

She was outside trying to have a snowball fight with Ponce and Georgie when she spotted the familiar SUV on the curve outside of town coming toward the lodge. Dropping the snowball she was trying to compact from the inch or two of dry powder on the ground, she lifted a hand to shield her eyes from the glare of the bright morning sunlight, jostling Georgie in the backpack strapped to her shoulders. He kicked to let her know that he didn't appreciate this interruption in their play, but then Ponce hit her a glancing blow off the side of her head, the "ball" of snow exploding into whisper-light powder that showered George liberally and sent him into gales of giggles. When she didn't immediately retaliate, Ponce paused to see what had caught her attention. She waved him off, her heart pounding so hard in her chest that for a moment she couldn't move. Then the truck turned into the gap in the fenced parking lot and her feet were suddenly moving.

The SUV was parked, and he was opening the driver's side door by the time she got there. The smile on his face rivaled the sun in brightness. She threw herself into his arms, feeling Georgie bounce against her back as she did so.

"Colin! You're here!"

"I'm home," he said, but his words didn't hit her right away.

"You didn't tell me you were coming."

"I didn't know until day before yesterday, and then there was so much to do—"

"Home!" she gasped, finally hearing him. "You're staying?"

"Eventually," he confirmed with a smile. "It'll take some time, but I think this is where we belong."

She threw her arms around his neck. "Oh, Colin! It's wonderful!" Suddenly she pulled back. "But how? What about your business? Your house?"

He laid a finger across her lips. "I'm dealing with the business now. Part of it can come with me. In fact, I brought work again. And I put the house on the market. It shouldn't take long to sell. It's in a good location, and I've made sure it's a good buy.''

Real. What had seemed at times in these past many days to be nothing more than a figment of an overactive imagination was real after all. Tears flooded her eyes. She blinked them away. He bent his head and kissed her briefly but firmly on the mouth, then reached around her to cup a hand around Georgie's head and kiss him above one eye.

''Hello, son.''

Lauren laughed, thrilled and excited. Reaching back, she jostled Georgie by pushing up on the seat of his sling. ''I can't believe this!''

''Believe it,'' he told her, reaching into the truck to pluck out his coat and shrug it on. ''That's a cold wind coming off that lake.''

''Aw, you just need some motion to warm up your blood,'' she teased, dancing back to scoop up a fistful of snow and hurl it at him. It was mostly powder, but it dusted his head and shoulders and goaded him into action.

''Hey!'' Lunging, he caught her by a coat pocket and then grappled for a grip at her waist. She could have slipped away but didn't, preferring to be pulled up close against his tall, powerful frame. He locked his hands in the small of her back, reaching beneath the backpack to manage it, and blew flakes off his eyelashes. ''We've had some snow, I see.''

We again. ''Not much,'' she said, more breathless than she had any reason to be, ''and the wind sweeps it away pretty quickly. That's why we ran out first thing this morning to play, isn't it, Georgie?''

''Is that so?'' Colin released her then and reached around her to pull George from his backpack.

''Now tell me about this playing-in-the-snow business,'' he said to the boy. Putting his forehead to Georgie's he pretended to listen intently. "Uh-huh," he said after a moment, "sounds to me like Mommy needs some instruction. What do you say we give it to her?"

With that, he lifted Georgie onto his shoulders. George grabbed fistfuls of hair as Colin dropped forward to scoop up snow in his bare hands. Lauren gasped, expecting Georgie to topple headfirst onto the ground, but he managed the maneuver well, grinning gleefully as Colin straightened and plastered her right in the chest with a giant snowball. Laughing, she backed up rapidly, then darted to the side as Colin bent to scoop up more snow, but he anticipated her movement and hit her on the top of the head.

Screeching with ruffled pride, she darted away again, then quickly stooped to scrape together her own weapon. Colin nailed her before she got back to her feet, then smoothly sidestepped the missile she launched in his direction, letting it splatter and puff against the side of his truck. For the next several minutes she darted side to side and back and forth, taking more shots than she evaded while trying to scrape together a defense, which more often than not fell harmlessly on the SUV against which Colin had taken his stand. Frustrated with her lack of success in either evading his missiles or landing her own, Lauren finally called truce and surrendered.

"I give up! You've won! I admit it, I'm a lousy snowball fighter."

Colin pumped a fist in victorious braggadocio and lifted an enraptured George off his shoulders and onto his hip. Jogging toward her, he huffed and puffed in an obvious effort to make her feel better, feigning exhaustion. "You almost had us licked. If you hadn't been quite so quick to throw in the towel…"

Lauren ruffled her hair to get out the snow and plucked free the slipping barrette. "Baloney. You've obviously had more practice with snowballs than I have."

He laughed. "I've had my share of dodging and throwing. What can I say? I was a boy." He shook his free hand then and jammed it into his pocket. "Man, that stuff's cold. It's real dry, though, good for the skiers."

"You ski?" she asked hopefully.

"I love to ski. I'm not exactly a stud on the slopes, but I sure have fun."

"Great! I can't wait to go. I'm darn good, if I do say so myself."

"Well, you can show me up on the slopes, then, and I'll pummel you with snowballs when we get home."

"Home," she said, sobering. "I still can't believe you mean to move here."

He slipped an arm around her shoulders and pulled her to his side. "It'll take some time to work it all out, but I think it's for the best."

"It's just such a sacrifice," she argued, "giving up your business."

"Oh, I fully intend to rebuild that," he stated, moving her toward the front door of the lodge.

She stopped in her tracks and forced him to face her. "Colin, Eagle Nest is a village of some two hundred permanent residents."

"I know it's small," he said, "but there's Angel Fire and Red River and Cimarron and Taos. Heck, I'll go to Espanola and Raton for business, if I have to. Someone within a reasonable driving distance has got to need advice on putting together, funding and operating a small business."

She laughed at that. "Where were you when I needed you?"

"You might find a use for me yet," he said huskily, cocking his head.

Her entire body heated, erupting into pink blossoms high on her cheeks. "Businesswise, I mean."

His grin was slow and lazy. "So do I. But even if no one in and around these mountains needs me, I've got other options. My publisher is interested in doing a series of self-help or how-to books aimed at small entrepreneurs."

"Hmm, maybe I do need you. Businesswise, I mean."

He chuckled. "Well, you've got me. Now let's get inside. I'm freezing."

"What about your things?"

"I thought I'd wait to unload until I know where I'm going to be."

She turned and led the way into the lodge, saying, "I knew I should've gotten the cabin ready. It's the weekend, so we're full up unless someone fails to show. Think you can handle the couch until then?"

"The couch will do fine," he said, letting the door close behind him. He shuddered, adding, "I should've brought my long johns. I don't think I'm prepared for this cold."

"It'll warm up later in the day," she told him. "Really, you can go out later in your shirtsleeves. Tonight it's supposed to snow again, though, and you'll want to stoke the fireplace."

"Stoke the fireplace. Will do." He carried George to the counter and placed him atop it, then began getting him out of his snowsuit. "Maybe I ought to borrow this outfit. Won't need to stoke the fireplace then, will we, pal? No need for hauling in firewood then. What do you think? Can I borrow this nice, warm suit?"

Lauren watched him struggling to unzip and unsnap and wrestle off the suit. Georgie was his usual compliant self, which meant that he was practically boneless, the next thing to a dead weight. It was amazing how little fingers could snag in seemingly smooth sleeves, and garments without hooks or sharp edges could cling to like surfaces. She knew from experience how difficult undressing an infant could be. She knew, too, real eagerness for the experience when she saw it. She'd been there. Often. A little shiver of unease fluttered through her. She couldn't put a name or a label to it, but something about the obvious, almost desperate plea-sure with which Colin performed this small task for Geor-gie struck her as unusual, not dangerous at all, not even wrong, but oddly intense. Indeed, it felt right, too right, somehow. It compelled her to step in and help him out.

"Here, let me," she said, walking around behind the counter to stand opposite Colin. She poked two fingers into the wrist of one small sleeve and spread them, widening the tube through which Colin was tugging Georgie's arm. The arm slid free. Together they worked free the other arm and then his legs, first removing his shoes, which had to be put back on afterward. Georgie squirmed and poked fin-gers in his mouth and scratched at a big button on the front of Colin's coat. Finally, his patience exhausted, he tried to roll over onto his belly and crawl away. Colin righted him and kept him in place, sort of, by tickling and tussling with him until Lauren got his shoes back on him. Then Georgie happily sat on the counter and drummed his heels against the side while Lauren attempted to smooth his hair. Sud-denly she had to know something.

"Why are you here now?" she asked Colin, beseeching him with her eyes for an honest answer.

"I couldn't stay away any longer," he said.

Lauren felt her heart pounding with that strength-stealing intensity again. "Why?"

Colin looked at Georgie and traced with his fingertip the little swirl of the omnipresent cowlick just to the side of the center of his hairline. Then he looked up at her and said, "You. I had to see you, to be sure."

"And?"

He smiled, his eyes filled with such tenderness that it was almost painful to see. "Will you marry me, Lauren?"

It was then that Lauren realized she'd been holding her

breath. Reaching across the counter, she hugged him, Georgie trapped between them, and laid her head on his shoulder. "Yes! Oh, God, yes! You don't know how much I needed to hear you ask. You didn't really the first time, you know."

"I know," he said, hugging her back. "All I can say is that this whole thing has just taken me so much by surprise."

"Me, too." She turned her face up to his. "But what a wonderful surprise."

He kissed her, long and deeply, until Georgie pushed and kicked and squirmed until he drove them apart.

"Dow," he said, attempting to slide off the edge of the counter.

"Down!" Colin exclaimed, catching Georgie and swinging him into his arms. "You want down, do you?" He then quickly convinced Georgie that he really wanted up—up, up and flying about the room like an airplane, arms outstretched and laughter filling the air as they swooped and swung and rolled.

Real, Lauren thought. It was real. He was real. Miracles were real.

Chapter Seven

It was cold. Colin crawled from beneath the covers and padded in his stocking feet to the fireplace, where he shoved another log onto the fire. He wondered if Georgie was this cold. His common sense told him that Lauren wouldn't let the child suffer, but he knew, too, how soundly George slept. It wouldn't hurt just to peek in on him. Quietly, by the light of the fire, he moved across the room and into the heavy darkness of the hallway, running a hand along the wall to keep himself oriented. At the door to Georgie's room, he located the knob and turned it carefully. The door swung silently inward. A night light burned softly on a shelf in the corner, illuminating the friendly form of a big-eared bunny. Colin tiptoed to the crib and stared down at his sleeping son, noting that this room was definitely warmer than the living area.

Lauren had dressed the child in a heavy-footed sleeper, but his little hands were thrown up above his head, free of any cover. Colin slipped a finger into the boy's tiny palm and found it invitingly warm. He should have known. Reassured, he dropped a delicate kiss on the boy's forehead and turned toward the door. He bumped into Lauren.

Backing up a step, she pushed hair out of her eyes and folded her chenille robe tight. "Is anything wrong?"

Colin shook his head. "I thought he might be cold."

"He sleeps really warm," she said softly, "like a little furnace. It makes regulating the nighttime temperature in the apartment difficult."

Colin shivered, despite the T-shirt, fleece warm-up bottoms and socks that he wore. "Why don't you tell me about it in front of the fire," he whispered, turning her and pushing her gently toward the door. He kept a hand on her shoulder as they moved down the hallway, then just naturally left it there, draping his arm around her as he moved to her side in the living room. The fire crackled across the room, almost as inviting as the warmth of her body at his side. Suddenly he was no longer cold at all. He decided that he was going to be downright hot before he let her leave him again.

The chair and the coffee table had been shoved away from the fire when the couch had been unfolded, so she allowed him to steer her easily toward the foot of the bed, where she perched almost primly while he tossed a couple more logs onto the fire. "I know it's an inconvenience," she said haltingly, "having to stoke the fire, I mean, but Georgie sleeps so warmly that I have to keep the temperature down. I've tried dressing him differently, but sometimes he kicks the covers off and takes a chill. On the other hand, if I dress him too warmly, he sweats and takes a chill from that. Part of the problem is that his room is the warmest in the house."

"I noticed that," Colin said, dusting off his hands and coming to sit beside her.

"I close the vent in there, but for some reason it's still warmer," she complained.

"These old buildings can be tricky," Colin said, "especially when you add modern conveniences like central heat."

She nodded. "It's expensive, too. You wouldn't believe the cost of propane in this valley, and electricity!"

"There are other ways to generate heat," Colin said huskily, sliding a hand up her back beneath her hair to her nape. This was the woman he was going to marry. He would sleep beside her, make decisions with her, comfort her fears, enjoy her smiles, touch her body. It was that last privilege that he was thinking of now. He heard her swallow, felt the elongation of her neck as she did so.

"I—I thought we'd agreed t-to wait," she whispered.

"We did," he said. "We will. But there's making love, and then there's making love."

She turned up big, green-gold eyes to him. "What if we g-go too far? I'm not using any birth control."

He massaged the back of her neck. "We won't go too far. I promise. Trust me."

She slowly lifted a hand and brushed her fingertips through the hair at his temple. "I trust you," she whispered.

He bent his head and kissed her, drawing deeply from her mouth. Much to his satisfaction, she melted into his arms. He held her for a long while, exploring her mouth with his tongue, then tasting her skin with kisses and tiny strokes with the tip of his tongue. After working his way to her ear, he used the edges of his teeth to trace its delicate contours before gently sucking the small lobe. She moaned and began to breathe heavily. Ah, but he had barely begun to touch her.

Drawing away, he slowly parted the front of her robe and pushed it off her shoulders and down her arms. Carefully, gently, he unbuttoned the shirt of her heavy flannel pajamas. Sliding his hand inside, he cupped her breast, exulting in its weight even as he eased her back and down onto the bed. Rising above her on one elbow, he folded open the front of her shirt and looked his fill in the flickering light as he molded and teased her breasts, bringing them to peaked fullness. She lay quietly, except for the harshness of her breathing, her hands resting beside her head.

"You have extraordinary breasts," he whispered, and began to suckle her, licking her nipple to moisten it before pulling it into his mouth. She moved restlessly, arching against him, gasping as he tugged and laved one breast with his mouth while massaging the other with his hand. He bucked at every undulation and moan.

The room was absurdly warm now, absolutely toasty. Rising above her on his knees, he ripped off his T-shirt and tossed it away. She immediately lifted a hand to run it over his chest, riffling her fingers through the light dusting of dark hair, scoring his flat nipples with her fingernails. He thought he would burst, the length of him distorting the front of his soft pants and pulling them taut across his buttocks.

Determinedly, he moved astride her on his knees, hooked his fingers in the waistband of her pajama bottoms and pulled them down. No panties. She trembled, her breath coming in ragged gasps. Moving to the side, he sat back on his heels. He wanted desperately to spread her legs, but he didn't dare. Instead he stroked the silky triangle of surprisingly light hair and watched as she shuddered. He slid his hand down between her legs, parted her with his fingertips and slid his middle finger deeply inside her. She convulsed, clasping him with her inner muscles, and he wondered if it was possible to drive himself insane by simply touching her. When he slid his thumb into place and began circling the sensitive nub, she cried out. He lay down beside her, cupped her face with his free hand and kissed her, taking her cries into his mouth until they ceased. She was crying softly when he turned her on her side and wrapped his body around hers.

"Did I hurt you?"

"No, oh, no. I'm just so happy."

He chuckled. He couldn't help it. "Good. I want to make you happy."

"This moment is absolutely perfect," she said on a sigh.

"Well, not perfect," he remarked wryly, intensely aware of the throbbing hardness in his groin. "I think we'd better marry quickly." He wrapped his arms around her lazily. "Before Thanksgiving, anyway."

"I guess we'd better," she said, giggling softly and turning so her cheek was against his chest. He pulled her tighter and flipped the edge of the blanket upon which they lay over them. "Do you know," she whispered after a moment, fingers stroking his hair, "that you have a cowlick almost just like Georgie's?"

"Umm," he replied unthinkingly. His cheek against the top of her head, he closed his eyes and slept.

Colin woke on Monday morning alone in the sofa bed in front of the fire. They had agreed since that first night that it was wiser to confine their intimacies to affectionate gestures suitable for public display, and while he looked forward eagerly to this marriage now, he was aware that he had never been quite so frustrated as he had been these past two days. The situation had some true rewards. Lauren positively glowed, and Georgie had actually called him "Da-da" yesterday, but Colin was finding it increasingly difficult to go to bed at night and wake up alone.

He heard Lauren in the bedroom with Georgie, speaking softly. Throwing back the covers, Colin sat up, adjusted his clothing and stood. He made a pit stop in the bathroom between the bedrooms, quickly washed up and joined Lauren and George. Lauren was dressed in a pair of mustard-yellow slacks and matching turtleneck, her hair swept up into a perky ponytail at the very top of her head. The color suited her perfectly, bringing out the golden highlights in her hair and eyes. A transparent ruby gloss made her lips so kissable that Colin couldn't resist. Even though she was struggling to dress their son, he turned her into his arms and captured her mouth with his.

Lauren lifted her arms around his neck and leaned into him, soft and willing and, oh, so womanly. Only when a half-dressed Georgie began to rattle the sides of his crib did Colin break the kiss. Lauren laughed deep in her throat. "Good morning, future husband."

"Good morning, sweetheart."

"Da-a-a," Georgie said, knowing exactly how to get the attention he wanted.

Colin swept him up and whirled him around. "Want Daddy to finish dressing you, hmm?"

Lauren took the boy from his arms. "Better Daddy should dress himself while Mommy finishes this and orders breakfast. We have a lot of plans to make."

Aware of his empty stomach—and the level of his frustration—Colin instantly agreed. "Meet you in the dining room."

He quickly returned to the living room to raid his suitcase. Armed with a pair of gray wool slacks, a soft black flannel shirt and the requisite paraphernalia, he locked himself in the bathroom. Twenty minutes later he carefully parted and combed his short, thick hair and went to meet his family.

When he arrived in the dining room, he found Lauren and Georgie at their customary table near the kitchen. Georgie sat in his high chair, a spotty bib tied loosely around his neck, oatmeal decorating his face. The room was empty otherwise, as the dining room was not yet officially open. Lauren called out to him.

"I ordered pecan French toast and Canadian bacon. Is that all right?"

"Excellent," he said. Coming near the table, he drew out his chair, then paused to run a hand over the top and back of Georgie's head. Just then Juan pushed through the swinging kitchen door, a cup of coffee in one hand. Colin looked up at him and smiled a greeting. Juan nodded in return. Not for the first time, Colin sensed an air of waiting and watching about the compact, older man.

George pointed his messy spoon at Colin and said matter-of-factly, "Da-da," as if informing Juan of Colin's identity. Juan simply looked at Colin, his brown eyes flat and cautious, and an unwelcome certainty hit Colin with the force of a blow.

He knows.

Fear shivered up Colin's spine. Somehow Juan knew, or at least suspected, that Colin was, indeed, George's father. He knew, and he was keeping silent, waiting to see if Colin followed through with this marriage. Was it possible that Juan knew as well how concerned Colin was with Lauren's happiness? Did Juan understand that it was too late to tell Lauren the truth now? She couldn't possibly understand that he wasn't trying to mislead her, that he could love her simply for what she had done for and meant to his son. She couldn't know the truth, not until they'd had a chance to build a life together.

Very much aware of Juan's watchful attention, Colin sat down in his chair, reached across the table for Lauren's hand and lifted it to his lips. "You look marvelous this morning. That color suits you."

"Thank you, kind sir."

Keeping her hand in his, Colin next turned his attention

to George. "Are you eating that cereal, champ, or is it eating you?"

Lauren laughed, but George just aimed a glob of oatmeal at his mouth with one hand and waved his spoon around with the other. Colin good-naturedly attempted to teach George how to actually eat with a spoon—and ended up with oatmeal on the knee of his gray slacks. Deferring to Lauren and her good advice, he decided to let George figure out the spoon in his own time. After cleaning his knee with a napkin dampened in his water glass, he smiled and maintained his jovial manner, but a cloud had shadowed the eagerness with which he had taken on the day, and no matter how wide he smiled or how often he laughed, it would not go away.

They lingered in the dining room, making wedding plans and greeting the guests as they wandered in by pairs and groups. Colin was taking a proprietorial air with everything around him lately, insisting on tending the front desk as the need arose and hopping up to refill coffee cups when the overworked new waitress found herself behind. Lauren found that she quite liked it. He was making himself a part of the lodge and everything else that had to do with her life, and it felt exactly right that he do so.

The last two days had been glorious, with Friday night falling into the realm of the unimaginably wondrous. Even more important, it had proven the strength of Colin's ardor and trustworthiness. The one thing that had made her slightly uncomfortable was his eagerness to establish himself in the role of Georgie's father, but she attributed that uneasiness to her own possessiveness of the child and her fears of losing him. Then she had realized that Colin's eagerness to parent the child could only aid her cause. Surely a caring, loving, two-parent family had a greater chance of adopting an infant than a single woman. The paternity test, she wouldn't even think about. She couldn't. It just couldn't be possible that after all that had happened some stranger could lay claim to her, *their,* child. Together, she and Colin would find a way to keep him. She just knew it.

When the front desk bell chimed, Lauren quickly stood, feeling that it was her turn to answer that particular summons, but Colin, bless him, was still ready to step in.

"You haven't finished your breakfast," he said, pushing aside his coffee cup. "I can go."

It was true that she'd been a little too dreamy this morning to eat, but she was finding that she could live quite well on love alone. "No, I'll take care of it. I guess I'm just too excited to eat." She dropped a kiss on his cheek as she skirted the table. "You take care of the baby. See if he'll let you do something about that face."

"Come on, youngster," he said to Georgie as she walked away. "Let's get your face cleaned before that cereal sets like concrete."

As she slipped behind the counter, she took notice of an oddly dressed man pacing beside it, his reddish blond hair ruffled from the crisp autumn wind. His expensive, camel-colored wool dress coat seemed inappropriate with the faded jeans, sweatshirt and ragged athletic shoes he wore, but the irritation on his boyish face transformed into an engaging smile the instant he saw her.

"Hello. Can I help you?"

"My name's Jeffrey Locke. I'm looking for a friend, a Mr.—"

"Colin Garret," she finished for him, recognizing the name of Colin's best friend. He didn't look much like a lawyer with his pale, splotched skin and rosy, almost feminine mouth, but Colin had told her that Jeff Locke was not only his best friend but also his attorney. She held out her hand, smiling welcomingly. "How do you do? I'm Lauren."

"Lauren Cole!" he exclaimed, taking her hand in his. "Colin has been singing your praises."

Lauren beamed. "Well, that's nice to hear. I'm quite a fan of Colin's, too."

"Oh, that's good. This is such a nasty business, it's nice to know that you bear him no ill will."

"Ill will?" Lauren echoed, chuckling. "Hardly."

Jeff Locke ruffled a hand through his hair and leaned against the counter, obviously relieved. "I don't mind telling you, I was concerned about it. He seemed so uncertain and worried when he was home last. That's why I'm here, actually. I thought if I rushed the blood test and got the court order he could finally relax. Where is he? I want to give him the good news."

Lauren could only blink at the man. "Blood test? Oh, for the marriage license, of course. But what's this about a court order?"

At that moment Colin stepped into the foyer carrying a fussing Georgie. "I think he needs his mom to tell him—" He stopped abruptly. "Jeff! What are you doing here?"

For a moment Jeffrey Locke seemed confused and hesitant, but then he rushed forward, exclaiming, "This must be the man! Good grief, he does look just like you." He slapped Colin on the shoulder, then reached up and caught one of Georgie's hands in his. "Hello, there, George Colin. I'm your uncle Jeff."

"Dalton," Lauren murmured, oddly numb. Neither man seemed to hear her.

"Jeff, you shouldn't be here," Colin hissed at his friend.

Jeff Locke backed up a step. "I brought the results of the blood test. Good news, pal! The boy is yours. You were absolutely right."

The boy. His. Results of the blood test. Lauren reeled, unable to accept the obvious implications, and yet, she had known. On some level she had known and refused to see, to acknowledge, to believe. It was so much easier to dream.

Colin was looking at Lauren with a worried expression. "I think we'd better discuss this in private," he said to his friend.

"What's going on, Colin?" Jeff wanted to know. "Why aren't you celebrating? And what's this about a marriage license?"

"That's enough, Jeff," Colin said sharply. "I don't want to discuss personal business in public."

"No," Lauren said, managing to sound only exhausted when she meant to sound stern. "I need to hear this."

Colin divided a desperate look between his friend and her. "Uh, Lauren, Jeff's driven a long way, and—"

"Oh, that's all right," Jeff interrupted lightly. "I, um, just wanted to bring you this." He extracted a folded piece of paper from his inside coat pocket.

Colin took the paper in one hand and tucked it out of sight. "Thanks. I appreciate your effort," he said lightly, too lightly.

A still-confused Jeff Locke rocked back on his heels. "I don't mind telling you, I went above and beyond the call of duty on this one. I may have even made some enemies."

"I'll remember that," Colin muttered, as if that put an end to the matter, but Lauren knew she couldn't let him sidestep this, much as she wanted to.

Digging deep, she steadied herself and looked at Jeff Locke. "Why?" she asked. "Why did you go to all this trouble? What does that paper say?"

Jeff glanced at Colin, then shrugged. "Just what we already knew, that Colin is definitely the boy's father."

The boy. George. Numbly Lauren looked at Colin, vaguely aware that he had gone pale.

"What about the court order?" she asked in a breathy

voice, dread warring with fear and disbelief and awful certainty.

"Lauren, it doesn't matter," Colin said gently, but she switched her gaze back to Jeffrey Locke, knowing instinctively that what she had to know would come from him.

"Why does he need a court order?"

Jeff licked his lips. "To take custody—"

"Shut up, Jeff!" Colin barked, but it was too late.

"—of the boy," Jeff finished lamely.

Colin swore, muttering curse words under his breath.

Jeff Locke had had enough. "I don't get this!" he exclaimed. "Colin, listen to me. You can take the boy home with you today."

The air left Lauren's lungs in a painful whoosh, as if someone had driven a fist into her chest. Colin was staring at her, Georgie held before him almost like a shield. "Lauren, listen to me."

But she couldn't listen. She didn't dare. All she could think to do was to clasp her son to her breast. "Give him to me!"

Colin handed him over without hesitation, while Jeff Locke asked, "What the hell is going on?"

"Let me explain," Colin said to her, ignoring Jeff. "I meant to tell you, but I wasn't sure."

"No," she whispered, her world crumbling around her. "No, no, no! Oh, God, no!" She was screaming at the end. Frightened, Georgie suddenly wailed, and she couldn't comfort him, didn't know how. Colin was Georgie's father. George was his. And he meant to take him away! No marriage. No love. Just a way to be around his son. She staggered, the pain of full realization almost bringing her to her knees. Colin automatically reached out, and that gave her the strength to jerk away. "Don't touch him!"

"Honey, listen!"

"You said, 'Trust me,' and I did!"

"You still can."

She didn't bother replying to that because it was so preposterous. "How could you?" she demanded instead. How could I? she wondered. "Oh, my God, I've done it again!" She took a step forward, realized that Colin was blocking the way and backed up again, desperate to leave this place, this truth.

"I didn't want to hurt you," he said slowly, as if she were a hysterical child. "You don't deserve to be hurt. You've loved and cared for him so generously, it didn't seem fair to repay you with loss and pain."

Tears poured down her face. "So you decided to marry me," she said bitterly, thinking her humiliation complete. "Or was that another lie?"

"No. It was just a misunderstanding," he blurted, then winced. "I was trying to tell you the truth, but I botched it, and you thought I was proposing. Later I decided it was the best thing for—"

The remaining words battered at her eardrums, but she couldn't take them in. Suddenly she was reliving every moment of that night there at the campsite, while at the same time seeing the worried faces of the two men with her. She wanted to faint, to close her eyes and let consciousness slip away. She wanted to run, to get so far away from the ugly truth that she need never face it and know the depth of her own foolishness. But there could be no escaping this. Colin was Georgie's father. He had come here to take him away. Her dream hadn't become reality. Her miracle was a nightmare. And she had trusted him. Once again she had trusted where she should not have. Once again she was the fool. Gradually she became aware of another presence, a familiar calming voice and sheltering form. Juan. Juan was safe, her good right arm, her friend.

She let him guide her from behind the counter, Georgie clinging to her like a frightened little animal, his runny nose wet against her chest. She knew that others were speaking, watching, following, but escape was all that mattered. He led her through the great room and toward the apartment. When she realized that refuge was in sight, she literally ran for her private quarters, and once there she locked the doors. With Georgie in her arms, she held the universe at bay and began taking stock of the shattered remains of her world.

She cried for hours. He stood with his head bowed, listening through the door. "Please give me the key," Colin pleaded one more time. He'd threatened and even shaken Juan, but the older man remained sadly adamant.

"She'll open when she's ready."

"I have to explain this to her. I have to make her understand."

"What does she not understand?" Juan asked, shaking his head and shrugging his shoulders. "You are the boy's natural father. You can take him away."

"I don't want to take him away."

"But you will."

"Only if she makes me," Colin insisted hotly. He wanted to hit someone, starting with Jeff. This whole thing was an unspeakable disaster, and Jeff had brought it all down on him. Oh, Colin knew that his friend had only meant to help, as well as he knew that he had been the author of his own destruction. But he'd had only the best intentions. He'd tried to do what was best for everyone. She need not have known the truth until he had proven that they could make the marriage work. They would have been happy then, Lauren and Georgie and him.

Suddenly the door to the apartment opened, and Colin at last found himself face-to-face with the person he most desperately wanted to see. She looked a perfect mess, her hair in disarray, eyes and nose swollen, skin splotchy.

"Thank God!" he said.

Her smile was brittle, ugly. She kicked his suitcase out into the hallway. "I want you out of here."

"Not until you listen to me."

"No, you listen to me," she said, folding her arms. "I'm going to fight you, all of you. I won't give up my son, and I won't be cheated out of my life!"

"No one's—"

"And I won't take your pity!" she cried. "You think I'd marry you now? You think I can love you now? If you meant anything you said about not wanting to hurt me, then you'll get out and leave us alone."

"Lauren, I can't—" She reached for the door to shut it, and he leaped forward, blocking it. But Juan leaped, too, and it quickly became obvious that if he was going to get into that apartment, he was going to have to fight his way in. He thought of Georgie and how he'd cried when Lauren had folded, and the will to fight ebbed. He stepped back. The door closed in his face. He pressed his fists against it, trembling with regret and worry. "I'll be back," he promised. "I'll go now, but I'll be back, Lauren, for both of you." A gentle hand clasped his forearm, and Colin looked down at the small brown man beside him. "It's the only way, Juan," he said despondently. "That hasn't changed. She has to marry me. She has to."

Chapter Eight

Lauren cried until she couldn't cry anymore, vacillating between humiliation and anger.

She had trusted him, loved him, offered him her heart, and once again she had only been grasping at air. What a fool she was. And yet, how dare he do this to her? After all she had told him about her past, after the intimacies they had shared, after she had bared her heart to him, he had lied to her. He had come to Eagle Nest to take Georgie from her—and stayed to betray her and break her heart. And the worst part was that she had welcomed him. Well, no more. He was no different from Larry, wanting what was hers. But he wouldn't get it. He wouldn't get Georgie.

Briefly, the idea of simply packing up the baby and disappearing into the night appealed to her, but she knew that was no real solution. Colin would merely hunt her down, and it would mean giving up everything she'd worked for. She had to do something, though, other than stand by in tears and watch her life be gutted. For now, she decided, she would lick her wounds. Tomorrow or the next day would be soon enough to decide what to do. For now she would rail against the unfairness of it. Later she would plan.

Unfortunately the afternoon mail brought more bad news. Juan, bless him, did not try to keep it from her. Instead he seemed to understand that an attack from another direction would put the starch back in her spine, and a letter from Larry's lawyer, insisting that she sell the lodge and split the proceeds—minus half the cost of renovations— with her spoiled, greedy brother, definitely qualified. By Tuesday morning she was ready to fight tooth and nail for what was hers.

Deep down, at the very bottom of the well of her soul, she knew that with Georgie, at least, the battle was already lost. Colin was Georgie's father. She accepted that. Perhaps, in some part of her, she had from the moment she'd first seen Colin. They were as alike as two peas in a pod, right down to the cowlick. Georgie even seemed to share many of his father's personality traits, now that she was alert to them. Every smile started in their eyes. Patience and a certain calmness seemed their natural demeanor, but she had glimpsed in both of them a private depth of emotion foreign to most people. Yes, Georgie was definitely Colin's son. She didn't need the blood test to prove that. But he was hers, too. In the end she supposed that Colin would win custody, but she meant to have a hand in the child's life if it took every penny she ever made and decades to secure her position.

The lodge was another matter. She simply couldn't afford to give up income. She was going to have to hire an attorney, anyway, maybe several of them, so she might as well fight fire with fire where her brother's demands were concerned. Meanwhile, life could only be lived day by day.

She still couldn't quite believe that she had been such a

colossal fool, but as Juan put it, "The heart sometimes cannot bear to acknowledge what the eyes see, and the mind sides with the heart." Well, her heart had taken its last battering, and her eyes were wide open and reporting to an alert brain for a change. All were in protect-and-fight mode. If she kept Georgie closer to her side than before, refused Colin's repeated phone calls and spent more time locked away with the baby in their private quarters, no one could blame her. She didn't let anything slip, though. She kept on top of everything at the lodge and even wrote Larry's lawyer a letter offering the cabin for Larry's sole ownership by way of compromise. She didn't expect that offer to be acceptable, but at least it bought her some time.

By the end of the week she'd gotten enough referrals to have picked an attorney in Taos to help her fight for custody of Georgie. She made an appointment and began a detailed list of all the arguments in her favor, with the reluctant help of Mercedes Allonzo, the social worker who had recommended her as Georgie's foster mother. With the lodge busy, especially on weekends, and Georgie growing more mobile and independent every day, Lauren had her hands full by day. Georgie had started to protest when she put him in his playpen. She was almost glad, and learned as never before to function with him perched on her hip. Only at night when her treacherous heart held sway over her slumbering mind did she suffer regrets and longings and grave doubts.

She continually dreamed of Colin's gentle smile, of the calm depths of his blue eyes, of the easy affection he had shown both her and Georgie. She remembered the pride with which he had watched Georgie take his first steps and the eager questions he'd asked, trusting her expertise. Even worse, though, were the imagined embellishments of their lovemaking, the remembered sensations heightened, or so it seemed, a hundredfold by dreams of completion and ultimate joining, words of love that were never whispered, pledges never made. These were the dreams that left her aching for what might have been. These were the memories she could not bury deeply enough and made her question the sense in fighting the inevitable.

Colin would not be swayed. "Nothing else is fair."

"Fair to whom?" Meg, Jeff's wife, argued. "Certainly not to you. What's fair about an unwanted marriage?"

Sighing, Colin pushed his hands through his hair and looked around the cluttered, comfortable den where he had passed so many enjoyable evenings. It was a home where children lived and thrived, the crowning achievement of an ambition shared by two people in love. It was exactly what he wanted, and he could see himself having it with Lauren, if only she'd work at it with him.

He pinched the bridge of his nose. "Listen to me, Meg. As much as I love George, *she* loves George. I can't just ignore that."

"But—"

"Forget it, Meg," Jeff said dryly. "You're wasting your breath."

Colin smiled to himself, recognizing both the tone and the ploy. "I'm not a complete fool, you know," he said lightly. "Believe me when I say that I have to do this."

"Is it really up to you, though? You can't just march her off to a preacher at gunpoint," Jeff pointed out. "How do you expect to get her to agree?"

"She'll agree," Colin said.

"How can you be so sure?" Meg pressed anxiously.

Colin met her gaze. "What would you do for your girls, Meg? Would you marry to keep them?"

Her eyes went wide. "But he's not even her son."

"Suppose someone came after almost a year and said, 'Oops, our mistake. You don't get to keep her after all.'

Would it really matter to you then whether or not she was really yours?''

Meg looked down at her hands. ''No.''

''But what kind of marriage can it be?'' Jeff asked. ''She'll never trust you again, not after the way I spilled the beans.''

''I think she will,'' Colin said, ''once she understands that marrying me will give her equal rights to George.''

''No, it won't,'' Meg said. ''Even I know that stepparents don't have standing under the law.''

''Stepparents, no,'' Colin said softly.

Jeff suddenly propelled his chair upright, nearly dislodging Meg in the process. ''You aren't thinking what I think you're thinking!''

Colin smiled wanly. ''It's the only way, Jeff. I've thought it all through, and it's the only way.''

''You're really willing to do this?''

Colin leaned forward on the couch and considered briefly, but he already knew the answer. Looking at Jeff, he spoke decisively, to his lawyer this time. ''It's the right thing, the only thing. Take care of it. Right away.''

Lauren turned over the rag and vigorously polished the front of the counter until no trace of oil remained except the sheen. Straightening from her crouched position, she set aside the spray can and the dust rag and placed a hand in the small of her back, stretching muscles cramped too long. It was then that the front door opened. She whipped around, prepared to offer a smile, despite the early hour. Her breath stopped in her throat. Colin. He held three large suitcases, one in each hand and another beneath one arm. She had known he would come, of course, but somehow she hadn't managed to prepare herself for this inevitability during the past two weeks. She turned her back to him.

''We don't have any vacancies.''

She heard the myriad small sounds of luggage being deposited on the floor and knew she was in for a fight. "That's too bad," he said, a little breathless from the cold morning air, "because I'm not leaving."

Lauren walked around the counter and went down on her haunches, intending to polish that side of the counter. She had spritzed oil on the grooved trim next to the floor when a flurry of footsteps warned her. Still, she was shocked when he grabbed her by the upper arms and easily lifted her to her feet, turning her to face him.

"Stop this!" he commanded. "You can't ignore me, Lauren. I'm George's father, and I'm not going away. Talk to me, damn it!"

She yanked free of him, stepping back, and smacked the oil can and rag onto the counter. He wanted talk; she would give him talk. "How could you lie to me?" she cried.

Wearily he ran a hand over his face. He hadn't shaved, and his hair was longer than normal and rumpled, making the cowlick immediately noticeable. "I didn't lie to you," he said smoothly.

"You didn't tell me the truth!" she retorted.

"Are you ready to listen to it now?" he asked so reasonably that she wanted to hit him. She folded her arms, steeling herself. She had asked for it, after all. He took a deep breath. "I had a foolish affair with an emotionally unstable woman named Thea Sanford. I told you about it the day we drove to Taos."

"Go on."

"She is George's biological mother."

Lauren recoiled from the thought of her Georgie being born of such a woman as Colin had described that day. Then a glimmer of hope danced before her. "The woman who checked into my inn was Doris Drew."

Colin shook his head. "Doris Drew is Thea's sister. She lives in Norman, Oklahoma, with her husband and family.

Thea must have stolen her identification and posed as her sister."

Crestfallen, Lauren turned away to lean against the counter.

"Thea is a small woman," Colin went on, "a little taller than you with brown hair that she bleaches blond and wears just above her shoulders. She has gray eyes and a little mole at one corner of her mouth."

Lauren closed her eyes. The same woman. "Go on," she whispered.

"When I realized what problems Thea has and how deep her instability is, I tried to get help for her, but it was just another round in the ongoing saga of Thea's illness. She resented any attempt to help her deal with her problems, so I ended the relationship. She hounded me for weeks, somehow thinking that would induce me to get back together with her. I won't go into details, but suffice it to say I had no trouble getting a restraining order. Then she found a way to punish me. She had deliberately stopped taking her birth control almost at the beginning of the relationship, even though she made a great show of continually taking it. After the breakup she had discovered that she was pregnant. To prove it, she sent me the results of a lab test. Then she left me a cryptic message on my answering machine telling me that I would never see my child."

Lauren swallowed, remembering all that Colin had told her of his childhood and how he treasured family because of it. "She knew that would wound you deeply."

"Yes," he said softly. "I want a family. I've always wanted a family of my own, and she knew that."

"What did you do when you found out about the baby?" she asked.

"Everything I could think of. I went to her apartment. She had moved out without giving notice. I called the school where she worked. She'd been fired about the time

I broke up with her for behaving erratically. I called her family, but they hadn't seen her. I contacted the police, but they couldn't do anything. It seems that a child does not belong to his father until he's born. Without Jeff, I don't know what I'd have done next. He helped me start a search, but we learned only where she'd been, not where she'd gone. Then one day around the first of March she showed up at my office specifically to tell me that my son was someplace where I'd never think to look and would never find him. She told me she'd given him up for adoption."

Lauren sighed, moved despite her best intentions not to be. "She came here to give birth because it's remote."

"No television or radio stations."

"And we asked the local papers not to print the story in order to protect the lodge," Lauren admitted. "We were so certain that the state system would uncover any family member willing to take over custody of the child."

"But she had given the wrong name," Colin said, adding quickly, "I don't blame you. Tourism is your living. You don't need stories circulating about women giving birth in your rooms."

"Still, if one of the larger papers had picked up the story—"

"You don't know how many infants are abandoned statewide," he said, "and we had no way of knowing she'd given birth in New Mexico. She has ties to Oklahoma and Texas, too, so we had to cast a wide net. We only had an approximate time of birth to go on. Then one day Jeff overheard a conversation at a table next to him in a restaurant. It was the subject of skiing that first caught his attention. Then mention was made of some woman giving birth at the lodge where these people had stayed during the Christmas holidays. He interrupted and questioned them. He wanted to call the proper authorities, but I decided to check it out on my own."

"And the rest is history," she muttered.

"I didn't expect to find the baby here," he said. "I just wanted to talk to someone, see if it might be Thea who'd given birth here. But the moment I walked in the door, I knew."

"I was holding him on my hip," she said absently, remembering. "I saw the look on your face and misinterpreted it. I thought you were looking at me."

"I was," he admitted. "As certain as I was in that first instant that he was my son, I also knew that you were his mother. You gave me my first and only twinge of doubt."

"So you questioned me."

"Rather subtly, I thought," he confirmed.

"Oh, you're subtle, all right," she quipped sarcastically. "I never suspected a thing."

"I didn't want to cause you unnecessary pain," he said softly but urgently. "I saw how you love him, what a healthy, happy baby he is. I can't tell you how grateful and relieved I was—and still am. All those months when I was looking for him, I prayed that he was with someone who loved and treasured him, and when I saw you, I knew you were answered prayer. I just couldn't blurt out that I'd come to take him from you. I decided to wait until I had real proof. And in the meantime, I found myself attracted to you."

She turned to face him then. She had to look into his eyes for this. "Because of Georgie," she said. "You were attracted to me out of gratitude for what I had done for your son and because I had still had him. I was your excuse to see him."

He opened his mouth to deny it, but then he closed it again. "This whole situation is so far outside the norm," he finally said, but she had seen all she needed to know and turned away again. "I tried to tell you!" he went on.

"That night at the campsite, I tried to tell you the truth, but I botched it, and—"

"And I was stupid enough to think I was the main attraction," she interrupted shakily, "stupid enough to think you wanted me for me and Georgie because he was mine."

"Lauren—"

Suddenly feeling trapped, she whirled around and pushed past him, exclaiming, "Don't bother! I already know how big an idiot I am."

He followed her from behind the counter, snatching at her arm. "You're not an idiot."

"Aren't I?" she scoffed, jerking away from him. "I was totally convinced you loved me."

"Lauren, please. I'll always—"

"Don't say it!" she demanded. "I don't want to hear how grateful you are!"

He writhed in frustration. "Isn't it enough that I want to marry you?"

She laughed, not that it was funny. "I *don't* want to marry *you!*"

A muscle ticked in the hollow of his jaw. "Well, you have no choice," he said through gritted teeth.

"The hell I don't! I'm going to fight you!"

Suddenly he rammed his hands into his coat pockets, yanking out two seemingly identical papers, which he slammed onto the end of the counter. "Fine!" he exclaimed. "You want a choice? Here it is!" He hastily unfolded first one paper and then the other. "You can fight me in court." He stabbed one paper with his index finger. "But this says that George goes with me until it's settled. And in the end, we both know who will win."

Lauren blanched and folded her arms. The court order. She hadn't wanted to think about it, hadn't wanted to believe he'd use it, but she knew that was nonsense. In his place, she'd use it in a heartbeat. Why shouldn't he? But to take Georgie from her, after all he'd done… She shook her head, unwilling to go there. "I—I've hired an attorney," she blustered. "H-he says—"

"I know what he says," Colin stated flatly. "Jeff talked with him yesterday afternoon, and he admitted that he couldn't get a judge to overturn my custody order."

Lauren shook her head. "No. He would've told me."

"I asked him not to. I asked him to give me one more chance to convince you that marrying me is the only way, and he agreed that it's the best solution, especially when I told him I'd sign adoption papers."

Lauren reeled, gaping. "What?"

"I'll sign adoption papers," Colin repeated. "Once we're married, you can adopt George. That will give us equal standing under the law."

She couldn't grasp it. "Why would you do that?"

"Because it's fair," he said. "Because it's what's best for George. He loves you. You're his mother, the only parent he's ever truly known. I never meant to shut you out of his life. I only want what's best for everyone. Now what about you, Lauren? Do you want what's best for our son, or do you want to punish me for not being the fairy-tale lover you always imagined?"

He was right, of course. Marriage, adoption, sharing custody, it was best for everyone, except for one thing. Colin *was* her version of a fairy-tale lover. He was everything she could possibly want in a man, except that he didn't love her. If not for Georgie, he would never have looked at her twice, and that hurt more deeply than she could ever have imagined, more deeply than he could possibly understand. How was she supposed to live the rest of her life knowing that he had married her out of pity and gratitude and a sense of fairness and duty? How could she sleep by his side night after night, knowing that he'd have chosen otherwise if circumstances had not conspired against him?

"I don't think I can do it," she whispered.

"Just give it a chance," he said, seizing her by the upper arms. "If it doesn't work out, you'll still be assured of a place in Georgie's life as his legal mother."

He was saying that in the event of a divorce, she would have more legal standing than she had now—and he was right. She licked her lips. "I—I have a few conditions."

"Name them."

She pulled free of him and backed up a step, thinking furiously. "I'm not moving. Georgie and I stay here."

"If you remember, I decided to move here over two weeks ago," he said. "What else?"

The skin prickled on her arm, and she rubbed a hand over it. "I won't sleep with you."

"You mean you won't make love with me."

"I mean, I won't have sex with you *or* share a bedroom with you."

"Why?"

She gaped. "Why? Because you don't want me and I don't want you!"

"That's not true."

She put her hands to her head, unable—and unwilling— to grasp the meaning behind his argument. "If you can't promise me this, the marriage is off. Period!"

He made a frustrated sound in the back of his throat, then took a deep breath. "I promise you that I won't force myself on you, but you can't expect me not to try to change your mind."

"Oh, yes, I can," she assured him determinedly.

"I'll agree not to share a room or make love with you until you're ready," he said placatingly.

She smirked. Good enough. She couldn't imagine that she would ever be ready after all that had happened. She was a fool, but she wasn't stupid. "Then it's a marriage in name only," she said.

"Until you agree otherwise."

But that wouldn't happen, she assured herself, which meant that the only question now was, who would call it quits first? Either way, she'd have a legal claim to Georgie, and given equal standing under the law, most judges awarded custody to the mother. He could always contest the adoption, of course, but by that time she'd have plenty of ammunition with which to fight him. She squared her shoulders. "All right."

He breathed out a sigh of relief. "Then it's settled? You'll marry me?"

"I said I would, didn't I?"

He nodded and swallowed. "Okay. When?"

She shrugged. No need to rush now that it was settled. "It'll take some time. I have to make arrangements."

"For the wedding?" he prodded doubtfully.

She scoffed. "Oh, I don't think we need to play out that farce."

"Then why wait?"

"There are formalities to be taken care of. The county seat is all the way up in Raton, and that's probably where we'll have to got to get a license and—"

He swept up the second paper and waved it under her nose. "Done."

"What?"

"I had Jeff make the arrangements."

She closed her gaping mouth. "And he's very good at expediting legal matters," she drawled sarcastically.

"That's right. He is. So we might as well do it and get on with making a family of ourselves."

"It's not that easy!" she argued. "Where are you going to stay?"

"With you."

"The apartment isn't big enough for the three of us."

"What about that cabin you mentioned?"

"You can stay there!" she exclaimed, delighted at the prospect.

He shook his head. "Not without you and George."

"But—"

"I'll sleep on the couch, if I have to, but sleeping apart and living apart are two separate things, Lauren, and I refuse to even consider the latter."

Miffed—and trumped—she sighed disgustedly. "I'll have Georgie moved in with me. You can have his room."

"Fine. Will this afternoon give you enough time?"

"This afternoon!"

"I brought everything I need with me. The truck is just waiting to be unloaded."

Lauren folded her arms. "What about the ceremony? Have you even thought about who's going to perform it?"

"There are three ministers and a priest in Eagle Nest. Are you Catholic?"

"No."

"Neither am I. Choose one of the ministers, and I'll call him while you get Juan and Ponce to start moving furniture. Jeff and his wife are on their way from Albuquerque, either to witness the ceremony or help me leave here with George. If you want anyone else, I suggest you call them."

Lauren took a deep breath, trying to find a way to stall. But what was the point? The sooner those adoption papers were signed, the sooner she and Georgie could start over. She flattened her mouth disapprovingly, just to let him know that she was unhappy about this. "Fine. I'm sure the Baptist minister will oblige us if you use my name."

Colin inclined his head. "The Baptist minister it is. Say two o'clock?"

"Say four," she replied flatly.

"I'll make the call and start unloading my truck."

She stared at him a moment longer, unable to believe that this was really happening. Then she turned around and walked into the lobby. She had work to do. It was her wedding day. Such as it was.

Chapter Nine

Lauren chose a simple wool dress of winter white in which to be married. In deference to the snow, she struggled into a pair of high-heeled, lace-up boots. She left her hair down and wore a minimum of makeup, along with her grandmother's pearls. Grabbing up her coat, she kissed Georgie, hugged Maria and swept out of the apartment before she could think yet again about what she was doing.

Colin waited for her in the great room, nervously rocking back and forth on his heels. He looked positively stunning in a black moleskin suit, a gray wool coat draped over one arm. Jeff Locke and a tall, slender blonde whom Lauren took to be his wife, sat on one of the couches, the picture of patience. Jeff rose to his feet as Lauren drew near, and the woman slowly stood with him. Lauren ignored them both, knowing she was being rude but somehow unable to stop herself. "Let's get this over with," she said to Colin.

He grimaced with annoyance and dropped his voice into

the intimate zone. "You look wonderful. I like the dress. It was a good choice."

"It needs cleaning," she said dismissively, slinging on her coat, "but it'll have to do. Ready?"

Colin stepped back and glanced pointedly toward Jeff and his wife. "You remember Jeff." She nodded without looking at the man. "This is his wife, Meg."

A pale, slender hand with pink oval nails came into view. Lauren couldn't be rude enough to spurn it. Clasping it lightly, she looked up into pale golden brown eyes that held both understanding and encouragement. Lauren looked away again.

"It's nice to meet you." She glanced at Colin. "We're going to be late."

He looked past her toward the door to the private area. "Where's Georgie?"

"Maria is watching him."

"He's not going with us?"

"Why should he?" she retorted.

"I just thought he should be there," Colin said.

"You're marrying me, not him," she snapped. "Or did you forget?"

He clamped his jaws shut, that muscle pulsing again in its hollow. Then he said, "Fine," and held out an arm. She walked past it as if she hadn't seen it. He caught up and fell in beside her. The Lockes followed at a slower pace, whispering together.

Juan was manning the front desk, a small, pink cardboard-and-cellophane box on the counter in front of him. "This came for you from Angel Fire a little while ago, Miss Lauren," he said almost apologetically as he pushed the box forward. Lauren stopped and opened the box. It contained a small nosegay of very pale pink rosebuds, white baby's breath, delicate greenery and narrow white ribbon.

"I thought you might like some flowers to carry," Colin said softly.

For a second Lauren considered pushing the box away, but in the end she opened it and carefully lifted out the small bouquet. She wouldn't have chosen this color or style, but then nothing about this wedding was as she might have chosen. Yet, a wedding it was, and the flowers helped her feel a little more the way she'd thought she'd feel as a bride.

"Thank you," Lauren said briskly, and turned her attention to Juan. "We won't be long."

She pointed toward the door and strode away, aware that the trio behind her were throwing on coats. Once outside she turned left instead of heading for the parking lot. Her little car was parked at the end of the building, and she went straight to it. Colin caught up just as she extracted her keys from her coat pocket and opened the door.

"Why don't we take my truck?"

"Do you know where we're going?" she asked smartly.

"No."

"I do." With that, she shut the door and poked the keys into the ignition. Jeff and Meg Locke came through the door just then, and Colin hurried back toward them, speaking and gesturing. They nodded and turned into the lot. Jeff hurried back to the car and around it to the passenger side. Opening the door, he folded himself inside the small, battered car.

Lauren put the transmission in gear and backed away from the building. They drove in silence down the hill and into town, the Lockes following in their European luxury car. Lauren pulled the car up in front of the small, white frame building. The pastor immediately opened the front door of the church and stepped out onto the narrow porch in his good suit and tie. Colin jumped out of the car and hurried around toward her door. Lauren took a deep breath and opened it before he got there. Nevertheless, he reached inside and helped her out, clasping her hand in his firmly.

She let him lead her toward the church, her nosegay clutched before her like a shield. Her heart was pounding so hard that she shook with the reverberations. Her wedding. Dear God.

Colin tried to loosen his grip on her hand, fearing he'd break her knuckles, but he had this insane notion that if he did so, she'd turn and run for her life. He couldn't blame her. He'd botched just about every aspect of this thing. He smiled bitterly as Lauren greeted the minister, wondering silently how many other men had to resort to court orders and coercion in order to get themselves married. He made the smile polite as Lauren introduced the man who would marry them, even though he had spoken to the gentleman on the phone. Jeff and Meg joined them, and they went inside.

The building was cold, even though the heater blew at full blast. "We could do this in my office," the minister suggested hopefully. "It's warmer in there."

Colin looked at Lauren, who nodded. The minister led them through the small, stark sanctuary and out another door at the back of the room. They followed him down a short hall to a room on the sunny side of the building.

It was a nice room, painted a warm gold and trimmed in creamy white with oak furnishings.

"Will in front of the fire be all right?" the minister asked, and Lauren again nodded. Quickly, the fortyish man with dark, lightly graying hair began setting aside chairs and blocking out space. When he had everyone out of their coats and standing in place, he picked up his Bible from the desk and asked for the rings. Colin reached into his pocket for the simple gold bands he'd purchased in Albuquerque. He wanted to tell Lauren that they could shop for something more to her taste whenever she wanted, but he doubted that now was the time to broach that subject or any other. Her face was already as grim as a bride's could be. He was glad that she'd left her hair down. It softened her, proclaiming her femininity. She had beautiful hair.

The minister began by saying how honored he was to perform this task for them, meaning Lauren, primarily, and then opened his Bible. Colin held Lauren's small hand in his and listened to the admonitions and advice that was part of the service. When it came time to repeat his vows, he did so in a smooth, firm voice. Lauren said hers in little more than a whisper, never once looking him in the eye. The rings were exchanged—hers was a little large—and the minister then paused to lead them in prayer. Colin closed his eyes and squeezed both her hands in his. A final admonishment, and the minister pronounced them husband and wife. Colin leaned in to kiss his bride, only to have her avert her face ever so carefully at the last moment, so that his kiss landed as much on her cheek as the corner of her mouth. He told himself that it would do—for the moment.

Congratulations were murmured. The minister offered them coffee, was politely refused, and they all got down to the business of signing the registry. They walked out into falling snow, the promise of a gray day come to fruition. The whole thing had taken less than a half hour. Now, Colin mused grimly, the real work began.

Jeff and Meg followed them back to the lodge, ostensibly for coffee. When they arrived, however, they found that Shelby, the cook—who looked as though he'd done hard time in maximum security, right down to the broken nose and tattoos—had made a lovely wedding dinner for four of grilled steaks, scalloped potatoes and asparagus with hollandaise. He had also baked a cake and decorated it with maraschino cherries cut into the shape of flowers. Juan had mulled some wine, to warm them, he said, and Maria had dressed Georgie in his best clothes, while Ponce and others had set a pretty table and strung up a banner that said simply, "Congratulations."

Lauren was ill at ease, but Colin was eternally grateful. He resisted the urge to take Georgie in his own arms, letting Lauren do it instead, and merely slipped an arm about her waist as Jeff and the inn staff, along with a few guests, toasted their happiness. Afterward, they cut the cake, without any of the usual wedding reception high jinks, so that those who wished to do so could go ahead and eat it, then they sat down to have dinner themselves with Jeff and Meg.

Conversation was stilted at first, but Meg did her best, complimenting Lauren on everything from the lodge itself to the hollandaise sauce. It was George who rescued the day, however. Lauren insisted on keeping him at the table with them, and Colin certainly had no objection. Maria had already fed him his dinner, but when the cake came to the table, his blue eyes lit up with greed. Snagging Lauren's sleeve, he demanded a bite. Lauren tied a napkin around his neck and obliged, explaining almost shyly, "He loves sweets."

"What child doesn't?" Meg asked. "It would have to be a special occasion like this one for me to let my girls eat sugar this late in the day, though. They bounce off the walls when I let them load up. You can forget getting them to bed if they eat sweets too late."

"Getting this boy to sleep is rarely a problem," Lauren said, "but with sweets he doesn't know when to quit. He'll eat until he makes himself sick."

"Now who does that remind me of?" Jeff asked teasingly. Colin felt his face heat, and Meg laughed.

"That wasn't really his fault," Meg said to Lauren. "The girls made a real haul during Halloween last year, and they tried to feed Uncle Colin everything they didn't like.''

"Does the slogan 'Just say no' mean anything to anyone here?" Jeff quipped.

"Oh, like you tell those girls no about anything," Meg scolded.

"That's different," Jeff exclaimed. "They're my angel babies."

"And they have you wrapped firmly around their little wingtips," Colin stated self-defensively.

"Darn straight," Jeff replied. "What are daddies for?"

George pointed at Colin. "Da-da," he said. Then he smacked his lips, looked pointedly at Colin's cake and said, "Bite." Everyone laughed as Colin fed his son off his own plate. When that bite was chewed and swallowed, George went back to Lauren. "Ma-ma, bite." And so it went until their plates were clean. It was then that George turned a speculative eye on Jeff's plate. When Jeff lifted an eyebrow in offer, George showed him his teeth and laughed delightedly.

"Oh, how can you resist that?" Meg exclaimed.

"He does tend to be something of a charmer," Lauren commented proudly.

"He's just delightful," Meg gushed. "Neither of our girls would have sat there so patiently, I promise you. We'd have hidden half the flatware and grouped the glasses in the center of the table out of reach long before now."

Finally Lauren warmed up enough to chat comfortably about the children. Jeff gave George one more tiny bite from his plate, then Lauren put a halt to the gorging. George tried charming and pleading and finally tears, but Lauren did not give in. When she reached to take him out of his chair, Colin got up and interceded.

"Here, let me. He'll ruin that pretty dress."

George came happily into Colin's arms. For a moment,

Lauren looked as if she would object, but then she turned back to her conversation with Meg. Colin sat down again, George standing in his lap, and carefully divested the boy of his napkin bib. To Colin's surprise and delight, George put his arms around Colin's neck and gave him a sticky sweet kiss. Colin hugged the child, a lump in his throat, and casually draped an arm around the back of Lauren's chair. Now if only his wife could be so accepting and affectionate, all might yet be well.

After a little while longer, the Lockes rose to leave. Lauren graciously offered them a room for the night. "Since it's a weeknight, we do have a vacancy."

Meg shook her head. "Another time, perhaps, but thank you for the offer. I want to get home to the girls."

"And I have to be in court in the morning," Jeff said.

Lauren accompanied Colin as he walked them out, Georgie sitting on the crook of his arm. Meg kissed Lauren on the cheek, and Lauren returned the gesture. Then Meg kissed Georgie, who tolerated but did not respond. Finally, she kissed Colin.

"You've done very well for yourself, handsome. You have a lovely family. Treasure them."

"I do, believe me. Thanks for coming, you guys. It means a lot to us, doesn't it, honey?" He dropped an arm around Lauren's waist and pulled her to his side. To his hopeful relief, she stayed there, smiling and nodding until all the goodbyes were said and the Lockes were out the door. Then she calmly pushed his arm away, plucked George off his elbow and walked away without a word. Colin bowed his head, suddenly feeling very much alone.

It was not an ideal arrangement. Lauren tossed and turned on her narrow single bed. The big bed had gone into Georgie's room for Colin since that bed and Georgie's belongings would not fit into Lauren's room together. She was surprised to find that she missed it. At least that was what she blamed her restlessness on, better that than the fact that it was her wedding night and she was sleeping alone just as she had demanded. Georgie was more disturbed by the move than Lauren had imagined he would be, too. For the first time, he seemed to have trouble settling down to sleep. Twice he sat up in bed and just looked at her as if to ask what he was doing there. She realized that this was the first time he'd spent the night anywhere except the room down the hall since he was six days old and she'd officially been named his foster mother. She knew that he must be terribly confused, poor baby.

Rolling over to face the wall, she closed her eyes, trying to block out the glow of Georgie's nightlight, but after a few minutes she resignedly opened them again. It was no use. She couldn't sleep. She wished that she could turn on the television. Late-night TV programming was guaranteed to put her to sleep, but with George in her room and awake, she dared not. She thought briefly of slipping out to the living room, but the danger of encountering Colin was too great. Disgustedly she realized that she was a prisoner in her own bed, another grievance she could lay at Colin Garret's door.

Garret. She was Lauren Garret now. Colin Garret was her husband. She had once expected to be happy about that—until she realized he had come to take Georgie from her. No, that wasn't true. It wasn't that he had intended to claim George that she resented so. He had every right to George, and heaven knew he'd gone far beyond what any other caring father would have done in order not to take his son from her. It wasn't that he'd lied to her, either. He'd had no reason for that other than to spare her pain. What she resented, what cut the heart right out of her chest, was that he didn't love her. Her husband felt only pity and gratitude and perhaps lust for her, but that was all. And he couldn't know how she grieved that lack. He could never know. She had to have some pride, after all.

When she thought how she'd thrown herself at him in the beginning, she just wanted to disappear into thin air. How he must regret having allowed himself to respond to her! What entanglements had followed. And yet, many men would have pressed for more and still have walked away with George without a second thought for her, which was a large part of the reason she loved him. Yes, she could admit it now, here, alone in the silence of her heart. She loved her husband, but she didn't know how to forgive him for not loving her in return. When the tears came, she let them fall silently into her pillow, grieving her wedding night, grieving her inability to rejoice in all her blessings, able only to focus on what she lacked.

The next thing she knew, she was jerking awake. Seized by a sense of panic, she threw back the covers and bolted into a sitting position, shoving hair out of her eyes. Colin was standing in her room, Georgie in his arms.

"What? What are you doing here?"

"The baby was fussing," he said simply.

She took another look and realized that Colin was standing there in nothing more than a pair of long, lightweight, form-fitting, insulated underwear that left little to the imagination. "You're not dressed!"

He looked down at himself. "I'm dressed. As dressed as I can stand to be in that room." He looked at Georgie. "Hey, maybe that's the problem. Is it too cool for you in Mommy's room, son?" He turned to Lauren again. "Want me to take him in with me?"

Shaking her head, she got up to go and take Georgie from him. "I'll put him back down. He has to learn to sleep in here." It was the look in Colin's eye that stopped her. She realized, belatedly, that she wasn't properly dressed, either. Why the devil had she put on this particular night-gown, anyway?

"You look lovely," he said softly. "Just like a bride on her wedding night."

Lauren looked down at the filmy white gown trimmed in delicate lace. It wasn't new or particularly revealing, but it made her feel foolishly provocative anyway, and she suddenly hated it. She took Georgie from his arms, muttering, "I'm sorry he woke you."

"He didn't wake me," Colin said softly. "I couldn't sleep."

She began preparing to change Georgie's diaper and put him down again. "If the room's too hot, try leaving your door open," she said.

"It doesn't have anything to do with the room."

She ignored that. He lifted a hand and skimmed it over the hair tumbling past her face. "Lauren, can't we just try for a real mar—"

She cut him off, stepping back. "Leave me alone, Colin," she whispered, closing her eyes. "For pity's sake, just leave me alone."

He dropped his hand and sighed. "All right, Lauren. If that's what you really want."

She nodded her head sharply, stepped up and began undoing Georgie's sleeper. "Go back to bed. I'll take care of him."

Colin hesitated briefly before leaning down and kissing Georgie lightly on the forehead. "Good night, son. Daddy loves you." He slipped from the room, never knowing he'd pierced her straight through the heart.

"Damn." Lauren shifted the letter out of Georgie's reach and continued reading, despite a marked reluctance to do so. Her little ploy to put off her brother and his attorney had neatly backfired. Now Larry was including the cabin in his demand for recompense. "Damn, damn, damn."

"What's the problem?"

She nearly jumped out of her skin at the sound of Colin's voice, and as usual, irritation flashed through her at her own reaction.

"Do you *have* to do that?" she demanded, rotating her desk chair around to face the office door even as she shifted the letter out of Georgie's reach again.

"Do what?" he asked, clearly puzzled.

"Sneak up on me."

"I didn't sneak up on you, Lauren. The office door is open, but I knocked before stepping through it. Now tell me what has you so upset."

"It's not your problem," she retorted, tossing the letter onto the desk as Georgie reached for it once more. As if life wasn't difficult enough, Georgie had never been more demanding than he had been these past few days. Juan said it was all the tension, which he declared was thick enough to cut with a knife—while implying that it was her fault. She knew it was; she just didn't know what to do about it.

Colin leaned against the door frame and slid his hands into the pockets of his khaki pants. "Lauren, you're my wife," he began reasonably. "Your problems are my problems. Please tell me what is in that letter."

"It's just another empty threat from my brother," she snapped.

"Who does not yet know that you're married," Colin said pointedly.

Lauren heaved a long-suffering sigh. "It hasn't even been a week. And I'm not close to my family, you know that."

"And I can't help wondering whose fault that is," he muttered.

Slapping her hand on the desktop, she came back with

a razor-sharp reply, more than ready for a fight. "What would you know about it? You've never even had a family!"

"I have a family now," he replied softly. "At least I'm trying to. You seem to be trying not to."

Lauren's breath caught in her throat. Ashamed, she looked away. "I'm sorry. I—I just have a lot on my mind right now."

"Sharing the load lightens it," he suggested hopefully, but she shook her head. He sighed. "At least let me look after the baby for a while."

Again she shook her head, telling herself that she wasn't being unreasonably possessive of the boy, but she couldn't shake the thought that if Colin should dissolve the marriage before the adoption papers were signed, she would lose George altogether. In a conciliatory tone, she said to Colin, "You need to get your office up and running. Just concentrate on that for now."

Reluctantly Colin nodded and pushed away from the door frame. "That's why I came in, actually. I know you mean to move the copy machine into the supply room, but I think we ought to go ahead and sell it. Mine is more compact and requires less upkeep. Jeff's offered to broker it for us. I can take it to him when I drive down to pick up the rest of my stuff."

She had resisted selling the copier, despite its bulk, age and the expense of maintaining it, simply because she wanted to be able to continue operating independently if Colin should give up and go away, but she simply didn't want to discuss it anymore. "Fine. Whatever you think best."

"In that case, I'll go tomorrow," he said.

The idea of having him out of the lodge for a day was disturbingly attractive. She waved a hand absently, so as not to give herself away. "Fine."

"I could be gone overnight," he pointed out.

Her heart skipped a beat, but whether in eagerness or reluctance, she couldn't have said. "No problem."

"I didn't think it would be," he muttered cryptically. She made no reply. He bowed his head and quit the room.

Lauren wanted to cry—again. She didn't want to be so cold to him, but she just couldn't afford to let herself warm up. No telling what stupid thing she'd do then or what she might reveal that was best kept hidden. The last thing she needed to do was give him the power to control and manipulate her. The last thing she needed was for him to know how she really felt about him.

Georgie leaned forward, reaching once more for the letter upon her blotter. She gently pushed his hand away. He stiffened, and his face crumpled as he began to cry. Lauren sighed. She knew exactly how he felt, wanting something he couldn't have, but this new behavior was tiring for both of them.

"Let's try for a nap again," she said, getting to her feet. She would decide what to do about Larry's newest demand later. Maybe she would even discuss it with Colin—just as soon as she found the energy and strength to face him again. This marriage, such as it was, had proven nothing if not exhausting. And she saw no way ever to go back to what had once been a peaceful, if solitary, existence.

She had to face facts. Her life would never be the same since she'd met Colin Garret. No matter what happened in the future, her life was forever changed, and right now she couldn't believe she would ever be happy again.

He stayed away the first night out of necessity. The real estate agent had an offer on the house. Should Colin's counteroffer be acceptable, the buyer wanted papers signed immediately. That meant sticking around to see if the buyer was willing to up the ante enough to satisfy both parties and, if so, get the papers signed. The deal was struck the next morning, and by midafternoon Colin had arranged for the movers to pick up his furnishings and transport them to Eagle Nest, where he and Lauren had agreed they would be stored in the empty cabin. He had intended selling them, but she had balked at the idea, saying that if they decided to refurbish the cabin they would need the furniture. He knew that she was merely attempting to hedge her bets, to give him a graceful way out of the marriage in time, but he had no intention of ending his marriage, and he knew of only one way to prove it to her.

Jeff counseled him to wait, but Colin reasoned that marriage required total commitment. He instructed Jeff to make the necessary filings immediately, turned down an invitation to dinner on the pretext of being anxious to return home and then deliberately sat alone in a house that he owned only technically and for which he no longer held the slightest emotional attachment. He wasn't certain why he chose to stay away a second night or why he delayed returning the next day. He didn't want to be in Albuquerque. He didn't want to be away from Lauren and George, and the business he conducted that next day could as easily have been done by telephone, and yet he hesitated to return to the lodge.

Was he hoping that they would miss him as much as he missed them? Or was he trying to give Lauren a break from his obviously troublesome presence? He only knew that a certain sadness accompanied his impulse to stay away and that it was somehow easier to be alone in Albuquerque than it was to be alone in Eagle Nest. For he was alone as yet. He and Lauren were legally married. George was legally his. Somehow, though, he was not yet the husband and father that he longed to be. His marriage contained no partnership; his fatherhood remained a mere adjunct to Lauren's parenting. And he didn't know how to achieve the sort of acceptance and bonding for which he yearned.

Nevertheless, by that third evening, he knew he couldn't stay away any longer. The need to see and be with his family, the urge to go home, was simply too strong. He loaded the last of his personal possessions in the SUV and set out, wondering what type of reception he'd receive upon his arrival.

When he coasted down into the high, broad valley, he felt the tug of home like a hand that plucked at his heart. Turning his back on the modern trendiness of Angel Fire and the ski slopes, he headed northward once more, slowing only when he saw the lake spread out at the foot of the mountains across the valley and the string of lights beyond it that decorated the rustic main street of the village. To the northeast, tucked below the curve of the road that trailed over the mountain to the Old West town of Cimarron, waited the lodge, its thick adobe walls gleaming like a smile of welcome in the night, its trio of chimneys smoking gray against the black bulk of the mountain. Lauren. George. Home.

For the first time since the truth had risen up and slapped them all in the face, Colin really felt that somehow, some day, it might really be all right.

Chapter Ten

Lauren gasped at Georgie's unexpected strength as he twisted in her arms. Another move like that and she'd drop him! Deeming it the safest course to sit down with him until he calmed, she hurried into the living area and scooted into the corner of the couch, trying to deposit him in her lap. Georgie stiffened and howled, downright angry at having the nasty-tasting medication poured down his throat, while she tried to convince him to wash away the taste with a drink of water. Very near tears herself, Lauren literally pleaded with him.

"Georgie, please, just take a drink. The bad taste will go away if you just take a—" A flailing arm knocked the cup out of her hand, spilling water across the carpet and splashing the two of them. Shocked, Georgie caught his breath, interjecting a shard of silence into the chaos. Lauren recognized the sound of the door opening across the room.

Twisting around to look over her shoulder, she could not

restrain her relief at the thought that Colin might be home. Georgie took it as an indication of more indignities to come and let out a scream of protest, kicking and bucking in a bid for freedom. Unprepared, Lauren lost him, watching in panicked horror as he slid from her lap to the couch and right off its edge to the floor, where he hit his head with a dull thwack. The blow momentarily stunned him. Lauren's breath caught in her throat. The next instant he screamed like all the hounds of hell were tearing at him, the sound gurgling with tears. Lauren threw herself down beside him, terror and relief swirling with guilt.

"George!"

With trembling hands she attempted to ascertain the seriousness of his injuries, but George was already rolling onto his belly and pushing up to all fours, as if he meant to escape her at all costs. Suddenly Colin was there, crouching and sweeping Georgie up into his arms.

"Here, now. Here, son. Calm down."

Lauren scrambled to her feet. "George, are you all right, baby? Are you all right?"

To her utter dismay, George pushed her away, turned his face into the hollow of his father's shoulder and sobbed his little heart out, his hand lifting to the back of his head. Lauren's eyes widened. Rejected. The one person in the world who had always adored her had just turned his back. He didn't know what he was doing to her, of course. He was just a baby, after all. But the sting of it almost brought her to her knees. She felt her lower lip trembling, and then she clapped a hand over her mouth to hold in the sobs.

Colin was rhythmically jogging George against his shoulder and speaking soft words of comfort in a soothing voice. Already, George was calming. Lauren turned away. Creeping back to the couch, she sat down in the corner once more and hid her face in the cradle of her arms folded against the arm of the sofa. Without a word to her, Colin carried Georgie into the bedroom and closed the door. Lauren had never felt so alone and unloved and miserable as she did at that moment. She bit her lips until she tasted blood, but still the sobs choked and shook her.

She was unaware of the slowly gathering silence as she concentrated on taming her own rampant emotions, until she felt the cushions beside her sag with the weight of a body and strong arms pulled her away from the corner and against a warm, solid chest.

"Shhh, shhh. It's all right now, sweetheart. Everything's fine. Hush. Relax now. Just relax."

She let him hold her because she simply didn't have the energy to resist. Gradually the sobs eased. She had cried so much lately that sometimes it seemed she never stopped. "H-how is the baby?"

"He's fine. I checked him over before I let him go to sleep. The bump on the head was nothing. Poor little fellow was exhausted."

"I know how he feels," she mumbled sourly.

"Want to tell me what's been going on?"

She imagined that she heard a note of censure in his voice and pulled back, exclaiming defensively, "I wasn't trying to drop him on his head, if that's what you mean!"

He gaped at her. "Did I say that? Did I say anything even close to that? I just want to know what had him so upset!"

"He has an ear infection. I've suspected for several days that he wasn't feeling well, but this morning he was running a temperature, so I called and took him in to the clinic at Angel Fire. The doctor put him on antibiotics and a mild decongestant."

Colin nodded thoughtfully. "That's pretty standard for a baby who's cutting teeth, isn't it?"

She sniffed. "That's what the doctor said, but it's the

first time Georgie's ever had it. In fact, it's the first time he's ever been sick.''

"And you had to take care of it all by yourself," Colin sympathized. "I'm sorry about that."

She shook her head. "It's just that he doesn't understand."

"Poor kid," Colin said, his hand coming to rest on her shoulder. "I'm sure he doesn't understand the reason for his pain."

"What he doesn't understand is that some medicines taste bad," she retorted, sniffing. "He wasn't happy the first time I gave them to him, but this evening he simply wasn't having any of it. I've never seen him like that before. He actually fought me." She pushed her hair out of her eyes, saying, "I didn't mean to let him fall, you know. That's why I sat down here on the couch with him. Then I wind up letting him crack his head, anyway." Dear God, if he should be truly injured... Her bottom lip trembled again as she asked, "H-he's really all right? He doesn't need an X-ray, does he?"

Colin's blue eyes were soft with compassion. "No, honey, he's fine. I saw him when he hit. It wasn't really hard enough to hurt him, but I checked his head anyway. I don't think he'll even have a bump."

"Honestly?" She dabbed at her eyes. His hand cupped the back of her neck.

"You know I wouldn't take a chance with something like that, now don't you?"

She nodded, reassured, but somehow the tears began to fall again. Other concerns crowded in. Where had he been these past three days? Why hadn't he called?

"I have something to tell you," Colin said in that soft, reasonable tone of his that had recently started to make the bottom drop out of her stomach. Was he leaving? Had he realized that he'd made a mistake in marrying her?

She licked her lips, uncertain she could take whatever he might have to say. She shook her head. "I don't think—"

"It's about the adoption papers," he said doggedly. "I signed them. Jeff filed them yesterday, and sometime around the first of the new year we should get a decree. But that's just a formality. For all intents and purposes, you are legally Georgie's mother."

She couldn't believe it. After everything she'd said and done, after her coldness and snappishness, he had gone through with it. She heard herself blurt, "Why?"

For a long moment he just stared at her. Then he blinked and began to speak. "Why did I sign the papers, you mean? Well, for one thing, I promised I would. And for another, it was the right thing to do. You *are* Georgie's mother, the only mother he's ever known and, God willing, ever will. You've invested everything in him that any good mother would or could. It's right that your relationship with him should be protected."

The right thing to do. A promise kept. Fresh guilt assailed her. He was so good, so kind, and she had treated him so shamefully. Suddenly her heart simply overflowed with love, and she was blubbering again.

"Oh, honey, don't. There's no reason for this," he crooned as he pulled her close once more.

"Y-you d-don't understand," she sobbed.

"Yes, I do. You've had this weighing on you for so long, and now that it's all settled you hardly know what to do."

She lifted her head, turning her face up. "You can't know what it's been like."

"I know what it's like to understand that you have a child out there somewhere in the world, to worry if he's needing you, if he's safe, loved. I know what it's like to wonder if you'll ever find him, if he'll ever realize that you love and want him. I know what it's like to be that kid, too, to wonder what it was that you'd done that would make your own father abandon you.'' He gently stroked the hair away from her face. ''I know what it's like to find your son at last, to find all your worst fears disappearing, to see him happy and healthy and safe and loved. I know what kind of relief that is, how it brings you to your knees and at the same time strengthens you to see beyond yourself. You gave me that, Lauren. You gave me all that. It wouldn't be fair to take him away from you or to take you away from him.''

Was it any wonder that she loved this man? Lauren slid a hand up and around to the back of his head. It seemed the most natural, reasonable thing in the world to bring his head down to hers, to lift her mouth to his. He was her husband, after all, the father of her child. Her child, thanks only to his generosity and selflessness. And this felt so good, so right.

He deepened the kiss, tilting his head and sliding his tongue into her mouth. It became a slow, almost lazy kiss full of long, velvety strokes and gentle manipulations, and then gradually it changed, becoming a series of kisses punctuated by experimental nibbles and nips. At one point he sucked her lower lip into his mouth, laved its sensitive underside with his tongue and tugged it with his teeth. She never knew such a thing could be so erotic, that such gentle, unhurried, thorough kissing could cause such mounting pressure and tension in other parts of her body. By the time he moved on to the curve of her jaw and the underside of her chin and the lobe of her ear, she felt drawn tight as a bow string. He worked his way down her neck and back up again, raising gooseflesh and delicious shivers merely to calm them again. When he finally came back to her mouth, she felt as though she'd been starved and suddenly couldn't get enough of those kisses. She practically devoured him, and he let her, yielding control as easily as he'd assumed it.

Kicking off her loose, soft slippers, she straddled his lap, took his face in her hands and kissed him with all her heart. He let his head fall back, his hands resting at his sides. Yet, his mouth met every engagement she launched, and when she instinctively rubbed her body against him, he groaned deep in his chest and briefly cupped her bottom, momentarily tensing. She felt the reassertion of his self-control as he relaxed again, yielding himself fully to her direction. It was incredibly emboldening; she was discovering the eroticism of power. Suddenly she wanted to feel his bare chest against the taut, swollen mounds of her breasts. She knew it was foolish, but she didn't care. He was her husband, and she loved him. And she needed this. She'd worry about the consequences tomorrow.

Reaching down, she grasped the hem of her pajama top and peeled it up, breaking the kiss in order to slip it off her head and arms. Tossing it away, she watched as he devoured her with his eyes, his breath quickening. She sat back on his knees and pulled him forward by the lapels of his coat, which she then pushed off his shoulders and down his arms. He didn't help her, just brought his face close to hers and licked across her lips. Desperate now, she grabbed the front of his shirt and ripped it apart, popping buttons and tearing fabric. Sound rumbled up from the deep well of his chest. She shoved up his undershirt and plastered herself against him, literally attacking him with her mouth.

He held himself perfectly still for a time, making her gyrate against him to elicit a response. Moaning, he began to move his body against hers, pushing his hips up between her thighs, rubbing his chest against her breasts, meeting her kiss aggressively with tongue and teeth and lips. She ground her hips against him, and that did it. His control snapped. His hands clamped around her waist, pushing her down as he pushed up. She wrapped her arms around his neck, undulating against him.

Suddenly he yanked his head back, breaking the wild kiss, and set her off his lap and onto her feet. Stumbling backward, she felt his hands at her hips, skimming down her pajama bottoms. Then he quickly stood and threw off his coat and shirt in one fluid movement. He yanked the undershirt off and tossed it, stepped out of his shoes and opened his jeans, shoving them down to his ankles. Within seconds he stood naked before her, and what a magnificent sight he was, all firm, molded flesh dusted in places with dark hair. Long-limbed and broad-shouldered with every muscle defined, he looked like a statue come to life. He lifted a hand, palm open in invitation, and she could no more have ignored it than she could have stopped breathing.

A voice in the back of her head whispered that there were reasons not to do this, but the clamorings of her body drowned it out. She stepped free of the loose pajamas puddled about her feet, and put her hand in his. His gaze locked with hers. Slowly, he pulled her to him, giving her every chance to back away. Mesmerized, she stepped close and let her body meet his. He stared down into her face for a long while, searching it for uncertainty. She almost hoped he found it but knew he wouldn't. All her fears and insecurities had deserted her. He stepped back and turned toward the hall, her hand clasped in his. Abandoning all doubt, she followed, willfully giving herself over to sensation rather than thought. For now she would forget both past and future and merely allow herself to love.

Colin expected at any moment that she would pull away and flee him. He kept looking back at her, at the incredibly luscious weight of her breasts, the trim rib cage that seemed too delicate to support them, the narrow dip of her waist that flared into nicely rounded hips, the flat plane of her belly that tapered into a triangle of dusky hair. Shapely legs, perfect legs. She was wonderfully made, unlike any woman he had ever seen or imagined, completely Lauren— and almost his.

He wanted to fill his hands with her breasts and push himself deep into her body. And he knew that there were no guarantees, that if she drew back or cried out a denial, he would stop, even at the last moment. It didn't matter that they were married, that he had given her equal rights with his son, he couldn't take what she wouldn't freely give, and he was very much afraid that the long trip down that darkened hallway would bring her to her senses, that she would change her mind.

When they reached the bedroom door, he pushed it open with a sense of growing hope, and when she followed him into the room and down onto the bed, he felt that hope burst inside his chest. He wrapped himself around her, holding her against his body with both arms and legs. Rocking her gently, he closed his eyes and savored the moment, unable to find the words to describe what he was feeling, afraid to speak lest the sound of his voice break the spell that brought them here. Some part of him felt that this night had been inevitable since the moment he had walked into the inn, while another part marveled that he was here with her like this. He had come to find a son and had found a wife, a family and a home, as well.

She sighed, her breath warm against his chest, and her small hand began to explore the contours of his body. He tilted her head back with a hand beneath her chin and kissed her with all the tenderness and hope and longing inside him. Her soft body melted against his, and she pushed a knee between his thighs, drawing closer still. He knew in that moment that if he let her, she would make love to him, but now was not the time for it, as much as he would have savored every touch and sensation.

Now was the time to make her understand how greatly

he treasured her, how deeply he needed and wanted her, how completely he was committed to this marriage, this joining. Now was the moment to make up for earlier disappointments and to clear a way to the future. Now was the moment to show her that he was hers and to make her his at last.

Rolling her onto her back, he pinned her to the mattress with his body, trapping her hands above her head. Using one hand to hold her in place, he cupped each of her breasts while licking and lightly sucking her nipples. Her response was rewardingly intense. She arched her back and caught her breath and rocked her pelvis against his belly. He lessened the pressure of his body, allowing her room to move in any manner that pleased her while he lavished her breasts with attention. When she began to pant and press her head back into the pillow, he knew she was close. Moments later, she lifted her knees, shoved upward against him and cried out. He continued pulling at her breasts with his hands and mouth until she collapsed beneath him. Only then did he reluctantly leave her breasts and move down her body to work magic with his hands and mouth in even more intimate ways.

She seemed embarrassed at first that he would direct such pointed attention to her most private place, but he held her legs apart with the weight of his body and one hand and did exactly what he wanted to, watching as he did it. When he first touched his tongue to her, she jerked and gasped. When he began to suckle, she grabbed handfuls of his hair and alternately tried to pull him away and push him closer. He gladly let her yank and shove while he sought the height of response from her. In mere minutes she had given up clutching his hair for clutching the bedcovers and screaming. He caught his breath and began again, patiently, determinedly driving her wild. Only when he'd reduced her to mindless, breathless sobs did he move upward to cover her body with his once more and take his own fulfillment.

It was not as easy as he imagined. She was wet but swollen inside, her muscles still pulsing deliciously. He had to go slowly, with small, gentle thrusts, for fear of hurting her. When she lifted her legs and wrapped them around his hips, tilting her pelvis to assist his entrance, he was finally able to drive himself to the hilt inside her. His head swam. Various muscles convulsed uncontrollably. He had to stop and hold still, fortifying himself with several strong, cleansing breaths, before he could continue. Even then the slow, smooth, perfectly timed strokes with which he had planned to bring her to climax yet again eluded him. She fought him with frantic bucks and grinds, her fingernails scoring his back and arms as she struggled to make him give her what she wanted. With a groan of surrender he yielded to her body and his, pounding into her with all the finesse of a raging bull, until the world narrowed to that one elemental exercise with the resulting sensation and finally exploded, shattering them both into tinkling bright shards that could never be wholly separated again.

They were no longer two individuals with separate lives and futures. They were one in more ways than he had imagined…more ways than he even understood.

Lauren shoved at the covers, warm to the point of perspiration, especially along her back, where it felt as though a hot, heavy weight was pressed to her. Absent with sleep, she prodded an elbow at it.

"Mmm."

The sound came from far away. The gust of warm, moist air on the crown of her head did not. Reflexively, she curled her head forward to escape it—and felt something soft, yet raspy against her neck, something familiar. Sitting bolt upright she came to two simultaneous conclusions—she was in bed with her husband, and he definitely needed a shave. The previous night's amazing events came slamming at her like three-dimensional images projecting from a movie screen. Hands, mouths, naked skin, and—

"Oh, my God!"

"What's wrong?" Colin asked groggily, stretching in the bed next to her.

Wrong? Her whole life was wrong! This wasn't supposed to happen, for numerous very good reasons that no one knew so well as she did. She was the one who had insisted upon a platonic marriage. She was also the one who had tried to rip his clothes off in the living room last night!

She closed her eyes, digging the heels of her hands into their gritty hollows. What had she done? And why, in heaven's name, had she done it all night long without once thinking of the morning and the consequences that could well come with it? Everything was changed now. She had completely lost control of her life. As the full ramifications struck home, she felt herself pale and begin to tremble. To her very great relief, Georgie called out from the other room.

"Ma-ma-da!"

"I'll get him," Colin said around a yawn, throwing back the covers and rolling up as he swung his feet to the floor. He stood, as naked as the day he was born, and called out, "I'm coming, George."

"C-clothes," Lauren choked, quickly averting her eyes and dragging up the bedcovers. "I, uh, it'll be c-cold."

He walked to the closet and pulled down a shirt and a pair of jeans. The jeans he slid into. The shirt, a brown plaid flannel, he tossed her way. She had it on and was doing up the buttons by the time he moved to the dresser, extracted a clean white T-shirt and pulled it on over his

head. On his way to the door he detoured to her side of
the bed, bent down and kissed her quickly on the mouth.

"Morning, wife."

She mumbled a good-morning as he went out the door.

"Da-da!"

"I'm coming, son."

Lauren closed her eyes and collapsed back on her pillow.
How could she have been so stupid? She could be pregnant,
for pity's sake! The thought woke a deep yearning in her,
but she shook it away. A single woman with one child to
raise had a difficult enough time of it. A single woman with
two children would never have enough time or energy to
devote to both, not to mention money. If Larry succeeded
in forcing her to pay him his share of the worth of the
lodge, she would see her income cut by far more than half.
How could she possibly raise two children on that, even
with child support? Ruthlessly she pushed that thought
away. It wouldn't happen. It couldn't. Just as she couldn't
be pregnant.

And why not? asked a small, rebellious voice in her
head. You aren't a single woman anymore. You spent all
last night making love to your husband!

"But he doesn't love me," she whispered. And I will be
single again. There. There it was, the whole reason she
couldn't be pregnant. This whole marriage thing was a
sham, a way for Colin to repay her for taking care of Georgie, as if she needed repayment for loving her own son.
The other, the sex, that was just a convenience for him. He
was a man, after all, a good man, but a man, nonetheless.
She dared not read more than that into it.

So be convenient, argued that rebel voice. He appears to
like it well enough. He might even like it well enough to
stay interested.

But she knew she couldn't do that. She couldn't learn to
depend on him in any way, and she couldn't give him the

upper hand—if she hadn't already. Chewing her lip, she tried to think what she'd said to him last night, what he had said. Had she told him that she loved him? She searched through her memories of the night before, flushing at moments as she recalled some of the things they'd done together. She hadn't known some of those things were possible, hadn't expected ever to experience some of them. Now that she let herself remember, however, she realized that they'd done those things, all of them, without a single word. Oh, they had made sounds. They had, in fact, communicated quite ably, but not with words. She breathed a small sigh of relief just a Colin carried Georgie into the room.

"Here's your beautiful mommy," Colin said, plopping Georgie onto the bed and following him down.

"Good morning, sweetie," Lauren said gently, feeling his forehead. "You still have a little temperature, poor baby."

Georgie rubbed the side of his head with his fist and looked around the room as if trying to figure out what was wrong with it. He mumbled something and held out a hand toward the closet.

"What do you want, honey?" she asked lightly. "All your toys are in the other room."

"Maybe he wants his toys and his other things moved back in here where they belong," Colin said cautiously.

Lauren gulped. Moving Georgie back in here naturally meant that Colin would be sharing a room with her, and she couldn't have that. She could only see one way to regain her footing in this marriage, and she might as well be about it. "Colin, I hope you don't think that last night changes anything."

"It changes one thing," he said after a moment. "At least the marriage has been consummated."

She sat up, crossing her legs beneath the covers. "Yes, but…that can't happen again."

He cocked his head to one side. "Why not?"

Georgie pointed at the window and mumbled something else unintelligible. Lauren looked in that direction, as much to make him think she was paying attention to him as to avoid looking at Colin. "Well, for one thing, it would be t-taking a t-terrible chance."

"Meaning?"

"I'm not, uh, using any birth control."

"That can be taken care of," he said softly.

"I—I just don't think it's a good idea. I'm not r-ready."

He was silent for several moments, but then he said, "Can I ask one question?"

"I suppose."

He sat up, legs folded, and lifted Georgie onto his lap. "Do you ever expect…I mean, do you want more children?"

She looked at her lap. "Someday."

"Then someday we have to have a normal marriage," he said. "I can wait if I have to, but not too long. I want Georgie to have siblings. I want us to have a baby."

She was torn between delight that he might truly mean to continue the marriage and despair that, because he did not love her, it could never be what it was meant to be. She was nothing more than a convenience to him, in every way, and she'd best not forget that, but it hurt. Oh, how it hurt. She threw back the covers and got out of bed, exclaiming, "I'm not a baby machine!"

His mouth dropped open. "I never said you were."

She truly didn't want to fight with him. In fact, she wanted nothing more than to get away from him. "I'm going to take a shower."

"Okay. Now let me tell you what I'm going to do. I'm going to move Georgie's things back into his bedroom,"

Colin said firmly. She opened her mouth to tell him that he was not going to do any such thing, but he looked up at her then with an expression as implacable as stone. "I'll leave my clothes in here and sleep in the living room, but you and the baby are going to have some normalcy in your lives."

"You can't—" she began, but he cut her off with a lifted eyebrow.

"Oh, yes, I can. This is my home, too, now. You can keep me out of your bed, but you cannot keep me from doing what I think best for you and our son."

She knew he was right, but she didn't have to like it. "Fine," she snapped. "Knock yourself out."

"I will," he promised softly as she swept from the room. "And I'll give Georgie his medicine," he called to her as she strode down the hall. She wanted to tell him not to bother, that she could take care of her son, but last night had almost been her undoing. The thought of Georgie being so angry with her that he would turn his back on her again chilled her. So let Colin play Daddy while he would. She'd get herself together soon enough, and when he finally walked away, she'd stand tall on her own two feet.

Chapter Eleven

As Lauren approached the table, Colin got up and walked around Georgie's high chair to pull out Lauren's seat. She flashed him a strained smile, but he wouldn't be put off. He had secretly overhead her remarking to Juan only yesterday that she wished he, Colin, would not be so "darn charming and attentive." He considered it proof that he was getting to her, and since that was exactly what he hoped to do, he wasn't about to back off now. She had pulled her hair up into a ponytail, leaving the slender nape of her neck bare. Bending forward, he pressed his lips to that sensitive skin before straightening and walking around the table to retake his own seat. She was lightly rubbing the back of her neck when he looked up.

"I took a look at the cabin today," he said brightly. "I think it has wonderful possibilities."

She smiled at Georgie, replying absently, "Do you?"

He nodded and reached for his napkin, shaking it out and

draping it over his lap. "It's larger than I thought it would be."

"Is it?" she murmured, unnecessarily loosening the napkin that Colin had tied around Georgie's neck.

"I think we can do three bedrooms," he said. "Two downstairs and a small guest room upstairs next to the library in the loft."

She finally looked at him. "Library?"

"Well, a small library. I think we can squeeze in a second bath beneath the stairs, too. Or, we can build onto the back of the building and use the loft for a combination library and playroom."

"I don't see the point in building on," she said dismissively, spreading her own napkin.

"I suppose there's time enough for building on before our family outgrows the place," he said, watching with keen interest as her face flushed a dusty rose. "If I start work now I can have it ready by the first of the year."

"You expect us to move *then?*" she asked incredulously.

"Better start thinking about what you want to do with the apartment," he affirmed doggedly. "We could always rent it, I suppose, or keep it for special guests, family and friends."

"You don't have any family," she snapped.

He let it roll off him, knowing that she was testing him more than trying to hurt him. "But you do," he said calmly, "and we both have friends."

The waitress appeared with the dinner he'd ordered, announcing, "Shelby says he's outdone himself with this shrimp and avocado fajita."

"Looks wonderful," Lauren conceded. "But who are the French fries for?"

Georgie was already helping himself to the platter, reaching across the table to do so. Colin chuckled. "Isn't it obvious? I had some in here the other day, and you know how he likes to eat off our plates. He loves the things."

Lauren bristled. Leaning forward, she chided, "You shouldn't have let him! He needs to eat a healthy diet."

"To offset all that sugar you give him," Colin said pointedly.

Anger flashed in her eyes, but she glanced at the hovering waitress before averting her gaze. "That's only until he stops taking that nasty medicine."

"So in three days the suckers disappear?"

She said nothing to that, just picked up her fork and stabbed a lovely pink shrimp the size of his thumb.

"Can I get you anything else?" the waitress asked brightly.

Colin smiled up at her. "No, thanks, Jemma. We're perfectly capable of getting ourselves anything else we might need. You save your energy for the paying customers."

"Thank you, Mr. Colin."

"Thank you."

Lauren stabbed him next, with a quelling, suspicious glare. "You've gotten awfully chummy with the help, or should I say, the female help."

He had to bite the inside of his cheek to keep from laughing at that inadvertent display of jealousy, which he did not dignify with a reply. Plucking a flour tortilla from the server, he brought the subject back to one he'd been meaning to investigate further for some time. "Speaking of family, what are our plans for Thanksgiving?"

Lauren shrugged. "We have several bookings, so the dining room will be serving the usual Thanksgiving feast. Why do you ask?"

"Jeff and Meg invited us to join them this year."

She looked startled. "I can't leave the lodge on such an important—"

"That's why I told them we couldn't, regretfully, accept

their invitation, but it was thoughtful of them to think of us.''

''I'll, uh, send Meg a note thanking her,'' she replied with a nod.

''That would be nice,'' he said, rolling his fajita. ''Now what about your family?''

She lifted both eyebrows. ''What about them?''

''Well, obviously we can't go there, but have you invited them here?''

''They wouldn't come.''

''You sure about that?''

Sighing, she laid down her utensils. ''You don't understand my family. Mother will be holding court, as usual, in her little house in Santa Fe. Larry and Randi will be there at daybreak and hang on every word she says, most of which will be criticism of everything and everyone but especially me. Mother will cook enough to feed an army and complain every moment about how tiring it is, but she won't let anyone else lift so much as a finger. Then after dinner she'll lie down on the sofa with a headache while Larry waits on her, hand and foot, until the kitchen is cleaned up—by me. Afterward, she'll convince him and Randi to spend the night, even though they live less than ten miles away, claiming her heart is acting up again, despite the fact that several doctors have told her and us that there is nothing whatsoever wrong with her.''

''Your mother sounds like a very lonely woman,'' Colin ventured gently.

Lauren rolled her eyes. ''Lonely? When she has Larry and Randi at her beck and call?''

''What if they did come here for Thanksgiving?'' Colin asked. ''Would they be welcome?''

''Of course they'd be welcome,'' she retorted, starting to eat again. ''But they wouldn't come.''

He said nothing more on the subject.

* * *

Colin was as nervous as a June bug roasting in a hot skillet. Lauren had never seen him so jumpy.

"Will you calm down!" Lauren insisted, glaring as he began jingling his change again.

He jerked his hands from his pants pockets. "Sorry. Guess I'm just anxious to get at that turkey. Sure smells good, doesn't it?"

Lauren nodded and went back to straightening the tiny bow tie beneath Georgie's plump chin. It was already damp with drool, but he looked like a perfect darling in his little suit, knee pants, long socks and all. When the outer door opened, Lauren turned a practiced smile in that direction, only to feel her jaw drop in a gape of shock.

"Mother?"

Hallie Cole smiled with uncharacteristic temerity, her white-gloved hand reaching up to pat her hair. The tint in her short, tightly curled hair bore a slightly greenish cast, demonstrating that she had yet again overprocessed it severely. God forbid that a hint of its natural gray should show, despite the fact that she was on the down side of sixty and sliding inexorably toward seventy, having married and borne her children quite late in life. Lauren managed to get her mouth closed, noting as she did so that her mother was wearing her good, dark-green suit with the rhinestone buttons beneath her black wool dress coat and its detachable fox fur collar. Her feet were wedged into brown pumps at least one size too small.

"Hello, Lauren. We were thrilled to get your invitation."

We, Lauren immediately saw, included her brother Lawrence in his ill-fitting charcoal-gray suit and her sister-in-law, Miranda, with her surprisingly big belly squeezed into a corduroy coat. Lauren had barely begun to consider the mystery of the aforementioned invitation when Colin stepped forward to offer his hand to her mother.

"Mrs. Cole, I'm Colin."

"Oh!" She laid a gloved hand on his cheek, gushing, "A son-in-law ought to call his mother-in-law by her given name, don't you think? I'm Hallie."

"I'm delighted to meet you at last," Colin said smoothly. "Lauren speaks of you often."

Hallie Cole actually simpered. "What a handsome, charming man you are." She smiled at Lauren. "I'm so happy for you, dear, and I understand completely why you couldn't wait for a proper wedding or inform us right away."

"All those legal complications," Colin chuckled, sliding a worried glance in Lauren's direction.

"Explained them all, did you?" Lauren asked slyly, suddenly understanding everything.

Colin met her gaze levelly. "I did my best, sweetheart."

"So I see."

Georgie grew tired of sitting quietly on the counter and twisted around to reach for his father, calling, "Da-da."

Colin quickly scooped him onto his hip and turned him to face Hallie. "George, I'd like you to meet your grandmother."

Hallie gushed all over the baby without actually touching him. "Oh, he does look just like you!" She glanced at Lauren. "What a lovely family you make." To Lauren's surprise her mother opened her arms and advanced toward the counter. Leaning over it, she actually hugged Lauren. "I'm so very pleased."

Larry stepped up then. "Yes, Laurie, we all are. Congratulations. Er, best wishes. And thank you for inviting us. It's very thoughtful, all things considered, especially since neither Mom or Miranda are in shape to prepare the feast this year."

Miranda patted her big belly. "It's just like Colin says. We can all sit back and let the staff pamper us."

Lauren lifted an eyebrow in Colin's direction. He had

the good grace to look flustered. "Uh, I'd like to pamper you all myself!" He chuckled uncertainly. "But rest assured that Shelby has done all the cooking."

Everyone laughed as if he'd made a very clever joke, everyone except Lauren. She smiled, though, and said, "Why don't you all go in and make yourselves comfortable in front of the fire? I have one or two more things to take care of here. Ah, you could help me, Colin. Dear." She nodded at her family. "We'll join you in just a minute."

Colin watched them file out of the foyer with something akin to desperation. When he turned back to Lauren, he visibly steeled himself. "I—I wanted to surprise you. They were very anxious to come, by the way. I thought, perhaps, you'd be pleased by that."

Lauren considered him wonderingly. She'd have bet her last nickel that her prickly family would have refused such an invitation with sniffs and complaints about her unwillingness to participate in the vaunted family traditions, not to mention her tardiness in reporting her impromptu marriage. Instead, Colin had managed to smooth over everything, and they had driven hours in their best clothing to share the holiday. Even if it did have plenty to do with the prospect of being pampered by hired staff, she recognized a peace offering when she saw one. And she knew whom she had to thank.

"I trust that Shelby and the Herreras know what is expected of them?"

Colin visibly relaxed. "They've been very supportive."

Lauren sighed. "You just never cease to amaze me, do you know that?"

He smiled, shaking his head, and whispered, "I just want to make you happy."

She wanted to believe that, and almost did, but now was not the time to contemplate the state of her marriage. She had family awaiting her. She walked out from behind the counter. Colin met her at the end, and she reached for Georgie, who came into her arms quite willingly. Side by side, they went in to see the family in the great room.

Hallie had made herself comfortable on the sofa closest to the fire. Miranda had lowered herself into a chair farther away from the flames, and Larry was walking around assessing the room as if judging its market value. He turned when Lauren and Colin entered the room with Georgie.

"You've done wonders with this place, Lauren."

She determined to take the compliment at face value and said graciously, "Thank you."

Colin took her elbow and steered her to the sofa directly facing the one on which her mother sat. Lauren lowered herself carefully, tugging with her free hand at the short skirt of her chocolate brown, crushed velvet dress. She had piled her hair up in a loose chignon that Georgie immediately began trying to undo when she stood him on the sofa next to her. She pretty much ignored him, moving her head and gently pushing away his hands from time to time as she made small talk with her mother about the drive up, while Colin gathered everyone's coats and deposited them in the apartment.

"Don't muss Mommy's hair," Colin said sternly upon his return. As he sank down next to Georgie, he captured those busy little hands. "It's not nice to play with Mommy's hair when she doesn't want you to, especially when she looks so beautiful."

Lauren couldn't help thinking that he looked pretty stunning himself in pleated black slacks, matching shirt and a cream white silk sweater, but she dared not say so. Instead, she glanced at her watch and then looked to her mother once more. "Appetizers and drinks will be served in about ten minutes, but if you like I'll be glad to go to the kitchen for anything you want now."

"Oh, no, we'll wait," Hallie said graciously. "Unless you'd like something, Miranda?"

Miranda shook her head as a family from Dallas entered the great room and nodded greetings to Lauren and Colin while talking excitedly amongst themselves about the possibility of skiing that afternoon. Lauren had posted a notice in the lobby earlier letting everyone know that the slopes at Angel Fire had been given an extra layer of man-made snow, so the slopes were ready despite a somewhat disappointing early snowfall season. A trio of young women already dressed in ski gear tramped in right behind the family and made for one of the window seats, laughing together.

"Business seems good," Larry said, sitting down beside his mother, who seemed anxious to smooth over the remark.

"Have Miranda and Larry told you their news?" she asked eagerly, then proceeded to do it for them. "They're having twins!"

Lauren gasped, turning an inquisitive gaze on Miranda, who smugly patted her belly as if to say, "Top this one!"

"Congratulations!" Colin exclaimed heartily.

"Yes, congratulations," Lauren echoed, wondering how on earth Miranda and Larry were going to cope with twins when they seemed barely able to cope with themselves. Would this impact her brother's demands on her?

"Isn't it something?" Hallie gushed on. "Here I am thinking I'll never be blessed with grandchildren, and suddenly I have three!"

"And it won't stop there," Colin said. "Lauren and I plan to have more children, don't we, sweetheart?"

Lauren's heart thumped hard in her chest. "Eventually," she muttered.

"Better be careful," Larry commented. "You know what they say about twins running in families."

"Is that true?" Colin asked of no one in particular.

Suddenly, Georgie grabbed Lauren's shoulder and all but shouted in her ear, "Bite, Mama!" He pointed past his father, who turned his head and chuckled.

"It seems that the appetizers have arrived."

"Leave it to this little eating machine to be the first to know when the food's ready," Lauren quipped, relieved to be able to change the subject.

"Why, that poor baby's starving," Hallie scolded.

"Perpetually," Colin said easily, getting to his feet. "Excuse me a moment."

"He's always had a hearty appetite," Lauren explained, wrestling Georgie into her lap, "but he had an ear infection not long ago and got these two new teeth, and since then he just can't seem to eat enough."

"He's about to take a growth spurt," Hallie predicted sagely. "Mark my word, a week or two from now you'll be putting long pants on him, and they'll suddenly be too short."

"You're probably right," Lauren conceded, grinning.

Colin returned with a tray of appetizers and a collapsible table, napkins draped across one arm. Maria followed with the drinks cart. Georgie stretched his little arm toward the tray.

"Ladies first, son," Colin said, gallantly serving Hallie and Miranda, then Lauren. Lauren sat George on the couch next to her, spread a napkin over his lap and fed him bits and pieces out of her own napkin. Colin put the tray on the table and sat down next to her, taking charge of the drinks end of business by carefully helping George sip from his cup of mulled cider, while Maria served the others then moved off to help Ponce take care of the paying guests. Colin also took charge of the conversation by engaging Larry in a detailed explanation of his job as assistant manager of a large grocery store. Before the subject was exhausted, Juan appeared in the doorway to announce that dinner was served.

Everyone got up and moved into the dining room, where Shelby had set up an elaborate buffet, complete with two perfectly roasted turkeys and all the requisite traditional dishes, with a New Mexico twist thrown in here and there for good measure. To Lauren's surprise, Juan had set a large table for her family, complete with covered serving dishes of everything on the buffet so they didn't have to stand in line. Hallie, Miranda and Larry eagerly allowed themselves to be ushered to their places. Lauren could only smile as her mother swept past the paying guests, nodding as regally as any queen. When they were all seated and their glasses filled with their drinks of choice, Colin proposed a toast.

"To family," he said, "with which I have recently been so richly blessed."

"Hear, hear."

They all drank, but then Hallie said rather censorially, "We really ought to say grace."

Colin surprised Lauren yet again by covering her hand with his atop the table and saying, "I'd be delighted, if you'd allow me the honor."

"Well, you are our host," her mother said reluctantly, casting a glance at Larry. Colin was quick to pick up on the byplay.

"Perhaps you'd like to do it, Lawrence?"

"Oh, no, go right ahead. As mother pointed out, you are the host."

Hallie smiled so graciously that Lauren wondered if she was as miffed as Lauren suspected. Larry, after all, had been saying grace at the family dining table since he was old enough to speak in sentences. Nothing Larry had ever mumbled out of duty could compare with Colin's eloquence, however. He began by thanking God for his wife and his son. He spoke of the place Jeff and Meg and their girls had filled in his life, and he mentioned the Herreras and other staffers by name. Then he praised God for at last giving him a mother, brother and sister by marriage. He asked God to protect the twins who had yet to make their entry into the world, and finally he gave thanks for the food and the bounty enjoyed by all in this country and asked God to keep him ever grateful for his many blessings.

Lauren felt truly humbled, especially when he closed his prayer and lifted her hand to reverently kiss her knuckles, and she could tell by the looks on the faces of her family that he had won a high degree of respect and approval from them. No doubt about it, he had done her proud this day, and she couldn't help a burgeoning, and dangerous, sense of gratitude.

Colin wasn't the only one to do her proud that day. The food was not just delicious, it was extraordinary, and Lauren felt that her sometimes intimidating cook should be publicly praised. When she sent for Shelby to come out into the dining room, however, she was uncertain whether or not he would actually appear, so she was surprised when he did so immediately, wearing a white coat and chef's hat over his usual blue jeans. He grinned but blushed bloodred when the diners broke out in spontaneous applause. When Colin rose to shake his hand and clap him on the shoulder, Lauren could have sworn that she saw tears in the cook's eyes, but he escaped back into the kitchen so quickly that she couldn't be sure. She made a mental note to include a generous bonus in his next paycheck, then included the names of everyone on the staff who had made this such a special day. How, she wondered, was she ever going to thank her husband, though, without risking the emotional distance she'd managed to gain?

After they'd all stuffed themselves shamelessly, Colin suggested they take coffee in the apartment, which he'd had prepared beforehand. It seemed he'd thought of everything. Since Georgie was showing signs of wanting his nap, she was especially pleased with the arrangements. She trusted that he had stashed any incriminating evidence of their unusual sleeping arrangements.

As soon as she walked through the door, she knew that he had, indeed, taken care of everything. The place was spotless. Extra chairs had been carried in, and a cozy fire had been lit. The aroma of fresh coffee filled the air. Noting that her mother was hobbling on her now-swollen feet, Lauren found a pair of her own house slippers for her to borrow. She then put Georgie down for his nap, the work of mere minutes, and joined the others in the living area, where they all relaxed around the fire with cups of fragrant coffee. All was well until Miranda made a somewhat catty comment about the apartment.

"You didn't put nearly as much time and attention into decorating this part of the lodge as the rest, did you?"

Even Hallie raised eyebrows at that tactless verbal jab, but Lauren merely replied that she hadn't had money to do everything at once, so she'd concentrated on making the lodge a success first.

"Very understandable," Hallie said in what appeared to be an honest effort to praise Lauren. "Besides, the place is clean and comfortable. It may be a little small for a family, but I'm sure you weren't thinking of that when you made your plans. I mean, who would've dreamed you'd manage to get a child and find someone to marry you, too? Uh, here, I mean."

Lauren gritted her teeth, trying hard not to take the absentminded disparagement more seriously than the deliberate praise. Colin, naturally, attempted to make everything all right by interjecting a new note into the conversation.

"Actually," he said brightly, "we're getting the cabin ready to move into."

That was when the hammer finally fell. "So you aren't intending to include it in the settlement?" Larry asked caustically.

Lauren felt her temper surge hot, but she took a deep breath and attempted to cool it, only to hear herself saying smartly, "What settlement would that be, Larry?"

Larry stared at her. "I naturally assumed that you'd come to your senses and called us here to make an acceptable offer."

"You assumed incorrectly."

"Then why the invitation?" Miranda demanded.

Colin was quick to answer. "To celebrate the holiday with family, of course."

Larry ignored this obvious plea for a change of subject. "Look, Lauren, you know perfectly well that you're going to have to settle with me."

"I know nothing of the kind."

Larry came up off the couch. "My lawyer has told me that you have little choice."

"And my lawyer has told me—" she began hotly.

"But I'd think," Larry interrupted, "you'd have the decency to do the fair thing on your own."

"Especially as we're expecting twins!" Miranda put in.

"How did that get to be my responsibility?" Lauren demanded.

Suddenly everyone was talking, or shouting, at once.

"Stop!" Colin roared, standing and lifting both hands, palms out. When the room quieted, he looked pointedly at each of them. "This is not the place or the time for this discussion, so let's all agree to just drop the subject."

"Why should I?" Larry demanded. "This has gone on long enough! Lauren knows I own a share of this lodge and how badly I need that money!"

"I built this place on my own," Lauren retorted.

"But you don't need the lodge now that you've got a husband," Miranda said inelegantly.

"*You* have a husband," Lauren pointed out.

"And I'm perfectly content to stay home and let him provide for me and our children."

"Let me provide for them, you mean!" Lauren snapped.

"Now, Lauren," her mother began in that hated tone that implied immaturity and selfishness on Lauren's part, "you know that your grandfather left this place to both you and your brother."

"I know you're going to side with Larry no matter how much hard work and money I've poured into this place!" Lauren cried. "Why, just once, can you not take my side?"

"I'm not taking sides," Hallie protested, "but fair is fair and—"

"And whatever Larry wants, Larry is supposed to get!" Lauren shouted. "Yea, I got that message a long time ago."

"Don't use that tone of voice with our mother!" Larry barked. "You're just as jealous and hateful as ever!"

"That's enough!" Colin shouted, again silencing all of them. He shoved a hand through his hair. "What's wrong with you people? This is supposed to be a day of celebration, of thankfulness, a day for families to enjoy one another's company. Instead, you're tearing each other to pieces! Don't you understand what you have in each other? You're arguing about money, for pity's sake! Families are supposed to help and support one another. That's what I want for my son, not this petty arguing over old sibling rivalries!"

Lauren stared at him in shocked offense. Petty. Sibling rivalries. Money. Didn't he get it? Couldn't he see that her mother always chose Larry over her?

He glared at Lawrence, dressing him down with his manner and tone as much as his words. "You're Lauren's brother, not her father. You don't have any right to rebuke her." Larry rocked back on his heels but said nothing. Colin targeted Miranda next. "And you have no business trying to tell Lauren what she can and cannot do with her life. She's worked hard to build up this place, and she has every right to continue working if she wants to."

Miranda stiffened. "But surely you don't want your wife—"

"What I want from my wife is none of your business," Colin declared sharply. "That's between me and her. You have no place and no say in it."

Miranda blinked and looked down at her big belly, frowning. Lauren allowed herself a smug expression, only to find Colin glaring at her next. The fact that he didn't address her directly didn't disguise the fact that he was criticizing her.

"I tried to give you a chance to be family today, to smooth over your problems and put them behind you, to be happy with one another. Why couldn't you just accept that and love one another?"

"Maybe there just isn't enough love to go around in this family," Lauren choked out, unable to take her condemning gaze from her husband's face. It was the same old story, she thought bitterly. It always would be. Turning, she fled into her bedroom and slammed the door. So much for family togetherness. And so much for expecting her husband to weigh in on her side.

Chapter Twelve

Lauren glanced at the newspaper shielding her from her husband's view, then quickly estimated the time it would take her to reach the front door of the apartment. Colin sat on a stool at the bar counter, enjoying a cup of coffee and the Santa Fe paper. He appeared to be absorbed in his reading, and she decided that if she was quiet she could make it through the door without his ever knowing she had done so. Carefully she stepped from her bedroom and turned toward the front door.

"Still not speaking to me, I take it."

She drew up short, his words seeming to form a wall of sound against which she was powerless. The newspaper crumpled as he lowered his arms, and Lauren winced at the disappointment still evident on his face. She had lived with that look for days, and somehow it had eaten away at her righteous indignation at his lack of support and understanding where her family was concerned, somehow it had made her think that maybe, just maybe, she wasn't as "right" as she'd thought. The things her family had said still smarted, but she couldn't help thinking more and more lately that her brother did have some claim to the lodge and that she ought to be able to find some fair settlement. What good did it do to stay angry, anyway? It only made everyone tense—and kept that look of disappointment on her husband's face.

She took a deep breath. "Actually, I assumed that you weren't speaking to me."

"Oh? And why would that be?"

She looked down at her Western boots and the hems of her faded jeans. "I know what you think of me."

"I doubt that." The warmth and softness of his voice made her look up again. He folded the newspaper and laid it aside. "I think the real problem is that you don't understand me and my motives. I invited your family here because I want you to be happy, and I see that your relationship with them troubles you."

She sighed. "You can't do anything to fix that."

"Maybe not. But you can."

Those last words carried the weight of a physical blow. She shook her head. "You don't understand. My mother has never been on my side. She tolerates me when she must, but she doesn't…"

"Love you?" he finished for her. She said nothing, just stared at him and hoped that he couldn't see the longing that rose up within her. He was shaking his head. "That's not what I see. I think she's puzzled by your assumption that she doesn't love you, and I also think she doesn't know how to make you understand her feelings. You keep her at a distance, Lauren, just as you do me."

"No, I don't." But did she? Suddenly she wasn't so sure anymore. She bit her lip. "I don't mean to, anyway."

"Larry was ill as a child," Colin went on. "Your mother

was overprotective. You took that as a kind of rejection, and when your father died, you must have felt that you were completely alone in the world.''

"Except for my grandfather," she said in a small voice.

"Which was why you held on to this place with all your strength after he was gone—and maybe why you don't want to admit that it was meant to be as much Larry's as yours.''

"But I'm the one who brought this place to life, who makes it work.''

"I don't deny that. What you've accomplished here all on your own is nothing short of amazing. And in no way could your brother have done it. He knows that, Lauren, and he's shamed by it. He can't hold a candle to you as a person, and he knows it. And now he's got a family that he's not at all certain he can support. He's frightened, and he's gone to the only person who he knows can take care of things.''

"Me," she whispered, both shamed and awed. "I never looked at it like that.''

"I'm not surprised," Colin said smoothly. "You sell yourself short in every way.''

Her gaze sharpened, and for some reason her heartbeat sped up. "What do you mean?''

Colin stared at her for a long moment. "Can you really believe I want you only for Georgie's sake?" he finally asked. "I assure you, I wasn't thinking of him when I was making love to you.''

Lauren gulped as memories swept her. "Colin, I... You're right. I—I haven't really given...my family a chance.''

He smiled, his face softening. "I'm glad to hear you say that. Family is more important than money or anything else." He slipped off his stool and came toward her. "At least it seems so to me. I know that the people in my family are the most important ones in my life." He stopped in front of her and lifted a hand to smooth back the tendrils of bangs wisping about her forehead. "I want every good thing for you and our son, including a loving relationship with your mother and brother."

Lauren looked away guiltily. "I'm sorry for the way I've been acting," she said softly. "I don't know why you put up with me."

Suddenly she found herself seized by the upper arms and hauled up against him. "Then let me remind you," he said, and his head bowed to hers, his mouth capturing her own with purposeful strength.

What began as fierce possession, however, soon gentled to ardent persuasion—and persuasive it was, alarmingly so. When at last he lifted his head, she was a little dizzy and gasping for breath. She gazed up at those bright-blue eyes wonderingly. Was it possible that he really cared for her? She no longer doubted that he wanted her. How could she, any more than he could doubt that she wanted him?

Realizing suddenly how close she was to total capitulation, she stumbled backward, reaching blindly for the doorknob. "I, um, I think I should go write a note to my mother. Maybe apologize a-and invite her, them, for Christmas."

He smiled, one corner of his mouth slowly hitching upward and then the other following suit. "A family Christmas," he said. "Sounds wonderful to me."

Suddenly she felt unaccountably giddy. Laughter just bubbled up from deep inside her. "I—I'll try to find some way to settle things with Larry, too."

His smile widened. "You won't regret that."

She nodded, absurdly delighted to have pleased him. "Maybe I should invite Jeff and Meg and their girls. After all, it's not just Christmas. It's our son's first birthday, too."

"I'd like that," he said approvingly. "I'd like that a lot."

"Consider it done, then."

He put his hands to his hips and cocked his head as if seeing her in a whole new light suddenly. She trilled him a wave and escaped out the door—before she declared feelings better left unsaid or threw herself into his arms once more.

So much to do. Lauren hurried into the great room, having just managed to get the payroll out on time, and opened her mouth to call for Juan, only to stop as she spied Colin atop a ladder, his hands and arms full of pine boughs as he balanced himself and waited for a similarly laden Ponce to climb a second ladder at the other corner of the wall. As Ponce did so, Lauren saw that the boughs were strung together into a long garland with a thin wire that made it possible to lift them all at once and secure them to the wall with evenly spaced hangers already in place. Colin's idea, no doubt, and much more efficient than the old one-bough-at-a-time method that she'd employed last year.

Sometimes this husband of hers truly amazed her. Despite all the work he'd been doing on his own lately—always on the phone, driving back and forth to Albuquerque, plunking away at his computer, faxing and copying and making almost daily trips to the post office, not to mention working on the cabin—he still found time to shoulder his responsibilities as a father and help out around the lodge. He was absolutely determined that Georgie was going to be walking by Christmas and spent hours working with the child, though she was sure that Georgie saw it only as play.

Much had changed lately. She no longer felt compelled to draw away when he sat down beside her and casually draped his arm about her shoulders or slipped his hand into hers as they walked side by side. She welcomed his touch when it came and realized that she was spending more and more time in his company. Some part of her realized, too, that he was patiently waiting for her to invite him into her bed, and she wasn't certain why she couldn't find the courage to do it.

It was what she wanted, and yet she hesitated, needing something more, something for which she couldn't simply ask outright. She needed to hear that he loved her. She needed to know that she wasn't just imagining that those feelings existed on his part. But she could be patient, as patient as he was.

Calmly she waded into the work at hand, calling out to Ponce that he had pulled his end too tight. Colin grinned down at her and proceeded to follow her directions to the letter. When the garland was hung to her satisfaction, Ponce went out to help his father bring in the first of the half dozen trees they'd cut from high up on the mountain, while Colin pulled her aside for a brief conference.

"Juan and I have a proposal to make," he said, leaning against one of the comfortable leather chairs scattered about the room.

"Oh? About what?"

"The cabin and the apartment."

"What about them?"

"Well, the cabin is about ready, but for simplicity's sake, I think we ought to move after the holidays."

She'd been of two minds about this move from the beginning. On one hand, the cabin had been her grandfather's last home. It held wonderful memories for her. But living there with Colin had seemed wrong somehow, as if doing so would legitimize this crazy marriage. Lately, however, it was making a lot of sense. Crazy or not, this was a marriage, and she was beginning to think they just might work everything out between them. Besides, Georgie deserved a real home, something more than a glorified suite in what was, essentially, a place of business, and Colin had done an amazing job with the cabin.

She folded her arms and said, "I agree. Once the holidays are behind us and the decorations are put away, the move will be easier."

He beamed at her and, snagging her folded arms with one hand, he began pulling her toward him. Just then Juan and Ponce staggered into the room with the tree. It was even bigger than last year's, if that was possible, and Colin immediately went to help them maneuver it into position. When the tree was securely fixed in place, Ponce announced an intention to get himself a soft drink, while Juan and Colin approached Lauren.

"Did you ask her?" Juan prodded Colin eagerly.

"Not yet. We were just getting to it when you brought the tree in."

Lauren shifted her position, sitting on the arm of the chair, one fringed penny loafer swinging casually above the floor. "Why do I get the feeling that there is a conspiracy afoot here?" she teased.

Juan rubbed his hands together but looked to Colin to take the lead.

"The thing is," Colin began, "we haven't decided what to do with the apartment after we move to the cabin, so Juan asked—"

"It's just a suggestion!" Juan interceded quickly, and Colin nodded.

"Right. Anyway, the suggestion is that he and Maria move into the apartment."

"You want someone here all the time, don't you?" Juan asked excitedly. "I could be, like, the manager, or maybe just the night manager, and the apartment would be, like, a raise for me, but it wouldn't cost you anything, really."

Lauren was stunned—stunned that she hadn't thought of

this herself. It was a wonderful suggestion, and Juan deserved what would amount to a promotion. She just had one problem with the arrangement. "What about Ponce? Since the apartment is obviously not big enough for all three of you, where will he stay?"

"We were thinking," Colin began...

Lauren listened as the two men outlined their plan. "Let me get this straight," she said. "You're proposing that we move the employee break room off the kitchen, put the vending machines beneath the stairs, convert that little rest room across from my office to a private bath, move Ponce into what is now the break room and let Juan and Maria have the apartment in payment for Juan taking over the duties of assistant manager of the inn. Is that right?"

The expression on Juan's face was a mix of ecstatic eagerness and painful hope. "That's about it," Colin confirmed.

Lauren rubbed her chin, pretending to consider. "Hmm." She shook her head, and Juan's face fell—until she announced, "I think he ought to get a raise, too. Just a small one, mind you. That's all the budget can bear."

Juan whooped, and Colin laughed, slinging an elbow at his elated coconspirator. "Told you she'd go for it."

Juan grabbed Lauren's hand and pumped it up and down. "I will work so hard! You will be so proud of me!"

Lauren chuckled. "I already am. You've been my good right arm around here from the beginning. You can't work all the time, though. We'll have to look at rearranging the schedule so your being on call at night won't place an undue burden on you."

"I can do that," Colin volunteered. "It's part of what I do professionally, after all."

"Then I'll leave it in your hands," Lauren decided, thinking that she had plenty on her plate already.

"I can't wait to tell Maria when she comes after

school!'' Juan exclaimed, backing away. ''But first I tell Ponce.'' He hurried toward the door, calling over his shoulder. ''We get that next tree in quick.''

Lauren laughed, pleased to see him so happy. She lifted an eyebrow at Colin. ''Was this really his idea?''

''I can't say I didn't welcome it, but yes, it was his idea.''

''Why do you say that you welcomed it?'' she asked, puzzled by his choice of words. If she had learned anything about this husband of hers, it was that he chose his words thoughtfully and carefully, sometimes thinking long before speaking.

He reached out for her hand, rubbing her knuckles with his thumb. ''We're going to have a real home, Lauren,'' he pointed out softly, ''and a normal family life, dinner at our own table, quiet evenings in front of the television. I can't tell you what that means to me. You've made me very happy already. Is it any wonder that I want to do the same for you?''

She felt a lump grow in her throat. Swallowing it down, she quipped, ''I hope you aren't counting on me to cook.''

''I don't care who cooks,'' he said solemnly. ''I only care that our family has a chance to bond and sustain itself.''

She gripped his hand in hers, telling him with action instead of words that she shared that hope. All this emotion made her feel awkward, however, and she quickly excused herself. So much to do! But somehow the load seemed infinitely lighter now.

Colin was nervous again. He couldn't forget that the last time this family had gotten together they had parted in acrimony. Lauren had extended this invitation to her mother and brother primarily to please him, he knew, and if this visit should not go well, she was apt to blame him, too. He was well aware how much he had riding on this holiday visit and how little he could actually do to ensure that all went as he hoped. He prayed that the one thing he had thought of would have the desired effect.

Whatever happened, though, at least he had Jeff and Meg's visit to look forward to. It had been decided that they and the girls would come on Christmas afternoon and spend Christmas night at the lodge. This way, the girls could have their Christmas at home and still get to visit Uncle Colin, Aunt Lauren and baby George, whom they were crazy to see. Meanwhile, Lauren's family would be arriving any minute to celebrate Christmas Eve.

Lauren, oddly enough, seemed cool as a cucumber. True to her organized nature, she had finished her Christmas shopping by the first of October, although a week or so earlier he had caught her slipping out to Taos with Maria on a mysterious excursion that she was unwilling to explain. He felt pretty certain that he'd have at least one package beneath the tree, labeled from Georgie, most likely. Still, she had been much more receptive to his overtures of affection lately. He only wished that was enough for him.

He slipped behind the counter where his wife was entertaining his son by allowing the little scamp to ride in her lap while she whirled around on the rotating stool that was kept there. Georgie giggled as the stool spun, then laughed aloud as Colin brought it to a sudden halt, jolting the baby thrill seeker against his mother's protective arms. Having seized Lauren by the waist to stop the stool spinning, Colin bent over them both, bringing his face close to Georgie's as the boy squealed in delight. Suddenly Georgie reached up and locked his arms around Colin's neck, smearing a wet kiss on his chin. Then when Colin attempted to straighten again, Georgie held on. Apparently, he thought it a great game. Colin was inclined to agree. If Georgie could hold on, so could he.

Thrusting one arm beneath Lauren's knees and the other behind her shoulders, he scooped her up and lifted them both onto the countertop. Surprised, Lauren shrieked, then lapsed into laughter along with Georgie, who maintained his hold on Colin's neck. Colin leaned down and smacked kisses all over Georgie's giggling face, then he straightened as much as his son's stubborn hold would allow and looked into his wife's beautiful eyes. To his delight he saw only welcome there. Even so he proceeded slowly, giving her time to pull away if she wanted. Apparently she didn't. Oddly enough, as he leaned in to kiss Lauren, Georgie at last relinquished his hold and stilled, tilting his face up to watch as their mouths met.

With one hand holding Georgie securely, Lauren reached up to sift her fingers through the hair on the back of Colin's head. He closed his eyes, savoring the contact, and loosely looped his arms around her. When the Cole family arrived, it was to find Colin kissing his wife most soundly, their son wedged between them contentedly.

"Looks like a Merry Christmas around here!" Larry observed heartily, grinning as a shocked Colin looked up at him.

"Oh! Uh, hello!" Colin managed as he helped an embarrassed Lauren get down from atop the counter. He took Georgie into his own arms, allowing Lauren to straighten her dark green sweater and long, matching skirt.

"Hello, Mama," she said meekly, "Miranda, Larry."

It was Larry who stepped forward first, offering his hand across the counter. "Hello, Sis, and thank you for your letter."

"Thank you for coming," she replied, briefly gripping his hand. Her mother stepped forward then, and Colin was pleased that Lauren hurried around the counter to take her mother into her embrace. "Mama, I'm so glad you're here."

Hallie Cole actually teared up. She had to clear her throat to speak. "Merry Christmas, dear. My, it smells like a pine forest in here."

Lauren laughed and turned aside. "Let me show you the decorations. We went all out this year. Shelby has mulled some wine and cider so everyone has something warm to drink."

They all trooped dutifully into the small lobby, where the stairwell was decorated with pine boughs, real holly and potted poinsettias. Small decorated trees were tucked into every nook and cranny. The dining room was done almost entirely in white and gold, with splashes of evergreen here and there, very elegant, very Lauren, to Colin's way of thinking. The tree there was decorated in lace and crocheted ornaments. The great room, however, was every inch a New Mexico Christmas, with its tall trees, each decorated in a single color—one red, one white, one terra cotta. The magnificent antler chandeliers were hung with spruce limbs interwoven with small twinkling lights.

Once the women and Georgie were parked in front of the fire with warm drinks, Colin went to help Larry carry in the gifts that the Coles had brought with them. He was a little shocked at the number of packages and as secretly excited as a kid to see his name on several of them. He was even more shocked to find that, while Hallie held Georgie on her lap, Lauren had hauled out easily a dozen packages of her own from some secret hiding place within the lodge and spread them beneath what had been dubbed the "family" tree. Since outside traffic was sparse in the lodge, the paying guests had been encouraged to use the other two trees in the great room for their own Christmas celebrations, and several packages already awaited opening beneath them.

Spying the spinet piano that now occupied the center of

the room, surrounded by poinsettias and candles, Hallie asked Lauren where it had come from.

"Oh, that's Juan's," Lauren said. Taking his place next to Lauren on the couch, Colin explained that because Juan and his family would be moving into the lodge when he and his family moved out and the apartment did not have enough room for the piano, Juan had insisted that it go into the great room, where it could be used as accompaniment for Christmas carols.

"Do we have anyone who can play?" Hallie asked hopefully.

"Actually, Ponce is quite a gifted pianist," Colin said.

"And he's already agreed to play for us this evening," Lauren added.

Hallie looked down at the child on her lap. "Wouldn't it be wonderful if Ponce could teach George?" she asked. "I mean, when he's old enough."

"That's some time away yet," Lauren said gently.

Hallie smiled down at George. "Oh, Granny would love her darling boy to play the piano for her someday," she crooned, hugging him, and Colin felt Lauren's hand creep into his. He gripped it tightly, knowing that he had never been happier than he was at that moment.

But many more delights were to come.

Ponce did play for them. The great room quickly filled with guests and the few remaining staff members who hadn't gone home to family celebrations of their own. With the lights lowered, the trees twinkling and the massive fireplace glowing with warmth, the whole assembly, about forty in all, sang carol after carol. Georgie crowed and clapped, obviously loving it. A simple but ample buffet of finger foods had been laid out in the dining room, and everyone was free to slip in and out, eating and drinking as the mood struck. Finally every carol of which everyone could think had been sung, and the lights were again turned up so those who were opening presents could see clearly what delights were theirs.

Colin was completely overwhelmed by the number of packages stacked at his feet by Lauren and Larry. Past Christmases for him had meant one or two gifts, if that. Every member of Lauren's family bought three or four presents for everyone else. He felt miserly for having bought only gift certificates at a fine Santa Fe restaurant for Lauren's family and single gifts for Lauren and George, not counting his and Larry's big surprise, of course. They each took turns opening their packages so everyone could see and appreciate what was given and received.

Georgie went first, and it was an absolute delight to see his little face light up as he realized these toys, books and articles of clothing were for him. He got an even bigger kick out of getting down on the floor and playing with the torn wrapping paper and ribbons, though. Miranda, by personal demand and mutual assent, went next, then Hallie and Lauren, who exclaimed loudly over the simple pearl earrings he'd bought, and Larry and, finally, Colin. Watching the others get what they wanted and loving what they got was almost as much fun as opening his own gifts, almost but not quite.

Hallie had bought him a perfectly awful sweater, which he immediately donned, pleasing her no end. The leather gloves, wool socks, cheap neckties and too-small shirts were equally treasured, but it was Lauren's big, lightweight package that truly intrigued him. When he lifted away the top and folded back the tissue, he found a luscious pair of dark blue-silk pajamas and matching robe. It didn't matter that he slept clothed only when the weather dictated or that Lauren might have had ulterior motives for choosing them. What touched him, what thrilled him, was that she had gone to the trouble to choose something so obviously costly and luxurious, so personal, especially for him, and that she'd had the shirt and robe monogrammed with the name "Daddy." The only package purportedly from Georgie for him contained a pair of matching slippers.

"These are wonderful," he said, indicating the opened packages heaped around him. "Thank you all so much." He leaned close to Lauren and whispered, "I especially love the monogram. Thank you, sweetheart." To his surprise and joy, she kissed him quickly, fingering the earrings he had given her.

"My pleasure."

"I have two more surprises," Colin announced, getting up to extricate his son from the heap of discarded boxes, paper and ribbons in which he had delightedly buried himself. Carrying Georgie back to his seat with him, he whispered in the baby's ear and pointed at Hallie. Sitting once more, he asked Lawrence to clear the way. When the holiday debris was shoved aside, Colin set Georgie on his feet, standing him between his knees. "Now," he said softly, "walk to Granny. Walk over to Granny."

Hallie's face lit up, and she bent forward, holding out her arms. Georgie immediately set off, slowly at first, but then faster and faster, until he tripped and fell just short of his grandmother's outstretched arms. Everyone made comforting noises, and both Lauren and Hallie moved to help him up, but Colin waved them back while speaking encouragingly to his son. Gamely Georgie got to his feet, smiled proudly and walked the remaining few steps to his grandmother. Colin and Lauren hurrahed and applauded, while the others made congratulatory sounds and Hallie hugged the boy. Sitting on his grandmother's knee, Georgie even applauded himself.

After several moments of this positive reinforcement, Lauren asked, "What's the second surprise? You said two surprises."

Colin nodded at Larry, who cleared his throat and

reached into his jacket pocket for a white envelope, which he presented to Lauren. "I want to say something before you open that." He cleared his throat again. "I want to thank you for being willing to deal with me. I know I didn't handle this thing very well. I don't seem to handle very much well, actually, but all that's changing now. I know that, with Colin and your help and advice, I can provide a comfortable lifestyle for my family now. Colin has made me see that instead of being jealous of your abilities, I ought to tap into them and let you really help me. The fact is, I'm proud of you, Lauren, and I'm going to make you proud of me."

Lauren looked at Colin as she reached for the envelope. "Larry, I don't know quite what to say, except, I never imagined that you might be jealous of me in any way. I guess I was too busy being jealous of you."

"For what?" Larry asked gently. "For needing Mom to hold me up all the time? For watching you do all the things I've never had the courage to do? For being the next thing to a failure?"

"That's not true," Miranda countered. "You're a fine husband, Larry, and you'll be a good father."

"I'll try," he said, looking over his shoulder at his wife. "I always have, but this is the first time I've really ever felt that I have a chance to really do something and do it right." He extended his hand to Colin then, saying, "No one's ever explained things to me the way you have. Mom's tried, I know, but somehow it makes a difference when it comes man-to-man. I'm grateful. For everything."

Colin smiled and shook his brother-in-law's hand, but he was painfully aware that Lauren had opened the envelope and was currently perusing its contents. The document consisted of only two pages. One was Larry's signed release to all claim on the lodge and its earnings, current and future. The other was an agreement for Lauren to buy out

Larry's interest in the lodge for a sum in the upper five figures. Colin felt that it was a reasonable amount, and Larry agreed. Everything had been taken into consideration: land, buildings—including the cabin—applicable taxes, current market value minus the cost of reparations, promotion and operation during the past fifteen months. It was much less than Larry might have gotten if he'd taken the matter to court, but more than he'd have received if Lauren had agreed to sell when he'd initially wanted to. Above all, it was fair to everyone involved, and Colin had given Larry some sound advice about investing the money and making it work for him and his family. Now all that remained was for Lauren to agree. Colin prayed that she would not feel he had usurped her authority or poked his nose in where it didn't belong.

Lauren looked at the papers time and time again, then lowered both to her lap. "Larry, this is great, except…I don't have any way to pay this. There's no provision for incremental payments, which would have to be small, especially if they're to be monthly payments. I might be able to get a loan, but I'd have the same problem paying it back. Still—"

"Sis, you don't understand," Larry finally interrupted. "That's the amount that's already been paid. It's a done deal. All you have to do is sign the agreement to make it all legal."

Lauren's mouth dropped open. "But how? Who?" She looked at Colin at the same time Larry did. "Colin? You didn't pay this, did you?"

He couldn't tell from the sound of her voice if she was glad or mad. He licked his lips. "It, um, seemed like a good idea at the time."

"Where did you get this much money?" she demanded, her voice rising alarmingly.

"Well, I, uh, closed on the Albuquerque house."

"You took the money from the sale of your house for this?"

"Part of it," he said a tad defensively.

"Part of it?" Lauren exclaimed. "How much was that place worth?"

He shrugged and muttered, "Quarter mil."

Lauren's jaw practically hit her lap. She stared at him for a full ten seconds, then she looked around her at the faces of her family. "Apparently I've married a wealthy man!"

"Not wealthy exactly," Colin mumbled uncomfortably, "just well-off."

"You're telling me that you gave up a two-hundred-fifty-thousand-dollar house for an eighty-year-old cabin!"

He was beginning to get a little miffed. "No, I didn't give up anything. The house was an investment, Lauren, and it paid off handsomely. This place and the cabin, they are home. I have a right to invest in my own home, you know, to secure my family's future. That's all I was trying to do. Maybe I should have consulted you, but Larry and I got to talking about it and—" When she threw her arms around his neck, twisting around in her seat to get it done, he finally got the message and shut up.

"You," she whispered, nose to nose with him, "are the most wonderful man I've ever known." When she kissed him, he was laughing, and so was everyone else.

No doubt about it, this was definitely going to be a Christmas to remember.

Chapter Thirteen

Lauren preened in front of the bathroom mirror, but she wasn't really looking at herself. Her thoughts were too full of the day past and the night ahead. She had never enjoyed such a remarkable celebration with her family. Larry was like a new man, and her mother seemed happier and more relaxed than Lauren could ever remember. Even Miranda had lost some of her smugness and spite. Just having the financial and legal threat to the lodge removed had rendered Lauren giddy with relief, but to at last feel the love and pride of her family brought to the surface emotions almost too rich to bear. And she had just one man to thank for all this joy, one man whom she had kept waiting much too long.

As her purpose crystallized, so did her vision. She took a good hard look at herself. She had brushed her hair to a high sheen, perfumed her body in a warm bath and put on her skimpiest, sexiest nightgown, a mere scrap of apricot silk and lace. Now all that remained was the seduction of her husband. Somehow, she didn't expect it to be much of a challenge, and yet she could feel herself trembling inside.

After taking a deep breath, she went from the bathroom into her, their, bedroom, where she turned back the bed, lit a candle on the bureau and draped a gold scarf over the small bedside lamp. She moved to the door into the living room and turned off the overhead light, using the wall switch. Then, very slowly, she opened that door and walked through it.

Colin had unfolded the sofa bed and crawled into it. She could see him shivering beneath the covers, waiting for the sheets to warm up. The fire glowed and flickered but really did little to warm the room. The chill made gooseflesh out of every exposed inch of her skin, but she wasn't concerned about herself. For weeks she had allowed, demanded, really, that her patient husband sleep alone in this cold room like an unwelcome interloper, while he had been quietly working to solve all their problems. The force of her gratitude helped her understand and appreciate the feeling she had so blindly denigrated in him. Now she was ready to coax that feeling into growth, to nurture and sustain it until it blossomed into the love for which she yearned.

Approaching the back of the sofa, she softly called his name. "Colin."

He raised up on one elbow, glancing over the back of the sofa. His eyes went wide as he took in the nightgown, and he sat up as she walked to the side of the unfolded bed. For a long moment he did nothing more than stare, but then he folded back the covers, silently offering warmth and the pleasures of his body.

Shaking her head, she offered him her hand—and her heart. "Come to the bedroom."

He swung his feet over the side of the bed, then paused, looking at her. "Are you sure about this?"

"Very sure."

He tossed away the covers and got to his feet, wearing the pajamas she had bought him. Their blue color did all the marvelous things to his eyes that she had imagined. He looked down into her face, carefully studying her expression. "No more sleeping alone," he said, and it was as much a question as a statement of what he expected this night to yield.

"We'll move your things into our bedroom tomorrow," she affirmed.

A smile broke across his face as he seized her hand, and he swept her from head to toe with his gaze. "You are," he said, every syllable a smoky, languid caress, "the most beautiful woman I've ever seen. I can't tell you how proud I am that you're mine."

"Finally," she added apologetically, blushing at his effusive compliment. His smile softened with understanding, and she literally melted inside. "No more sleeping alone," she promised, "and no more holding back."

He closed his eyes as if savoring the moment, but when he spoke, a playful, teasing quality edged his voice. "Then this must be where I finally get to carry the bride over the threshold," he said, and swept her up into his arms.

A few long strides carried them through the bedroom door, which he closed behind them with the backward shove of one foot. When he bent to place her upon the bed, she wrapped her arms around him and pulled him down on top of her. Chuckling, he braced his upper body weight upon his forearms and bracketed her face with his hands. He opened his mouth to speak, but she blocked the words with her own lips, anxious to experience again the delights to which he had earlier introduced her, delights she would no longer deny either of them. He seemed extremely willing to comply, and soon Lauren had reason to be thankful, indeed, that their now-year-old son slept so very soundly.

When the alarm went off, Colin was dreaming of intertwined bodies and yards of revealing lace. Surfacing, he groaned, then smiled as his wife snuggled closer to the warmth of his body, reminding him that everything in his dream had not been the product of his imagination. Sleepily he tightened the arm about her waist and kissed the top of her head, but still the alarm screeched.

"Take a baseball bat to that thing," he grumbled, well aware that the alarm clock sat atop the table on her side of the bed.

Instead, she reluctantly snaked an arm out from the warm cocoon of the bedcovers and slapped the snooze button. "We have to get up," she said around a yawn.

Colin blearily eyed the clock. Six o'clock in the morning. Closing his eyes once more, he protested, muttering, "Three hours sleep just doesn't cut it for me, Mrs. Garret."

"Perhaps not, Mr. Garret," she said with a sigh, "but Santa doesn't get to sleep in."

Both bleary eyes popped open at that, and an instant later he was on his feet and yanking on his pajamas. Lauren laughed, but he didn't care. This was his son's first Christmas, and he wasn't going to miss it. The possibility that he might have had been very real only a few months earlier.

"Well, hurry up," he said, grinning back at her. "You know George won't sleep past seven."

Groaning, Lauren threw back the covers, and Colin's mouth went dry. She no longer seemed uncomfortable with her nakedness, and he congratulated himself for it. God knew she had no reason to be anything other than proud of her body, but apparently she was just learning that.

"Next year," she said, hauling herself out of bed, "we're going to do things a little differently."

Colin had to clear his throat before he could ask, "How so?"

"Well, for one thing, we're going to be in our own

house, so we can do Santa before going to bed on Christmas Eve,'' she said.

Colin pointed a finger at her. ''You are brilliant.'' He reached down for his shirt and threw it on.

She chuckled as she shimmied into her gown, the slinky fabric floating over her luscious curves and momentarily causing his fingers to forget how to button his shirt. ''For another thing,'' she said, ''we are going to cut our son's birthday cake on his actual birthday, Christmas Eve, and not the day after Christmas.''

Colin managed a nod and got back to work on those buttons. ''I think that's a good idea, too. It won't matter this year because he won't remember, but next year we'll do it the way it should be done.''

''Having our own home will make it easier to do the family stuff,'' she muttered, moving around the bed toward the closet. He knew he ought to let her pass without interruption, but he just couldn't help himself. He caught her about the waist and pulled her to him as he turned and sat on the edge of the bed. He brought her to stand between his legs, his hands sliding up the backs of her thighs to cup her buttocks.

''This 'family stuff' has made me a very happy man,'' he said before pushing his face into the hollow of her belly. He nuzzled her, and it occurred to him that once again they had used no birth control. Might they have made a baby last night? A feeling of such wealth and warmth swept over him that it brought tears to his eyes.

''Merry Christmas, sweetheart,'' he said, looking up at her.

She brushed back the strands of hair that had fallen over his forehead and smiled down at him. ''Merry Christmas.''

Colin moved to kiss her lips, but she backed away, wagging a finger at him.

"Ah-ah-ah. Santa wouldn't lie around making love to Mrs. Claus when toys needed to be put out."

Santa. George's first real Christmas. Colin sighed. "He would if she looked like you," he grumbled. Reluctantly he got up to go after his robe and slippers. Lauren appeared in the living room wearing a robe and fuzzy house shoes. His excitement about playing Santa had reasserted itself, and he allowed her to lead him from hiding place to hiding place, pulling out the toys she had purchased for their son, one of which was an old-fashioned wooden rocking horse. Colin read the mantra "some assembly required" on several boxes and went into panic mode, demanding hammers and pliers and screw drivers. He was still bolting the runners onto the rocking horse when Lauren carried a sleepy-eyed Georgie into the great room, which, for the moment, they had all to themselves.

For a time Georgie was more interested in the bowl of cereal that Lauren had brought with her, but as he ate he watched Colin "play" with the toys beneath the tree and soon was bucking to get down and join in the fun. By the time Colin put him on the rocking horse, George was having the time of his life. It took a few tries for him to successfully maneuver the horse without sliding off, but he soon got the hang of it, and Colin loved watching him "ride." He couldn't wait for Jeff and Meg to come and witness his child's extraordinary skill on the rocking horse. He loved posing for pictures, too, and trading places with Lauren to take snaps of her with their son. It was as if his joy knew no bounds on this special day, as if his every dream had come to rich fruition.

Gone were the years of impersonal institutional holidays. No longer was he the outsider in a foster home meant to be merely a temporary stop or a guest in the home of a well-meaning friend. The solitary existence that he had known in Albuquerque seemed far behind him now and more bleak than he had even realized. That lonely little boy who had lived with grief and abandonment had finally been put to rest, and the man had come home at last, alone no more but a father and a husband who finally knew what wonder and joys could be found beneath a Christmas tree.

An hour later Lauren said hello to several guests lolling about the great room, adding hearty season's greetings, then passed on through the lobby and into the dining room. They were halfway through a late brunch when the Lockes came in, their heads and shoulders dusted with fresh snow. The girls, both adorable little strawberry blondes, squealed hellos to their uncle Colin and ran to throw their arms around his neck and make cooing sounds over Georgie, who recognized that these little people were more his size than the bevy of grown-ups surrounding them.

"They were up at 5:00 a.m.," Jeff explained, groaning as he dropped onto a chair at the table, "anxious to see Uncle Colin's new baby."

"He isn't new," the elder of the girls protested. "He's a whole year old already."

"Well, excuse me, Miss Methuselah."

"Oh, Daddy!"

Lauren accepted hugs from Meg and the girls and got up to pour coffee. The girls announced that they wanted what Georgie had to eat, and Colin went to deliver the order to the kitchen in person, while their father wondered aloud how on earth they could eat again after breakfasting first on cold cereal then egg sandwiches from the only drive-through in Albuquerque open on Christmas morning. Jeff said it while filching bacon off Colin's plate, though, and Lauren was soon ordering him a full breakfast and a plump cinnamon roll for Meg.

They sat around the table, laughing and talking for a long time before the kids begged to be allowed to go play. Lauren cleaned up Georgie, despite his protests, and they all adjourned to the great room, where the girls delighted in showing Georgie how to play with his own toys and Georgie delighted in having children in his audience. When the girls ran around behind the tree, Georgie got up and started after them, apparently forgetting that he was none too steady on his feet yet. The result was a bumped noggin, which every adult in the immediate area rushed to check out. Lauren had just hoisted him onto her hip so they could all get a better look at what was obviously a nonissue, since Georgie's tears were already drying, when Juan and his two near-adult children appeared in the door to the great room. They, too, were wearing heavy dustings of snow, but it was the signal Juan sent her, a thumb hooked toward the foyer, that really caught Lauren's attention.

"What is it, Juan?"

"Seems we have a guest without a reservation."

"Really?" On Christmas day?

He nodded and began carefully peeling off his outerwear. "Want me to take care of it?"

"No, I'll do it." Officially, none of the Herreras was working that day, but Lauren was hoping that if she took care of the registration someone else would make up the room. "I'll be right back," she said to the others. Then, without so much as a thought, she went out to greet their unexpected guest, carrying Georgie with her as she had hundreds of times before.

She slipped behind the counter just as a small woman with short, light brown hair turned from the single window in the foyer. Something about her struck Lauren as familiar, but that often happened, and Lauren instantly dismissed it. Smiling, she asked, "How can I help you?"

The woman walked toward the counter, her gaze trained on Georgie so exclusively that Lauren felt a prickle of unease. Then the woman lifted her gaze to Lauren's. And Lauren knew.

"Is that him?" the woman known to her as Doris Drew asked. "Is that my son?"

The bottom dropped out of Lauren's world. She physically recoiled, shaking her head. No. This couldn't be! Thea Sanford, otherwise known as Doris Drew, was safely ensconced in a mental health care facility in another state. The woman stepped closer, her gaze once more targeting Georgie.

"Oh, he's beautiful," she said. "I knew he would be, even though he was just a little wrinkly thing last time I saw him."

Lauren was unaware of screaming for her husband. She only knew that he was suddenly there, wrapping his arms around her and Georgie, expressing concern. She knew the moment he realized what was wrong and who was standing before them. Thea shouted just one word, and every muscle in his body went rigid.

"No!"

Colin literally stepped in front of Lauren and Georgie. "What are you doing here?"

"You weren't supposed to find him!" Thea shrieked. "He's my secret! You weren't supposed to find him!"

Jeff appeared then, and Colin spoke directly to him. "Call the police."

Squeezing behind the counter with Lauren, Georgie and Colin, Jeff grabbed the telephone receiver. "Do you have 9-1-1?"

Lauren shook her head. "Y-you'll have to c-call the village m-marshal."

Jeff started dialing the operator. Meanwhile, Colin was trying to reason with Thea.

"You can't stay here. You have to go. Lauren and I don't want you here."

"Lauren and I?" Thea echoed shrilly. "Lauren and I? You have no right—"

"I have every right," Colin broke in calmly but firmly. "We have every right. George is our son. He's mine by blood, and Lauren is my wife. She's legally adopted him. So you see, there is nothing here for you now."

Thea tore at the hair she'd obviously returned to its natural color and lunged forward, pounding the counter with her fists. "I trusted you!" she screeched at Lauren. "I trusted you to take care of my baby."

"And she's done that," Colin said, standing in front of Lauren protectively. "She's loved him like her very own."

"No! No! He's mine!" Thea screamed. "You're mine! She was just supposed to keep him for me. And you were supposed to marry me when I showed him to you!"

Colin tried to calm her. "Thea, where's your medication? Have you been taking your medication?"

"Yes, I'm taking my medication," Thea mimicked. "Not that I need to. I had this all planned out, you see, only as always you messed everything up!"

"You can't plan other people's lives, Thea," Colin pointed out. "You can only control your own life."

"That's what I'm trying to do!" she insisted. "Only no one will let me!"

Jeff finally hung up the phone, announcing, "The marshal's on his way. He's radioing the sheriff's office out of Raton for backup." He looked at Colin then and said baldly, "I told you we should've pressed charges."

Colin sighed. "I don't want to hurt you, Thea. I never have, but I must insist that you leave."

Thea shook her head. "Not without my son!"

Jeff picked up the phone again. "Okay. I'm calling for a protective order." He began dialing numbers, mumbling, "Nothing like calling on Christmas to make enemies out of friends, but so be it."

Colin tried again to reach Thea. "Please go. Please don't make us do this."

"Just let me hold him," Thea begged, and the pitifulness of it nearly cracked Lauren's resolve. Sensing this, Colin put out a restraining hand.

"No. I'm sorry, but George doesn't know you, and we don't want him upset. Now please go before the marshal arrives to arrest you."

All at once the pitiful, hurting mother disappeared and a fierce, angry virago stood in her place. "I'll get you for this. I'll get my son back, and you'll never see him again. Then you'll be sorry. You'll all be sorry! You'll suffer every day, just like I do. You'll have to take pills all the time and go to hospitals and have people tell you you're sick when you know it's all a lie!" Suddenly she started to blubber. "It's not fair! You should suffer for not loving me. Everyone should suffer for not loving me. I just want what's fair!" In the blink of an eye her tears disappeared and she asked almost conversationally, "Does he ever ask about me?"

"No," Colin said gently. "He can't remember you. Lauren is the only mother he's ever known or ever will know."

Thea frowned. "That's not right. I'll have to speak to my attorney," she mumbled.

"You'll all be sorry. Oh, yes, you will." She peeked around Colin and waved at Georgie. "Bye-bye, little boy," she said sweetly. "I have to go now, but I'll come back to get you."

With that she turned and walked out the door as if she didn't have a care in the world. Lauren shuddered. If Thea should ever get her hands on Georgie… Colin turned and pulled Lauren and Georgie into his arms, whispering apologies.

"I'm so sorry, honey. I should have known this would happen. I should have known."

"H-how did such a sick woman get out of the hospital?" she wanted to know. Colin shook his head.

"There's no way to keep her inside, I'm afraid. Once she's on the medication she levels out, and they have to let her go. Then she gets off the meds again and winds up on the street. She'll end up back inside again, and the whole cycle starts over."

"What if she does get custody of Georgie?" Lauren asked, trembling from head to toe.

Jeff covered the receiver of the telephone with his hand and answered that one. "Never happen," he vowed. "No way. Her parental rights have been terminated due to abandonment and mental incapacity. Even if she suddenly got healed, no judge is going to yank a baby away from a settled home with a natural and an adoptive parent. Plus, we're refiling all the old harassment charges and adding a new one. She'll never get near this kid, I promise." He wagged a finger under Colin's nose. "I won't listen to any arguments, either. I know you feel sorry for her, but you have a family to think of now."

Colin pulled Lauren and Georgie even tighter against him. "No arguments," he agreed, but Lauren could tell he was worried, and so was she. Protective orders and legal charges were fine, but who was to say that Thea wouldn't slip in some night when they were all asleep and simply take George?

She looked up at her husband. "Could we get a security system installed?"

"I'll take care of it first thing tomorrow."

"At the cabin, too."

"Cabin, too, and we can keep George in with us until it's done, if you want."

She blinked back the tears. "I don't think I'll sleep at all, if we don't."

He nodded and smoothed a hand over her back. "I'll sleep better, too."

They stood together listening while Jeff pleaded and argued and bullied with various officers of the court until he got his way—or as much of it as he was going to get. Lauren was amazed at how tough and uncompromising the seemingly affable, boyish Jeff could be. Finally he hung up the phone.

"Okay," he said. "It's all done but the inking. If she shows up around here again, you call the cops, and we put her away until all the charges are answered. Are we clear about that?"

Colin and Lauren both nodded. Jeff sighed, then determinedly smiled and rubbed his hands together.

"Okay, so when do we cut the birthday cake?"

Georgie immediately perked up at that. He didn't have an inkling about what was going on, but he knew the word cake, and as usual he was more than ready for his share of the sweet. "Kagk," he said, nodding enthusiastically. Lauren laughed along with the men, but it was stilted. The sparkle had gone out of an otherwise wonderful holiday.

Still, it was Christmas, and their darling boy had a first birthday to celebrate. The lodge was safe, and soon they would move into a lovely home all their own. Last night had been a beginning for her and Colin, and tonight promised to be a continuation. She wasn't going to let one sad, sick woman ruin it all. She let Georgie go to his father and turned to Jeff. "Thank you for your help," she said. "Now we have celebrations to make and friends to share them with."

"My sentiments exactly," Jeff announced. Then he reached for Georgie. "Come on, son. Let's go hunt up that cake."

"Kagk," Georgie said, going straight into Jeff's arms.

"Boy, you're easy," Jeff said, carrying him away. "Wish a piece of cake could get me this far with some judges I know."

Colin placed his hands on his wife's shoulders, and she

gladly leaned into him, her cheek against his chest. "It'll be okay, I promise," he told her softly, wrapping his arms around her once more.

"I know," she whispered. But would it? Would it really? She slid an arm around his waist, and together they went in to celebrate with a bit less joy and a tad more desperation than before.

Chapter Fourteen

Lauren struggled to open her eyes, determined not to over-sleep again. Beneath the covers she placed a hand on her stomach, wondering how much longer she could maintain the fiction that nothing had changed—and if she should even try. The weight of her own guilt told her that she should confess what she suspected, but for all the joy she had found in this full marriage, she had yet to hear her husband say that he loved her, and the new worries brought on by Thea's reappearance were causing second thoughts for Lauren. What if Thea somehow managed to gain cus-tody of George? Would her marriage hold then, or would Colin consider it void? A woman of more courage would simply ask him, but Lauren was too afraid of the answer to take such a chance, so she kept her secrets and wallowed in guilt because of it.

Lauren rolled over, momentarily disoriented to find her-self in a room other than that in the lodge apartment she had occupied for so long. Even after a month she still marveled at the home Colin had made for them here. Strangely, Georgie had adjusted readily to his new room, perhaps because they had been careful to recreate the look and feel of his old room. Beside her, Colin stretched and sighed and reached for her.

"Good morning, sweetheart."

"Good morning."

He kissed the center of her forehead, then snuggled her against him, fitting her body to his and wrapping himself around her. "Sleep well?"

"Umm-hmm. You?"

"Like a rock. Or should I say a log?"

Considering the log walls surrounding them, the latter seemed appropriate. Lauren smiled at the thought that she was waking in the room where her grandfather had lived out his life after the death of his beloved wife had led him to close the lodge. Lauren had loved visiting him in this homey, cozy cabin, and it felt good to be here, even if her grandfather would hardly recognize the place after all the renovations that Colin had pulled off.

"Are you okay, honey?" Colin asked, forcing Lauren to realize that she was once more drifting off to sleep.

"Hmm? Yeah, I'm fine." She rolled away from him and stretched her arms over her head, inhaling as much mind-cleansing oxygen as her lungs could hold.

"You sure?" Colin pressed, sounding genuinely concerned.

"I think I'm just still tired," she said, lowering her arms, "from the move." It was perfectly true, as far as it went. It had taken days to move her belongings and Colin's into the cabin and weeks to fully integrate them. She had learned much about her husband in the process. For one thing, he was a virtual clotheshorse, and for another, he possessed unusually fine taste and had chosen his furnishings with meticulous particularity.

When she had first seen the expensive, white, butter-soft leather sofa that was now the centerpiece of the living area, she had felt a pang of regret at the abuse it was going to suffer with a child in the house, but then Colin had plunked down onto it several heavy boxes, a grocery bag full of fruit juice and a greasy funnel that he used to add oil to his truck. When she expressed concern, he had told her not to worry, that he had carefully researched before buying the thing some six years earlier. In his opinion, it was indestructible, and he had reinforced that notion a few minutes later when he'd climbed up on its arm to hang a houseplant from an exposed overhead beam. He hadn't blinked an eye since, not when Georgie had spilled the juice from his sippy cup, dropped a sticky peppermint cane or knocked over a cup of hot tea on that luscious, and still unstained, leather.

He continued to dote on Georgie and seemed to relish every tear as dearly as every giggle, every catastrophe as wholly as every triumph, and he was the most naturally affectionate man Lauren had ever known. Yet at times Lauren wondered if she knew him at all, if his most true self was not buried so deeply that she would need years to burrow her way down to it. But did she have those years? If Georgie was taken from them, would Colin stay in the marriage?

She knew that a second child would keep Colin at her side, but she had to know that he would stay for her and her alone. So she kept quiet about the possibility of pregnancy and tried to be happy in the moment.

"I'll make the coffee," Colin said, pecking a kiss on her cheek and preparing to get out of bed. "Why don't you stay home today and get some real rest, hmm?"

She shook her head. "No, I have to get up."

"Whatever you think best."

She rolled onto her side, waiting until he left the room. Then she made herself sit up and swing her legs over the side of the bed. Her body felt as if it had weights attached to it. Slowly she stood and made her groggy way into the lovely private bath that Colin had installed.

The glass shower revealed the original log walls on two sides, and a tall pebbled glass window let in sunlight without compromising privacy. She turned on the hot water in the shower, marveling at how quickly the water steamed, disrobed and stepped inside. Feeling like a new woman, she stepped out again several long minutes later and reached for a towel, only to halt as she caught sight of her reflection in the antique mirror over the sink. Was her belly starting to bulge just a bit? Had her breasts firmed noticeably? She really couldn't tell, and if she couldn't then Colin couldn't. She wrapped one towel around her body and another around her head. Feeling surprisingly energized, she walked out into the bedroom, and found her husband sitting on the edge of the bed, his hands between his knees. A frisson of unease shivered over her.

"Colin, what is it?"

He looked up, smiled in appreciation of the picture she presented and held out a hand, inviting her to join him. "We need to talk," he said gently as she sat beside him.

Something told her that this was a conversation she didn't want to have. "I need to get dressed."

He nodded almost absently and baldly said, "Jeff called."

She knew from Colin's tone that it hadn't been a friendly call to pass the time of day. Gooseflesh broke out all over her body. Fear chilled her clear to the bone. "What did he say?"

Colin looked her square in the eyes and said, "Thea has

hired herself a very high-profile attorney, a real big gun in the capital, and he wants an early court date.''

Lauren closed her eyes. How could she deal with this? After all she had been through, all they had been through, how could this be happening? Acid welled in her stomach. She jumped and ran for the bathroom. When she had heaved her last, Colin was there to bundle her into her comfy terry cloth robe, help her rinse her mouth and tuck her back into bed.

''It's all right, sweetheart. It's all right. Don't worry. Everything will be all right, I promise. Just sleep a little while. Then we'll talk this through together. Just sleep now.''

Tears filled Lauren's eyes, but she dammed them behind closed lids and huddled into the warmth and comfort of the big, pillowy bed Colin had brought from Albuquerque. Within moments she sank into a deep, desperate sleep, confident that when she woke, her strong, thoughtful husband would still be there. For now.

Colin sat down on the edge of the bed and stared at his sleeping wife. This thing with Thea had really knocked the pins from beneath her, and he didn't know how to help her deal with it. He felt certain that they could win this fight, but they had to do it together, and yet lately he felt Lauren pulling back from him again. She puzzled him, this beautiful, passionate woman who had become the center of his world. She puzzled and pleased and thrilled him, and he wanted to wrap his arms around her and hold her forever at his side, protecting her from every ugly, unpleasant thing in life. Instead, he continually sought that comfort from her.

He reached a hand up to smooth back the crinkled, snarled tendrils of damp hair webbing her face. She inhaled sharply through her nose, muttered something unintelligible and finally opened her eyes a crack.

"I thought you'd like to see this," he said, holding up the photograph that had come in the mail.

She struggled up from beneath the covers, murmuring, "What is it?"

"The very latest photo of your charming nieces. That's Molly with the pink bow and Holly with the white."

Lauren sat up and reached for the photo, drinking in every detail of the cherubic twins who had made their entry into the world on New Year's Eve, just in time to furnish a much-needed tax write-off for their proud papa. Lauren smiled wistfully. "They hardly have enough hair for bows, but aren't they beautiful?"

Colin chuckled. "Randi writes that they hardly sleep, eat constantly, and have already figured out how to wrap their daddy around their tiny little fingers. Larry writes that Randi and your mom have spoiled them already, and your mother says that she wants a formal portrait soon of all three grandkids."

He offered the letter, addressed to the both of them, for Lauren to read, but she suddenly flipped back the covers, exclaiming, "The mail has already come? It must be past noon!"

"Relax. Everything is covered. You aren't expected at the lodge today."

"But—"

"Juan promised to call if he needed anything."

Lauren subsided, but she was frowning. "I don't know what's wrong with me lately. I must be coming down with something."

"Stress, most likely," he said on a sigh, "and I'm about to add to it, I'm afraid."

"Jeff," she said succinctly.

Colin nodded. "He's here."

"Here?" She hopped from the bed, completely unaware that her robe hung open to reveal the luscious body beneath. His reaction to such casual intimacies still shocked and slightly amused him. Would he never get enough of her? Why was it that, with familiarity, his desire for her grew rather than diminished?

Clearing his throat, he set aside the letter and got to his feet. Calmly, he took the photo from her hand, placed it with the letter, wrapped her robe tight and tied the belt. Only then did he cup her face in his hands and kiss her with all the longing and need she had awakened in him. She wrapped her arms around his waist and leaned into him. He broke the kiss, wrapping his arms around her and laying his cheek against the top of her head. After a moment he said, "You'd better get dressed, sweetie. Jeff's driven a long way to talk to us."

Nodding, she pulled back. Her eyes glistened with unshed tears. "How bad is it?"

"I don't know. He wants to talk to both of us."

She lifted her chin. The tears receded, and she said, "I'll only be a minute."

With that assurance he left her, returning to the living room, where Jeff sat perched on the edge of the sofa, Georgie on his knee. "She'll be out in a sec. How you doin'?"

"We're fine," Jeff said, glancing over his shoulder. "He's filling me in on what it's like to have a son."

Colin chuckled. "Is that so? Wonder how he would know?"

"Good point."

"Listen, if you don't mind keeping an eye on him a little longer, I want to be sure Lauren has something to eat when she comes out."

Jeff waved him away with a flip of his hand and began speaking in earnest to George. "So, what's this line of guff you've been feeding me, my man? You got a kid of your own stashed away somewhere, hmm?"

Chuckling again, Colin went into the kitchen, which was

separated from the living and dining areas merely by a wraparound bar and counter. He loved the open feel of the place. The windows and the peaked ceiling and the lack of walls gave the impression of great size and space and made the most of what they had. He turned the burner on beneath the skillet on the brushed steel stove and popped toast into the stainless toaster. He was just folding over an omelet when Lauren opened the bedroom door and stepped out.

Her hair had been piled into a loose froth atop her head, the kind that looked as though it would tumble down with the least provocation—provocation, he mused happily, which was his to give. She wore a big, baggy T-shirt in bright yellow over tight, black leggings that fit so well they made his mouth water.

"Is that for me?" she asked timidly. "I'm starved!"

"All yours, angel," he said, sliding it onto a plate and setting a fork atop it. He placed it on the counter and added, "Why don't you take it into the living room? I'll bring the toast and coffee."

"Uh, just juice, I think," she said, snatching paper napkins from the dispenser as she picked up the plate.

It occurred to him that she'd been laying off coffee for a while, and he approved, considering how uptight she was lately. He buttered the toast, poured the juice and carried both into the living room, placing them on the table next to the chair she'd chosen opposite Jeff. George was demanding to be let down, his eyes on his mother's plate. Colin picked him up and held him in his lap as he perched on the arm of Lauren's chair. Lauren took "morning" kisses and hearty hugs from the baby before digging into her omelet, occasionally feeding Georgie a bite from her fork when he tired of gnawing on the corner of toast clutched in his fist.

"You're going to have to get a second job to feed that kid," Jeff said teasingly to Colin.

Lauren dropped her fork to her plate with a clunk. "You really think we'll get to keep him, then?"

Jeff blinked and leaned forward to clasp his hands together, elbows balanced on knees. "I do think that, yes. But it may not be as easy as I'd hoped."

Lauren set aside her plate and picked up her juice glass, sipping from it thoughtfully. "Because of this high-powered attorney Thea's hired?"

Jeff nodded. "He's made a reputation championing the handicapped. My guess is that she's sold him on the notion that her mental illness is a handicap just like anything else—or vice versa."

"What does that mean, Jeff?" Colin had to ask.

Jeff shrugged. "Maybe nothing. In my opinion, he can't prove, according to current statutes, that Thea is in any way fit to parent a child, certainly not as a custodial parent. For one thing, her parental rights have already been terminated, and for another her record of failing to take the medication that helps control her condition is extensive. But I have the feeling that he may be trying to rewrite the law through the courts here, and if that's the case, there's no telling what he's got up his sleeve."

"What do you suggest we do?" Lauren asked.

"If it were up to me, I'd wage a well-documented case based on current law, and go in well armed with precedent that spells out in rhyme and reason why the law reads as it does."

"In other words, some handicaps make safe parenting impossible," Colin surmised.

"That's what I'd argue in Thea's case," Jeff confirmed. He looked from one to the other of them and added, "Then I'd offer an olive branch in the form of strictly supervised visitation with the proviso of court-ordered counseling on Thea's part."

The very thought chilled Colin. He didn't want Thea

anywhere near his family, but he knew that he might not have a choice. He looked at Lauren, uncertain how she would take the idea, but to his relief she seemed unruffled by it, asking only, "Her parental rights would remain suspended, wouldn't they?"

"That's the idea."

Lauren shrugged. "Georgie has to know about her someday, anyway," she said to Colin. "It might be better if he could see for himself, in safe, carefully controlled circumstances, who she really is."

Colin shook his head. "If she would stick with it," he said, "but Thea's record is nothing if not erratic. She never maintains her equilibrium for long. She'll drift in and out of his life if we let her, seemingly well one moment and deranged the next."

"You don't have to let her," Jeff said. "Like I said, it would be contingent on her staying in court-monitored counseling and taking her medication. If she doesn't do that, the agreement would be rescinded."

"And she'd be out of our lives for good," Lauren murmured.

"Might work," Colin said after a moment, hoping it was true.

"Might," Jeff admitted, "but I gotta tell you both, I'm small change compared to Thea's rep. You might want to consider hiring on some real fire power to face him down."

Colin was shocked. "Are you asking us to let you off the hook?"

"No!" Jeff exclaimed. "I can take this guy. I know I can, but this isn't just another case, this is you and your family, man. I just want you both to know that I understand completely if you want to play it as safe as possible and go with a big name on this."

Lauren shook her head. "To me, safe as possible is going

with someone who loves you like a brother and will fight with every breath in his body.''

''Ditto,'' Colin agreed, delighted that the sentiment had come from her.

''So what you're saying,'' Jeff clarified, lawyerlike, ''is that you want me to stay on this, to argue the case in court.''

''You are our lawyer, Jeff,'' Lauren said, placing a hand on Colin's thigh, ''not to mention our very good friend.''

''You heard the lady,'' Colin confirmed, covering her hand with his and giving it an approving squeeze. He grinned, quite proud of this wife of his.

Jeff clapped his hands together and rubbed them briskly, grinning. ''Okay. Let's get to work then.'' He pointed at Lauren. ''You and I have some serious talking to do. I need to know everything you can tell me from that visit last year when Thea gave birth to our boy until now. I've documented every detail of Colin's dealings with her and have reams on her past.'' Jeff added, ''There's certainly no record of mental illness in her family, which is good news for our boy here. Frankly, I think it's pretty much self-induced on her part, but I don't really want to get into that kind of chicken-first-or-egg argument in court.''

Lauren took George onto her lap and hugged him close.

Colin smiled down at the pair of them. ''George already has the best of moms.''

She turned her face up for his kiss. ''Thank you. Since he also has the best of dads and the best of lawyers I guess we're covered on all fronts, aren't we?''

Colin chuckled, feeling tons lighter than he had when Jeff had first called that morning. ''You could say that.''

Jeff was busy retrieving his briefcase from the floor, opening it on his knees and extracting what he needed to get down Lauren's story. ''You ready?'' he asked, all business now, and Lauren nodded.

Colin got up and lifted Georgie from his mother's arms, saying, "Why don't we walk over to the lodge and see what Juan's up to, hmm?"

"I'll come over as soon as we're through here," Lauren said.

"Don't forget to bundle up warm," he said, bending to kiss her once more. "The wind's sharp as broken glass out there today."

"I'll drive her over as I go," Jeff said.

"Excellent." He turned and smiled at his friend and attorney. "Stop in and I'll treat you to Shelby's rum pudding and a strong cup of coffee."

"Count on it."

"See you later," Lauren called as he carried George toward the back door and the coatrack. He tossed her a wink over his shoulder and went on his way, confident that she was up to the grilling to which Jeff was about to subject her. It felt good to know that she and Colin were in this thing together—and even better to think about pulling her hair down and delving beneath that roomy T-shirt when they were alone later. In fact, despite the coming court battle, life had never felt so good.

Chapter Fifteen

Lauren was so nervous that she felt sick to her stomach. At least, that was what she told Colin on those three mornings before the early March court date when she bolted from the bed to throw up. After all the home studies, physical and psychiatric examinations, not to mention a virtual sea of documentation written in nearly incomprehensible legalese and the depositions, they both had a right to jittery nerves. However, as she stood with Colin and Jeff in an antechamber off the courtroom waiting for the bailiff to call them to the docket, she wondered if the half lie wasn't coming back to haunt her by proving itself wholly true. Any moment now she expected to have to bolt for the ladies' room.

To calm herself, she whispered in her mind to the child growing beneath her heart. *Be calm, little one,* she thought. *Mommy's holding you safe. I love you dearly. Just be patient a little while longer while we fix things for your big brother.*

It was certain now. She'd done not one but two pregnancy tests, and both had proven positive. She'd followed up that with a visit to an obstetrician's office in Taos, but she hadn't yet confided the truth to her husband or anyone else.

When the door opened, Lauren's heart leaped into her throat, but the bailiff was merely admitting someone else. Hallie crossed the room at a near gallop and enfolded Lauren in her stout arms.

"I was so afraid we'd be late."

"Mama," Lauren exclaimed in surprise, "you didn't have to come."

"Oh, yes, she did," her brother commented wryly, "and so did I."

"We couldn't let you go through this alone," Hallie said in that scolding voice Lauren had once hated but was beginning to treasure.

Lauren smiled, a hand on the middle of her moss-green column dress. With its white-cuffed sleeves and lace-trimmed Peter Pan collar, it made a prim, feminine impression, while its lack of a waistline hid the imagined bulge of her belly. Colin wore his best black pinstripe suit, a royal blue tie with a tiny black design accenting the stark whiteness of his shirt. Next to him, Jeff looked slightly rumpled in dark brown. Meg was there to sit with Georgie and Mercedes Allonzo, the social worker, who, bless her, had offered stalwart support.

"I'm hardly alone, Mom," Lauren said, smacking a kiss on her mother's papery cheek, "but I'm glad you came, anyway."

"Randi thought it best to keep the girls at home," Larry said, "but her thoughts are with you."

"We appreciate that, Larry," Colin said, coming to stand beside Lauren and slip an arm about her waist.

"If that judge has an ounce of sense, he'll send that

woman on her way," Hallie huffed, shifting her weight from one swollen foot to the other. "Anyone can see that the boy belongs with you. Just look at him! He's perfect, happy, healthy. What a little darling. Come to Granny, sweet boy."

"Why don't you get off your feet, Mom," Lauren suggested, pulling around a stiff aluminum chair for her. Hallie promptly sat and took Georgie onto her lap. He got his fingers in her hair and had her ear clip off within the first second, but Hallie merely cooed and smooched.

Lauren was deeply thankful that Georgie did not seem to sense the undercurrent of worry that directed her days. She could only pray that when they left here, he would still be oblivious.

Jeff pushed back the cuff of his sleeve and checked his watch. "I think I'll step out and see what the holdup is."

Lauren wasn't sure that was what she really wanted, but she nodded along with Colin as Jeff slipped out the door. Colin turned to take her into his arms. "It'll be okay," he whispered. "It'll be all right."

She slipped her arms around his waist inside his coat and smiled up at him, trying to take and give courage. The door opened and Jeff reentered the room.

"Something's up," he said. "We're going into the judge's chambers. The other lawyer is already in there."

Lauren looked up into her husband's blue eyes, her heart in her throat. He smiled, but nothing could disguise the worry clouding his countenance. Almost at once the door opened again and the bailiff gestured to them. "This way, please."

"Just Colin and Lauren," Jeff clarified.

"The rest can wait here," the bailiff confirmed.

Hallie got up to kiss Lauren's cheek, while Larry clapped Colin on the shoulder encouragingly. When Georgie reached for her, Lauren had to hold him off. "Mommy will be back in just a minute, sweetie. You stay with Granny."

He immediately turned his attention back to Hallie's hair.

Lauren quickly headed for the door, Colin's hand a welcome, steadying weight in the small of her back. They walked across the small courtroom to a door on the opposite side, through it and down a short corridor to the judge's large but surprisingly Spartan chambers. She was standing behind her desk, hands on her hips as she spoke quietly to the small man standing in front of her. The judge slid a blank, impersonal look over Lauren and Colin, nodded at Jeff and sat down.

"Mr. and Mrs. Garret, counselors, I've reviewed all the materials provided the state for this hearing and am ready to render judgment in the custody issue of the minor child—"

"Forgive me, Your Honor," Jeff interrupted in a mystified voice, "but when are we going to be allowed to argue our case?"

The judge looked at the small, nerdish man in the pale suit standing beside Lauren. He shook his balding head. "There's been no time to speak with opposing counsel, Your Honor. I came directly to you."

The judge sat back in her chair, eyed the lot of them consideringly and nodded at the little man, who cleared his throat, hooked his thumbs in his belt and puffed out his chest as if about to deliver the Gettysburg Address. "My client has withdrawn her petition for guardianship."

For a moment, Lauren expected him to say more, much more, but then the impact of what he had said finally hit her. Her breath expelled in a whoosh. At the same instant Colin asked of Jeff, "What's going on?"

Jeff looked at the judge, saying, "We're stunned, Your Honor. My clients are understandably concerned—"

The judge silenced him with a lifted forefinger and

turned her attention to the other attorney. "I do believe we are entitled to a full explanation, Counselor."

He fingered his upper lip, then pompously said, "I am not blind to the seriousness of my client's disability. In point of fact, I accepted Ms. Sanford's case with the understanding that she would maintain with religious precision her schedule of prescribed medication. The longer she did so, the more she came to recognize the depth of her disability, which led her to believe that the best interests of the child are served by his remaining in the home of his father. Ms. Sanford has checked herself into a private institution for intense further treatment."

"And I'll bet that just chapped your old do-gooder backside raw," Jeff chortled unrepentantly.

"Mr. Locke," the judge scolded, but Lauren detected a glimmer of humor in her intelligent eyes.

The little lawyer harrumphed and looked down his nose at the carpet. "I did advise my client that her personal rights were of importance to others beside herself," he intoned. "However—"

"However," the judge said impatiently, "we are not concerned with personal agendas. Now, if everyone is up to speed, let us dispense with this matter and get on with business." She sat forward suddenly and opened a file on the top of her cluttered desk. "Having studied the documents presented me by the state and attorneys for both sides, and in consideration of the wisdom shown by petitioner Thea Sanford," she said mechanically, "I see no reason to act in the matter of custody, which is retained by the boy's father, Colin Garret. I also see no reason not to grant joint custody to his wife, Lauren Garret, in answer to her approved petition to adopt said infant child. Also, I hereby grant a permanent change in the birth certificate of this child to reflect the name, George Colin Garret, as petitioned by his father." She picked up a pen and signed several papers, closed the file folder and picked it up, plopping it atop a pile in one corner of her desk. She waved a hand dismissively. "That ought to take care of matters. Congratulations and goodbye."

Lauren became aware that Colin was crushing her hand in his. The other attorney had turned and was slapping his feet across the floor toward the door. Jeff shoved a hand through his hair. "Your Honor, I— Thank you!"

"Don't thank me, Mr. Locke," the judge said, flipping open another file folder. "This one was simple. Now get out of my office and go celebrate."

Jeff took Colin by the arm and literally dragged him toward the door. Lauren, however, stood her ground, her arm pulled out to her side by Colin's clasp on her hand. She felt suddenly swamped by affinity for the woman sitting behind the desk, and it seemed terribly important to say so. In the end, however, when the judge once again looked up, her irritation unconcealed, all Lauren could think to say was, "Thank you. You can't know what this means to us."

"Oh, I think I can," the judge said, smiling slightly. "In my business, Mrs. Garret, you learn to sift the wheat from the chaff. There was no question here about who the real mother is." She suddenly propped her elbows on the desk and leaned forward conspiratorially. "Tell me something, is the boy as adorable looking as the father?"

Lauren barked a laugh. "His spitting image."

The judge sighed and picked up her pen. "Some women have all the luck," she muttered. "Good day, Mrs. Garret."

The firmness of the farewell left no doubt that the conversation was definitely finished. Lauren finally allowed herself to be pulled toward the door. "Goodbye, Your Honor."

They went out into the hallway and through the door into the courtroom, which was empty, with Jeff leading the way. Colin was gulping air, as if still trying to take in all that had happened. Lauren felt surreal, almost outside of herself. It was as if one part of her exulted, while another reeled in shock. Jeff opened the door to the antechamber where the others waited. Colin and Lauren filed in after him. He closed the door, looked at the anxious faces trained on him and pumped his fists in victory, whooping like a wild man.

"We won! We won! It's all over! George is going home with his papa and mama!"

The room had erupted into celebratory exclamations before he was through. Meg rushed to embrace her exuberant husband. Mercedes clapped her hands, while Hallie hugged a wide-eyed George and Larry raised his eyes heavenward in obvious relief. Lauren felt her husband's hands on her shoulders, turning her to fully face him. Relief and jubilation warred with disbelief on his handsome face. Lauren thought of what the judge had said about him and felt a pang of dismay at the notion that popped into her head. She was lucky, of course. She was legally George's mother now. But how, she wondered, would she ever know whether or not her husband could ever truly love her? She let herself be pulled into his arms, laughter bubbling up from that relieved, grateful part of her, and hugged him every bit as tightly as he held her. She could tell him about the baby now. Everything was, finally, as it should be. Why, then, were the tears coursing down her face as sad as they were elated?

Colin sighed in pure relief and clutched the porch post. He felt too light to trust his feet to the ground. Everything felt too light, including the very air that surrounded him and with which he filled his lungs. He had believed all along that everything would be okay, but the nightmare of Thea Sanford had gone on for so long that the stray doubt had slipped in from time to time. He hadn't realized, however, just how many of those doubts he had harbored until they were gone. Standing on his mother-in-law's doorstep, he watched the sun setting over the mountains and felt unbearably grateful. A small but oddly shrill creaking alerted him that his moment of solitude was coming to an end, but he did not regret the intrusion, especially when he glanced over his shoulder and saw that it was Jeff who had joined him. The sting brought by the hand that Jeff clapped onto his shoulder felt unusually sharp. It was as if every stimulus had been heightened by his relief.

"How's it going, buddy?"

Colin shook his head, beyond words. He didn't even try to explain how he was feeling, so he talked about something else. "You know, the very last thing I expected was for Thea, of all people, to come to her senses."

Jeff chuckled. "Yea, talk about your shockers. I've gotta tell you, though, I think it would have come out the same if she hadn't. The judge made it pretty obvious which side the case study supported."

Colin chuckled. Jeff had been blowing his own horn, one way or another, all afternoon, with good reason. "You are really pumped about this."

"You betcha. I did a damned good job putting that case together."

"Never doubted it."

"In fact, I'm feeling so good about me right now that I'm gonna take on another project."

"And that would be?"

"Your marriage."

Colin almost fell over. "What the hell?"

Jeff huffed a deep sigh and shoved his hands into his pockets. "Listen, I've gotten to know Lauren pretty well lately, and I know you like a book, my friend, cover to cover and backward."

"What are you saying?"

"Think about it, Colin. You've always been supremely careful, and since this thing with Thea blew up in your face, you've given new meaning to the term thinking things through. But as astute as you are, old buddy, you sometimes don't see what's right under your nose."

"And you do?" Colin asked, incredulous that he was being taken to task.

Jeff fixed him with the patented let's-not-be-stupid-here Jeff Locke look and said baldly, "Why haven't you told that woman that you love her?"

Colin blinked, a growing sense of horror overtaking him. "I...she..."

"You're the sort who always thinks before he speaks," Jeff went on, "and that's what first clued me." He shook a finger at Colin. "You fell for that woman the instant you laid eyes on her, but even if Thea hadn't burned your fingers up to the elbows, you wouldn't have admitted it even to yourself. If you let Lauren think you were proposing marriage to her, then it's because you *wanted* her to think it. So all this pondering and studying and analyzing was nothing more than an attempt to justify to yourself what you were doing. Meanwhile, she's left thinking she was the fool for picking up on your signals and returning your feelings."

Colin frowned, partly to let Jeff know that he didn't appreciate being analyzed this way and partly to tamp down the riot of emotions percolating inside him.

"She loves you, dammit, as much as you love her, and she, at least, was brave enough to say so. Don't you think it's time you paid her back in kind? Don't you think it's time she knew?"

Colin could feel himself trembling. How blind could a seeing man be? he wondered. Defensively he said, "I've shown her in every way I could think of."

Jeff rolled his eyes. "Are you really that dumb? No wonder you were single so long! Women have to hear the words, Colin. You can bring 'em home roses and diamonds every day, burn candles every night, foam at the mouth every time you see 'em, but if you don't say the words—and often—they're going to doubt you. Hell, I came home bearing gifts more than once, I tell you, and nearly got my head handed to me on a platter before I understood just how often my Meg needs to hear me say it."

"So you really think it's that important?" Colin said, half teasing now.

"Damn straight. Let me save you a world of hurt and confusion here, old buddy. Take my advice. Tell the woman."

Colin stood staring into the waning sunset, the cerulean of the sky painted with swathes of milky-pink near the earth's horizon and deepening to night-blues above. It wouldn't do to let his interfering friend think that he was giving up his thoughtful, careful ways, however right the good attorney was. Nevertheless, one corner of his mouth hitched up into a rebellious smile. He swallowed a lump of sheer fear and said, "You argue a good case, Counselor."

Jeff scratched his head and rocked back on his heels. "Yeah, I do, don't I?"

Colin laughed and turned to offer his hand. "Thanks, Jeff. For everything."

Jeff clasped his hand in one of his own and threw a glancing blow at his shoulder with the other. "Let me know how it goes, will ya? I have a feeling you just may be about to discover what marriage is really all about."

Colin hoped that the nervousness he was feeling did not show, that the cold fear coalescing in the pit of his stomach did not grow large enough to choke him. He also hoped that Jeff was right. "Okay. Just don't expect a play-by-play."

Jeff chuckled and rubbed his hands together. "Wouldn't dream of it. That's another thing about women. They get squeamish about the private details."

Colin shook his head. "Never realized you were such an expert."

"Hey, when you're good, you're good."

They bantered a little longer before Meg came out to inform Jeff that it was time to rescue the baby-sitter. They were heading home. Colin took it as a cue. Time to drive his own family home. Time to face the rest of his life.

She was going to tell him tonight, Lauren decided. Delaying made no sense, and he had a right to know that he was going to be a father again. Yes, she would tell him tonight. Drawing a deep, fortifying breath, she stepped out of the bathroom. The golden glow of candles illuminated the bedroom with a softness that was almost tactile. Colin was in the mood to celebrate, after all. She had wondered on the drive home if his silence was from residual shock or something more sinister. Perhaps he had realized once and for all that he was trapped in a marriage he could never learn to appreciate, and here she was, about to double the locks.

Colin entered the room from the kitchen, carrying a tray laden with fruit, cheese and champagne. Yes, she would definitely have to tell him about the baby. Otherwise how did she explain refusing to drink the wine? He set the tray down on the foot of the bed and came toward her, his robe open to reveal his bare chest.

"There you are. I was beginning to wonder just how long you could soak, but I see that it was, as always, worth the wait. You look scrumptious, Mrs. Garret." His hands skimmed over her bare arms and lifted to cup her face. "I love the way you look and smell and feel," he whispered. "You know that, don't you?"

She nodded, smiling wanly, and brushed past him to the bed. "I wasn't sure what you were feeling this afternoon."

"Relief, shock and, in an odd way, utter exhaustion."

She could identify with that. "I know what you mean. When it first happened, I wasn't sure if I could believe it. Then the worries lifted away and the relief rushed in, and I realized that I was finally able to relax."

"Except you haven't," Colin said, stepping close again. "Neither of us has, and I think I know why."

She looked away, wondering if he had somehow discovered her secret. Did it show? Could he tell just by looking at her? "Colin, I—"

"Wait," he said, snagging the champagne glasses from the tray with one hand. "Let's do this right, shall we? I want to propose a toast." He filled the glasses and held one out to her. She hesitated a moment, realizing that he didn't know about the baby or he wouldn't have offered her alcohol. She took the glass, the golden wine sparkling and bubbling enthusiastically. "To the future," he said, lifting his glass to his lips. She raised her drink, intending to pretend to sip, then let it down again. No more deceit.

"I have to tell you something."

"I have to tell you something, too," he said, "something I should have told you a long time ago." He placed his glass back on the tray, took her glass from her hand and placed it next to his, then transferred the tray to the dresser. "Sit with me," he said, coming to stand beside her. He didn't seem to be giving her a choice. Taking her by the shoulders, he literally pushed her down on the side of the bed and sat next to her, holding her hands in his. "Lauren, I'm a careful man. I suspect you know that about me by now."

Dread mingled with curiosity inside of her. She bit her lip and nodded her head, deciding to hear him out, praying silently that he wasn't about to end their marriage now that his claim to his son was secure. "Go on."

His thumbs rubbed across the backs of her knuckles. "I made a terrible mistake with Thea," he began. "It made me even more wary than usual, or so I've been told. Anyway, when I met you, the very first time I laid eyes on you... Boy, I'm really no good at this."

"Just say it," Lauren snapped, feeling her nerves about to do the same thing.

He bowed his head, then lifted it again on a deep breath. "Lauren, you knocked my socks off. You bowled me over. It was fixed in stone right at that moment."

Lauren blinked at him, uncertain what she was hearing. "What was fixed in stone? What are you talking about?"

"You," he said, squeezing her hands. "The most beautiful, caring, sexy, intelligent, determined, hardworking, sexy—I said that, didn't I?" His mouth twitched a smile. "You were, are, the most incredible woman, everything I'd ever imagined, ever hoped for. I don't think I wanted to admit it even to myself, but I assume it was obvious or you wouldn't have, uh..."

"Thrown myself at you," she supplied wryly, warming to the thought. "I didn't mistake the matter then? You really were—"

"Am," he said. "I still can't keep my hands off you. Call it attraction, if you want to, but it seems a tame word for what happens to me when you walk into a room. You turn me inside out, babe. You always have. I can't think of you without wanting to make love to you."

She closed her eyes, smiling as the words soaked into her like gentle raindrops on parched ground. "I'm glad you told me," she whispered. "It helps more than you know because—"

"Oh, that's not it," he said. "That's just the warm-up for what I have to say."

Disappointment slammed through her. Here it came, the bad news, so to speak. "I see. All right. Well, let's get this over with, then."

He was silent for a moment, then he sighed. "I don't know why I'm so lousy at this. Yes, I do. I'm scared to death, that's why."

She looked up sharply. "Scared? Of what?"

He licked his lips. "Lauren, you once told me that you loved me."

She closed her eyes, mortified. "Oh, boy."

"I'm hoping, after everything's that happened, that some part of that feeling is still left in you."

She winced. "Colin—"

"Let me finish."

The conversation was downright painful, but she nodded, aware that the only way to get it over with was to hear him out. And yet he stalled, sitting silently at her side, her hands clutched in his so tightly she could feel the bones grinding together. Finally he chuckled, a self-deprecating, almost sad reflection of his state of mind.

"You are my wife. I schemed and pressured and blackmailed you to make it happen, but you are my wife, the mother of my son—and I'm still scared to death to tell you how much I love you."

Lauren's eyes popped open in the same instant that her jaw dropped. "What did you say?"

He was studying her face intently. "I said, I'm scared to death—"

"Not that!" she shrieked, yanking a hand free only to have it flap about like a fish out of water. "The good part! Get to the good part."

A grin began to grow on his face. "I love you. I love you so much it—"

She never learned just how much because she was just too thrilled to hear the best of it. She threw herself at him.

She had a habit of doing that. Why change now? "Oh, Colin! I love you, too! Oh, Colin! I love you! I do!" Her arms were around his neck, and they were falling backward, but she tried to plant kisses on his face, anyway, hitting mostly air but the occasional chin and nose also. Colin was laughing, his arms sliding around her waist.

"Jeff was right. I should've said it long ago. I'm sorry. The truth is your husband's a coward."

"Baloney." She drew back, looking down at him. "My husband is the most adorable, lovable…" He lifted his mouth to the curve of her neck, sucking gently at her skin, and she completely lost her train of thought. "Er, I, um. Oh. Oh, my."

His hands slid over the silk of her gown restlessly. "I love this gown," he murmured. "Take it off."

Obediently she shrugged the tiny strap off one shoulder and slid her arm up and out of the way, while he played havoc with her senses, rocking his hips against her, skimming his hands over her bottom to clasp her and press her down against him while he nibbled a path up her throat to her chin and finally her mouth. A ravening hunger seized her, and she was dimly aware that she had been holding it at bay for several weeks now. Perhaps it was true, what they said about pregnant women having increased libidos. Pregnant. Whoa.

She pulled back, sitting on her heels astride him. Her nightgown draped low over one breast, just barely clinging to the tip, and that's where his gaze went, followed an instant later by his hand.

"I haven't told you yet."

"Hmm?"

"I have to— Oh!" She sucked in her breath as her nipple hardened beneath his plucking fingertips. She closed her eyes, gulped and opened them again, determinedly shoving his hand away. "It's my turn. I have to tell you something."

He seemed genuinely puzzled for a moment. "I'm sorry. What were you saying?"

She couldn't help smiling lazily. "Better pay attention, Mr. Garret. I have an important news bulletin for you."

He blinked at her and propped his head on his folded hands. "What are you talking about?"

She took a deep breath, baring her breast in the process. Once more his gaze went there, as if attached by an invisible string. She stifled the urge to giggle and lifted her gown to cover herself. "This is important, Colin."

He straightened the frown on his face and gave her his full attention. "I'm sorry, sweetheart. You just make such a tempting picture sitting there like that." Suddenly he pushed up on one elbow. "Are you're breasts swollen?"

She derailed his hand, clearing her throat. "Uh, yes, I imagine my breasts are swollen. I may be gaining a little weight in the tummy, too." She smoothed her gown, outlining her belly. "It happens, you know?"

His brows furrowed. "What happens? What are you talking about, honey?"

Lauren squared her shoulders, her hands going to her abdomen. "I want you to know I didn't plan this," she began, but then she just jumped into it. "I'm pregnant."

For a moment he seemed not to get it. He tilted his head. "What?"

"I said, I'm—"

"Oh, my goodness!" He sat up. The bomb had finally hit. "We're having another baby?"

Lauren nodded, pushing her hair back. "I'll admit that I've known for a while. And I didn't tell you because I was afraid, in case they did take Georgie away from us."

"Afraid I'd leave you?"

She nodded, then rushed to justify herself. "Maybe I should have known, Colin, but you never said—"

He reached for her, pulling her close. "Hush, now. I understand. I should have told you sooner. Georgie brought us together. I suppose it was reasonable to think that without him I might not want the marriage, but surely you wouldn't have kept the child a secret from me?"

"No, of course not. To tell you the truth, if it hadn't turned out the way it has, if you'd wanted to go, I'm not sure I wouldn't have used the baby to hold on to you. I guess I just needed to know first if you'd stay for me."

"I'll never let go of you," he said, sliding his hand beneath her hair. "Never."

Tears filled her eyes. "I'm so glad you told me how you feel first. I know it's selfish of me, but I needed to hear it."

"Not selfish," he whispered, shaking his head. "Not selfish at all. Now, listen to me. How do you feel about having this baby?"

"Feel?" she echoed, knuckling tears from her eyes. "I'm so happy! Even in the worst moments, I had this baby to hold on to, to dream about. It wasn't so long ago that I wondered if I'd ever have a family of my own. Now I have the world's best husband, a child and another one on the way. I'd be a fool to be anything but ecstatic!" She laughed, rubbing her hands over her belly again. "I've been talking to her."

He was grinning. "Her?" He chuckled, his hands covering hers on her belly. "It's a girl, is it?"

"I don't know, but I figure, hey, we have a son."

Suddenly his chin trembled, and tears flooded his eyes. "I love you!" he whispered. "Oh, my, how I love you!" He pulled her down atop him, chortling. "We're going to have a baby! This morning I didn't know for sure if we were going to have one child, and now we have two!"

He cupped her face, pulling it down to receive his kiss. They were careening between extremes of emotion. At the moment she was almost laughing too hard to fix her mouth to his. The next instant they set fire to their bed.

It seemed true, after all, that pregnancy did supercharge the libidos of some women, some lucky, lucky women. The case could be argued, in months to come, that pregnancy was a special time in the lives of a couple unlike any other. Through good and bad, through swollen ankles and feet that disappeared beyond swollen stomachs, midnight cravings and sexual acrobatics, tears and laughter and the wonders of creation and love, through exploding myths and exploding waistlines, no two happier people ever weathered the joys and the inconveniences of gestation with greater relish. Oh, and it turned out that twins do run in families, after all.

* * * * *

Silhouette Stars

Born this Month

Bryan Adams, Joan Sutherland, Richard Burton, Demi Moore, Prince Charles, Meg Ryan, Boris Becker, Jodie Foster, Calvin Klein

Star of the Month

Scorpio

An interesting year lies ahead, there could be some major changes occurring especially in the second half and although you may feel apprehensive the outcome will be positive. Romantically this is an excellent time and you should find out just how strongly those around you feel about you.

Sagittarius

Career matters are highlighted and you should feel pleased with the options on offer. A shopping spree mid-month could produce some real bargains.

Capricorn

The recent hectic social whirl slows down and you can take time out to recharge. A relationship that has given you concern seems at last to be on firm ground.

 Aquarius

Family matters occupy your time and you could feel torn in several directions as those close refuse to take responsibility for their actions. However, late in the month the tension should start to fade and you will see a happier time approaching.

Pisces

A short break away from the routine will bring the romance back into your life. Finances look good and you may indulge in a little more than window shopping.

 Aries

Time to think about changing your environment either by moving home or planning some improvements. Your artistic talents will be working well and others will be impressed by your efforts.

Taurus

Recent financial gains have taken the pressure off and allowed you to make a few much needed changes in your life. This is the ideal time for new relationships or for making a stronger commitment to that special person.

Gemini

Your faith in those around has been shaken and you are unsure about who exactly to trust. Remember not to assume everyone is the same as you as you'll find you have some very good friends. A party late in the month gets you in the mood for socialising.

Cancer

Romance is in the air and may come from an unexpected direction. Socially too it's a happy time and someone close may have a good reason to celebrate.

 ## Leo

You may have reached the end of the road with a relationship but don't allow your disappointment to stop you seeing the other good aspects that are happening, especially in the workplace.

Virgo

Travel is well aspected especially when related to work where it could lead to some new openings. Romance should continue to go well as long as you are careful to include those close in your plans.

 ## Libra

An interesting month in which you may feel the aspects are working against you. However, you can turn it around by seeing the positive side and being open to the suggestions made to you.

Look out for more
Silhouette Stars next month

The Romance
Collection

Prince Joe
Suzanne Brockmann

The Five-Minute Bride
Leanne Banks

Molly Darling
Laurie Paige

Only £3.99

On sale 23rd December 2000

0101/SH/SH6

THE MacGREGORS

4 BOOKS ON THIS WELL-LOVED FAMILY

BY

NORA ROBERTS

Book 1 - Serena and Caine - September 2000

Book 2 - Alan and Grant - December 2000

Book 3 - Daniel and Ian - May 2001

Book 4 - Rebellion - August 2001

*Don't miss these four fantastic books by
Silhouette's top author*

0009/115/SH4

FREE!

2 Books

and a surprise gift!

We would like to take this opportunity to thank you for reading this Silhouette® book by offering you the chance to take TWO more specially selected titles from the Special Edition™ series absolutely FREE! We're also making this offer to introduce you to the benefits of the Reader Service™—

★ FREE home delivery
★ FREE gifts and competitions
★ FREE monthly Newsletter
★ Books available before they're in the shops
★ Exclusive Reader Service discounts

Accepting these FREE books and gift places you under no obligation to buy; you may cancel at any time, even after receiving your free shipment. Simply complete your details below and return the entire page to the address below. *You don't even need a stamp!*

YES! Please send me 2 free Special Edition books and a surprise gift. I understand that unless you hear from me, I will receive 4 superb new titles every month for just £2.70 each, postage and packing free. I am under no obligation to purchase any books and may cancel my subscription at any time. The free books and gift will be mine to keep in any case.

EOZEB

Ms/Mrs/Miss/Mr ....Initials..................
BLOCK CAPITALS PLEASE

Surname...

Address...

....

....Postcode ....

Send this whole page to:
UK: The Reader Service, FREEPOST CN8I, Croydon, CR9 3WZ
EIRE: The Reader Service, PO Box 4546, Kilcock, County Kildare (stamp required)